D1430755

SCHEMERS

Betrayal knows no boundaries

Edited by Robin D. Laws

Published by Stone Skin Press 2013.

Stone Skin Press is an imprint of Pelgrane Press Ltd. Spectrum
House, 9 Bromell's Road, Clapham Common, London, SW4 0BN.

ISBN 978-1-908983-04-6

A CIP catalogue record for this book is available from the British
Library.

1 2 3 4 5 6 7 8 9 10

Printed in the USA.

This book can be ordered direct from the publisher at
www.stoneskinpress.com

Contents

Introduction

Robin D. Laws

It's no coincidence that we use the same term for constructing a story and for overthrowing a regime. Like conspirators, writers are always plotting.

The Western narrative tradition rests on foundation of corruption, of forsworn oaths and subverted loyalties.

One of its pillars comes to us from Mount Olympus, via the classic Greek dramatists who transformed myth into literature. Analyzing their prototypes, Aristotle codified the core techniques of storytelling we still refer to twenty-three centuries later.

Look at that coziest of families, the House of Atreus. King Tantalus, scheming to test the omniscience of the gods, ambushes his son Pelops, murders him, dismembers him, cooks him in a stew, and serves him up as the main course at a divine banquet. Only Demeter, absent-minded with worry over her imprisoned daughter, falls for the ploy. The other Olympians helpfully resurrect Pelops, his devoured shoulder proving scant impediment. Still, the stain of betrayal has now permanently attached itself to Tantalus's descendants and will drip down through the generations.

As is typical in the wake of a political dustup, multiple narratives make competing claims to the truth. An alternate story, preferred by authors tracing their lineages back to Tantalus, has the gods cursing him for stealing their food, impregnated with secret knowledge, and distributing it out to the people. Here he's still sticking a knife in the Olympians, but for the benefit of the common mortal. In the mythic era as now, one observer's terrorist is another's liberator.

Yet a third thread casts Tantalus's betrayal of the gods as mere foreshadowing of the real curse. It makes Pelops recipient of the fateful imprecation, delivered as he kills his confederate in a chariot race–fixing scam. Leaving aside that tale's convolutions and ambiguities, an overarching point remains: the shift from betrayed to betrayer is never more than a story turn away.

Whatever the curse's origins, it establishes a pattern of violence and treachery enmeshing Tantalus' heirs. Pelops's twin sons, Atreus and Thyestes, murder their half brother, Chrysippus, in a botched bid for his throne. Banished by their father, they finagle their way to joint possession of the Mycenaean crown while its rightful wearer is off fighting a war. Thyestes then breaks faith with Atreus by conducting an affair with his wife. Following the family culinary tradition, Atreus retaliates by feeding Thyestes his own sons. Thyestes takes the long view on vengeance, incestuously conceiving a son destined to murder Atreus.

A generation later, Atreus's son Agamemnon betrays his daughter by sacrificing her to the gods in a bid for good fortune in the Trojan War. So his wife, Clytaemnestra, decides to murder him when he gets back. This incident provides the grist for Aeschylus's Oresteia, wellspring of Greek tragedy and thus of Western literature.

The other major wellspring, the Bible, devotes its first half to a cycle of betrayals, mostly perpetrated against God by his worshippers. Its origin story for the human condition turns on Adam and Eve's broken promise to God, with the serpent as unindicted co-conspirator. Bearing a curse similar to that of the version of Tantalus who stole awareness-laden food from the gods, their son Cain commits the primal murder. From that day on, the descendants of the original family keep turning their backs on God, earning punishment, and returning to the fold. After a suitable interregnum, they go back once again to subverting the terms of their contract with the Almighty.

The redemption narrative that ends the cycle nonetheless depends on treachery for its inciting incident, as Judas collects his thirty pieces of silver. Only in revisionist versions of the Crucifixion story does the cosmic necessity of this prototypical act of snitching earn him any mitigating sympathy.

It's Chaucer who starts the process of turning the influences on English literature into English literature itself. As you might expect from his raw materials, his *Canterbury Tales* abound with schemes, from the sinister to the comic. In The Man of Law's Tale, pious Custance is set adrift on a raft by her prospective mother-in-law, to stop her son the Sultan from converting to Christianity. Arcite of The Knight's Tale returns to Theseus's household in disguise to woo the object of his love. In The Miller's Tale, two apprentices vie to bed their master's wife, with a third candidate for the task lurking in the wings.

Traitors and plotters fill the boards of Shakespeare's stage. Claudius and Macbeth kill kings to usurp their thrones. Regan and Goneril slide their proud father's out from under him with transparent but strategically applied flattery. Brutus and Cassius conspire to assassinate an unsuspecting Julius Caesar. Romeo and Juliet meet their dooms due to a communication breakdown in a faked-death plan.

The activities of Machiavellians grow only bloodier during the subsequent Jacobean era, as political machinations spiral into cycles of outlandish vengeance in the *The Revenger's Tragedy*, *The Duchess of Malfi*, and *The White Devil*.

These motifs move to the prose page with the rise of the popular novel, most especially in the disreputable thrills of the gothic tradition. It in turn bequeaths its concerns, energy, and plot devices down through the decades to pervade most of today's popular genres, from romance to horror to science fiction to the spy novel.

Talk of spies ushers us from the product of writing to the extracurricular pursuits of writers themselves. History's relatively few writer/murderers tend to commit the act through passion or misadventure, rather than conspiracy. Their sallies against government generally occur in the public square, not behind the curtains. And, so far at least, none of us have cooked people and served them up to others. It is in the secret precincts of the intelligence world that life and art meet.

As both authors and secret agents lie for a living, it's unsurprising to see top literary names trafficking in tradecraft. Christopher Marlowe famously spied on Catholic rebels for Elizabeth's spymaster, Francis Walsingham.

Crossovers between the two fields thicken in the last century. In World War II, British Intelligence recruited Dennis Wheatley, author of rollicking spy thrillers and dashing occult adventures, to help fashion their disinformation campaign against Hitler. One of his juniors was his future literary equivalent, Ian Fleming. Graham Greene and Somerset Maugham also worked for MI6.

Meanwhile, in Washington, the Foreign Service ran inveterate ladies' man Roald Dahl as an agent of influence, seducing society ladies as part of their campaign to rally America to enter the war. Among the chief targets of this plan was the isolationist playwright and US representative Clare Booth Luce, whose ardors Dahl found sufficiently exhausting as to fruitlessly request a change of assignment.

None of the contributors to this book are presently engaged in covert operations. That I know of. Instead their schemes unfold on the page, as they engage you in the mutually agreed-upon deception at the heart of all fiction. With them you will enter into a conspiracy, to be tricked by an arrangement of black marks on paper to fill your mental stage with perfidy, whether delightfully devilish or authentically troubling.

Given the centrality of scheming and conspiracy to the literary tradition, we can't be surprised to see writers asked to write on the motifs to reach back into the past. Jesse Bullington whisks us back to the intersection point where those themes begin to build the foundations of modern genre with "The Devil's Tontine," an adroitly conjured gothic pastiche. It scrapes away our post hoc assumptions about that tradition to reveal the surprisingly light touch that characterized its initial wave.

In the knowingly theatrical "A Scandal with Bohemians," Jonathan L. Howard twirls a finely kempt Victorian mustache, playing on the super-villain iconography that coalesces in that era. His mock-Moriarty reminds us that the easiest target for deception is always oneself.

Likewise in sly dialog with the past, Elizabeth A. Vaughan ventures further in time, to the medieval, to brandish "The Weapon at Hand." In its focus on a royal household and the need for an heir, she sets us up to expect a classic court intrigue, but then…

Gareth Ryder-Hanrahan takes us to the near past and the crumbling days of Soviet Russia, where everyone is a conspirator and the spies know less than anyone, in "Buried." He immerses us in the greasy panic of a massive reordering of betrayers and betrayed.

Other contributors from our cross-disciplinary roster examine the state of betrayal in the ever-present, electronic now. Kyla Lee Ward's "The Character Assassin" enters the headset-wearing, trash-talking arena of obsessive MMO video gaming to propose the fresh category of murderer it might spawn.

With the rhythmic snap of verse, Laura Lush's "Pink Azaleas" crawls inside the consciousness of a cyber-stalker colonized by the online tool that most defines our decade.

Robyn Seale jumps us into the future with "Pipping Day," taking on what is perhaps the most emotionally resonant of popular apocalypses. Like all stories about robots, it's about us.

The protagonist of Tobias S. Buckell's near-future bio-thriller "A Pressure of Shadows" may or may not be us anymore. With taut control, Buckell suggests the imminence of the moment when questions of identity and of survival fuse into one.

If to perform the act of reading is to enter into a conspiracy with the writer, certain stories remind us of the danger of trusting professional dissemblers. Nick Mamatas slashes the art world with a rusty razor in "If Graffiti Changed Anything, It Would Be Illegal." The disconnectedness of its collective voice declares a destabilizing wrongness from the start, leaving the reader to unravel its nasty truth.

The narrator of Tania Hershman's "The Plan *or* You Must Remember This" addresses us in our time's default voice of deception, that of deliberately bland bureaucracy. Its reversed chronology gives us a puzzle to unlock, though perhaps not one as great as the easy suppression of conscience at the center of its driving social experiment.

With all this trickery to deal with, the simple pleasures of genre play supply us with a needed palate cleansing. We know from the title of crime yarn "Victimless Crime" that it will prove anything but. John Helfers takes the anxiety summoned by that dramatic irony and boils it hard. It will teach you to always carefully inventory your surroundings when stealing an expensive vehicle.

Molly Tanzer's fizzy shot of neo-pulp, "Qi Sport" declares its contemporary bona fides by tossing a classic set of tropes in the pop-cultural Mixmaster. Underlying her collision of cowboy hats and Chinese vampires is one of the canon's classic ruses.

Speaking of classic treachery, you don't come closer to the roots of the tradition than an assassin in a royal court. What distinguishes Ekaterina Sedia's "Protector of Ascheli" is not only the smoky evocation of its fantasy setting, but its focus on the emotional consequences of betrayal.

A like concern suffuses Kathryn Kuitenbrouwer's "The Bridgehouse Game," where the power of desire fuels an exercise in psychological domination and transformation. A cruel tale recalling Edogawa Rampo, its moral horror becomes all the more acute through the fugue-state lyricism of Kuitenbrouwer's prose.

Together these writers, hailing from the disparate precincts of poetry, fantasy, science fiction, comics, gaming, crime writing, and literary fiction have entered a dark room to put their knives on the table for you. Here's a goblet of wine, to parch your thirst. Don't worry if it tastes slightly off.

You can trust us.

— *Robin D. Laws*

A Pressure of Shadows

Tobias S. Buckell

Kikoru, despite her name, is definitely British. Maybe her parents raised her in Japan, or just took a strange fancy to the name. Marcus pulls at his handcuffs, and wonders how she gets blonde-silver hair like that? Are the roots dark?

No. It's natural.

She's striking, his drug-addled brain tells him. Things he normally leaves swimming around beneath his conscious mind are just on the edge of his tongue. She is something that haunts his typical midnight fantasy. Sitting in front of him for real.

"Marcus." She even talks to him.

A huge cockroach flies in through the metal shutters and lands by a guard. It's crushed by an absentminded boot stomp.

"Sitting right here," Marcus says.

"Where is the suit?"

"I'm not going to tell you." She doesn't expect that. "Scopolamine is a limited drug." Marcus smiles, his mind clearing. Little bacteria, itty-bitty inventions of the lab he worked in, run around his blood looking for truth serums, poisons, whatever.

Marcus ran off with more than one major industrial secret from the lab.

Kikoru leans forward, and Marcus feels a rush of heat. He expects something dramatic.

It all seems so irreal. Not at all like the humdrum research lab, or the long days spent hunched over a computer.

She sits back down.

"There are many options that I have here, Marcus. I can use modern methods, painless methods, or something more medieval. I personally would like to start with the medieval…"

What would be a snappy reply? Marcus wonders. "Medieval?" he asks. No, that's awkward.

The clammy thing she put on his neck triggers again. Marcus spasms. Drool runs down his neck. His vision blurs, and he drifts into unconsciousness. But it doesn't hurt.

Kikoru, though, isn't done. Marcus snaps back awake to see another needle pulled out of his forearm.

Marcus thinks this is fun. He's never been tortured before.

He wipes his chin and neck clean on the side of his sweat-soaked shirt. Outside a light tropical drizzle starts to patter off of the tin roof.

Grenada, during the rainy season. Marcus wonders why everyone considers islands paradise just because of a few beaches. It's more like hell, he thinks: too hot. But with palm trees.

"Marcus. Talk to us."

Marcus looks around the room again. Resistance equals uselessness, yada yada, he knows the routine. Watched enough movies…

"What do you want to know?" he asks Kikoru.

"What are you doing here?"

"I came to kill someone," Marcus says. Kikoru turns to get a better look at him. This is probably the only way he would ever get someone like her to pay attention to him. Pathetic, he tells himself.

♦

He'd landed at the Point Salines airport and stepped out into waves of heat that rippled off the tarmac. He couldn't understand what the taxi drivers yelled at him, so he randomly chose one wearing a yellow and red bandana.

Marcus carried two suitcases and pulled a large box on a trolley. The taxi driver shepherded him towards the back of a bright green van with an airbrushed painting of an outrageously busty brown nude languidly sprawled across the side.

"I'll hold that." Marcus lifted the large box up onto the seat.

"Yeah, man." Not "mon" like the T-shirts said. The vowel sat in the back of the throat. The taxi driver slid the door shut. A small cross swung on the rearview mirror.

"So," the taxi driver asked Marcus, clearly toning down his accent. "Where we going?"

"A hotel."

"Any hotel?"

"Any."

"Hard finding free room this week. Lot of tourists running around."

"But you might be able to help me," Marcus leaned forward, "for the right price, yeah?"

"Right," the taxi driver smiled. "We find you a hotel, eh?"

"Good." Marcus sat back and put a hand on the box, feeling the slight hum and cool of refrigerant seep through to his fingers.

♦

Kikoru unzips a small black case in front of him. It reveals many sharp-edged tools. "You had the suit with you?"

Marcus leans back. How does one get out of a place like this? In a movie you overpower everyone, then walk out. But in reality any movement outside of a certain range results in an epileptic fit. That is what the cold, clammy thing on the back of his neck does. Another neat invention by the company they both worked for.

"Yes."

"You used it that night?" Kikoru's pale skin probably doesn't do well in the tropics, Marcus thinks. Are those freckles? What is a deadly interrogator doing with freckles? He empathizes with her pale skin. People belonged in buildings, with air conditioners, and computers around them, a web of communications. He hasn't checked email in weeks. That couldn't be healthy.

♦

The suit caressed Marcus. Smooth and durable, it protected him from the outside world. Mimicked colors played across the surface, blending him into the background. Invisible, he balanced on a six-inch-wide ledge stained white with seagull droppings and looked at the beautiful woman. Below, the ocean pounded at rocks, throwing salty spray up into the wind.

The beautiful woman gripped the solid plastic railing firmly, the cold wind persistently tugging at her kimono. She swung over the railing, the balls of her feet wedged between the spokes, and leaned out over the edge.

Eighty feet to go, Marcus thought. She would free-fall for quite a few seconds before she hit the rocks and exploded all over the uncaring but surprised seagulls. But she hadn't jumped. Instead, she hung there for a small eternity.

"Are you going to jump?" Marcus asked, and regretted it.

She almost lost her grip, then turned in his direction.

Trapped by his impulse, Marcus tipped his head in acknowledgment. As if this was no stranger than a chance meeting in the elevator. She could see him now that he wasn't just the shadow on the wall her eyes assumed. What were the chances of meeting a pretty woman on a hotel balcony here? Marcus hoped he was a mystery to her, shrouded, unattainable. Maybe that way she would desire him.

"I... it was just a little thrill," she said. But Marcus wondered what would happen if he tugged at her? Would it still be a thrill then? Or would she realize how precious her life was?

"Ever come out here just to watch the sun set?" she continued. "You know, it's beautiful, the colors on the horizon. I want to see the green flash."

"Yes," Marcus said. "I like sunsets."

He wondered if there was anyone in the room behind her. No. So say something. The wind tugged at her kimono, not quite strong enough to pull her over, but strong enough to give Marcus a glimpse of deeply tanned muscular thigh. The woman pulled herself back over the railing.

"My name is Jennifer, who are you?" she asked.

Marcus stood up, knowing that she could see the outline of his body emerge from the constantly shifting colors and hues that blended him back into the background. His face, he knew from mirrors, was a featureless mold with eyes.

"Marcus," he told her. He leaned over the railing and touched her fingertip. Through the suit he could feel her fingernail press against his skin. He slid his forefinger down towards the webbing between her fingers. A professional swimmer? Similar webs folded between her toes. Beautiful.

"I think I took too much LSD." She shivered.

Marcus leaned forward. "You have an address, a number, a last name?"

She smiled. "All of the above." She was actually flirting with him. His heart sped. "I'm glad I met you," she laughed.

If he could touch her with his real skin, underneath, with his right ring finger, the electrical contact would give her his virtual business card. But he couldn't.

He gave her one of his many email aliases. She walked back in to write it down, and Marcus thought it would be quite dramatic if he disappeared by the time she came back. He tiptoed across away, using the pads on the palms of his suit to adhere to the wall. They had suckers in them that kept him attached to things. Another piece of engineering he'd worked on. Hundreds upon hundreds of hours of mandatory overtime.

Marcus never had a life. He'd been born in a machine, progeny of anonymous parent donors who'd sold their DNA. He'd been a child of the company. Beholden to them for shelter, education, work. Until he ran away.

To touch a woman… he wondered what more than just her hands felt like. Her thighs?

◆

Marcus stepped into his small hotel room, and his second skin took on the hue of the walls: a vague off-white.

A small vat filled with saline sat in the bathroom. Marcus dug his thumb into the chest, and the milkiness covering his skin slipped apart. It revealed pale, irritated skin beneath.

Marcus dropped the suit into the saline, hooked it up to a nutrient flow with IV, then took a shower.

He walked out to the balcony in a robe. The air outside still tasted salty. In the cool windy night, Grenada could be seen as bearable. Marcus retreated back inside, turning the windows opaque with a command. The air conditioner thrummed, trying to bring the room down into acceptable temperature. On top of the controls sat his little Spider-Man figure, posed in red and blue. Its vacant white eyes looked straight ahead, ready for any action.

◆

Marcus feels a bead of blood trickle down his cheek and pause, then fall to his lap. It splotches his khaki shorts. More follow. Kikoru stares at him.

"It doesn't hurt," Marcus says. God, this is fun. They can't torture him. Just like in the movies, the hero can sit there and take it. This is science at its finest. They have no clue about the little things in his blood.

"You want to know more?" Marcus asks. He'd get through to Kikoru yet. Her employers, who were probably his employers, wanted to know why he, a mere lab scientist, stole the suit. After a life of thankless work, he'd known more about the security at his lab than anyone else. Why not? Marcus wanted to see the outside world for himself. Simple. He was tired of having it piped into him as official company media.

"I never hurt anyone," Marcus says when Kikoru cuts him again. Marcus wonders what it would take to fix his face now. Mexican black market, no doubt. He doesn't mind his destroyed face though. No one really cared for his looks anyway.

The knife flicks again. She wants him to keep talking, and Marcus is tired of resisting even if it doesn't hurt. Some of the things she has done to his skin are making him intellectually sick. Seeing his own skin peeled away and muscle tissue laid bare by a scalpel is nothing like TV.

♦

Speckled slightly to blend in with the building, Marcus made his way up from balcony to balcony. The sun shimmered as it was sliced by the razor-thin edge between the blue ocean and even bluer sky. Hand by hand he inched up. The slower he moved, the more invisible he stayed. Two hotel employees in bright Hawaiian shirts, the American idea of Caribbean clothing forced on them, passed underneath him.

"She was drunk off her ass…"

"No shit?"

"I kid you not. So I let them out the door, and she can't even hardly stand up, and I'm like 'have a happy hangover'…"

Their laughter dwindled away. Marcus slithered up onto the roof and looked around.

From here he could wait, and then pick someone out on the road, and kill them. Then he would leave, go back north, sell his stolen secrets, and retire rich. Everything would make sense then. He was sure of it.

♦

Kikoru stops cutting at his forearms. When she leans out of his way, the bright light makes Marcus blink. His eyes tear. He is getting tired and sleepy, but they won't let him nod off; they slap him awake every time. He's sure he's hallucinating, because Kikoru looks like his supervisor, and Marcus has jumped back in time all those years to when he's first assigned to the bio-camouflage department.

"What do you know about chromatophores, Marcus?"

"A little, sir." What he wants to tell his supervisor is "fuck off." Marcus had been working on a project for three weeks. He wants to be left alone. Instead he nods. "Squid have them. It makes them invisible."

"Nature's camouflage, yes. I'm transferring you out to a special project that works with them."

Marcus wants to object. In retrospect he's glad he doesn't. Because now he has the suit.

Kikoru leans forward and wipes blood off of Marcus's chin. "What is it that lets you handle all this? Something in your bloodstream?" Kikoru draws the small knife across his jaw, looking straight into his eyes. "You don't even flinch."

Marcus feels something gnawing at the pit of his stomach. Fear. It makes him queasy. "It's a nice trick, to not feel pain," Kikoru says. "I wish I had it. You should not have been so obvious. You should have screamed a bit." Marcus's stomach churns. Something awful is going to happen. "It is just too hard to believe that a little lab slave could become a steel-eyed bastard in a matter of weeks, isn't it?" She grabs his left hand and splays it out on the desk.

"Don't you want to hear the rest of the story?" Marcus asks.

"Not just yet. When I tell you to."

Marcus closes his eyes as his hand spasms. He no longer has a thumb. He keeps his eyes closed, thinking of air conditioners and email. Kikoru's breath tickles his ear. Marcus can feel the edge of a long blade on his right wrist.

"It would be so hard to write without this hand, Marcus... or take a piss. You'd have to learn how jack off with your left. And we can chop that off if you're still uncooperative. So tell me where the suit is?"

"I hid it," Marcus moans.

"After you killed. To see what it was like."

Marcus hangs his head. "I didn't kill anyone," he whispers.

♦

The gun needed assembly. Sitting behind the lip of the roof near a noisy ventilator, Marcus slowly snapped it together.

Sighting was academic physics. Like a computer game. He'd tested the gun on a watermelon from the same approximate distance. Just line it up, squeeze…

Marcus zoomed the scope in on a random person, their dark features scrunched up in irritation at something. The evening wind shook the palm trees. It was a woman with a basket of laundry balanced on her head. What life did she lead? A hard one? Her neck muscles strained from the weight. Her clothing was bright and well kept, but the shoes were old and tattered. Marcus suddenly understood that he had more choices and luxury then she would probably ever see.

He could feel the rough concrete under his belly even through the silky flesh hugging his body.

All he had to do was pull the trigger, and then maybe he would understand why people asked him to make things that killed other people. Because all these things he designed sat on his shoulders and had pressed down so hard, and for so long, something inside him had broken. Making them was as horrible as using them, right?

He had to know.

Pull the trigger.

It would be just like a game.

The plan stopped making so much sense. Marcus put the gun down.

♦

Two voices. Two females.

"It was never like that. I told him I was just a friend."

"And…"

"He started pawing me, he says 'sure we're just friends' and then he wouldn't let me go."

"He didn't…"

"Oh no, I kicked him in the sack."

"Ha." Laughter. Marcus smiled along, enjoying the voyeurism, but didn't move. Weight had been lifted from him.

"He hopped all over the place, he was still squeaking when I walked out the door."

The two women walked out of the store beneath him and started down the road. Marcus stretched and got up. In the alley, far back behind the dumpsters, he had his duster.

He lowered himself to the street and kept to the shadows until he reached the niche.

No duster. Marcus looked around, heart pounding. Nothing happened. He put a hand to the greasy wall, and he caught his breath. He hadn't been caught. But he needed the duster so he could walk back to his hotel. It would take forever to sneak back.

An old bag lady huddled against the gutter. She had the pea-green duster wrapped firmly around her.

"Lady," Marcus shook her awake.

Her eyes flickered open. She screamed. Marcus jumped back, and the bag lady staggered up.

"Joombie," she cried. Her gray hair swung in ratty clumps, matted with runoff rainwater from the gutter.

"I need my coat," Marcus said.

"I am a child of God, and you canna touch me!"

"… don't want to touch you, I just need the coat."

"I fear you not," she said, still holding herself to the wall protectively, eyes wide.

Marcus hesitated. "I need it back."

She threw an old beer can at him, grabbed a shopping cart hidden behind the dumpster, and tried to push it out of the alley. Outside, on the street, they would be seen, so Marcus stepped up behind her and pulled the coat from her.

"Please," he muttered. "I'm sorry."

The old lady struggled and tried to grab it back, but Marcus already had it. He leapt up onto the dumpster and scaled up out of her reach. She looked up at him with disgust. "Evil spirits stealing raincoats. It a sad thing."

Marcus held the duster to his side and climbed away.

His duster now stank of dumpster garbage, he found at the top. He ran his fingers over the concrete until the suit tore and he could bloody his fingers.

A super hero would never be in this situation. Some people had good causes. They never corrupted themselves. He wished he had that willpower and poise that attracted him to those slick books. Marcus thought he was a good person, but all his life he made things. Horrible things. He knew what they would do. Like flesh-eating bacteria. Someone would deploy it. If you made it, someone would use it. Every project killed thousands of abstract people.

Marcus wanted to actually see someone's eyes fade, and look right into that person, at that dying moment, so they could see that he did it, that he took their life, that he was directly responsible. It was his fault.

♦

Marcus still has his right hand. He wants his life. Kikoru wants the suit.

"Lance Aux Epines Bay," Marcus says.

Kikoru sits on the edge of the table, giving him a closer look at her muscled thighs. She has a mole, just a small thing, where the white skin meets tan. "Really."

"But that's a quarter of a mile of sand. The suit could be anywhere," Marcus continues.

"Ah."

"So you would have to take me there."

"Where you would no doubt try to make your spectacular escape." Kikoru laughs. "So you didn't have the balls to kill that woman?"

Marcus looks at a corner of the room. He failed. He still doesn't understand it, but he has a feeling Kikoru knows why all those people force him to create death in the lab.

"No," Marcus admits. He wasn't like the people he'd seen on TV. He had an empty, hollow feeling in the pit of his stomach.

◆

Marcus slipped back into his apartment, threw the duster in the trash, and peeled off the suit. The ripped fingers would heal quickly, the suit being designed tough. Almost combat tough. He watched it sit in the saline; an amorphous clear blob, sucking up nutrients.

Chromatophores. Squid had them. Octopi had them. Nature's underwater solution to camouflage. What developed military nation did not perceive a need for efficient camouflage? Cephalopod DNA was stripped free, replicated, grown, and fashioned with a new decentralized nervous system.

Before he could wash himself clean he noticed his laptop checking email through anonymous redialers and global-link bounces. It blinked "mail."

The almost jumper, three doors down, wanted to meet again. In her apartment.

Marcus's fingers trembled. Was she really interested in him? He sent a reply. Two hours. That was enough time for him to hide the suit. He had to bury it somewhere. On a beach. People would be hunting for him soon.

Two hours and several minutes later, he walked in through the door to her room. He was toweled dry, in fresh clothes with no sand on them. But Jessica did not stand alone. Two men in blue suits waited for him.

The man on the left fired a dart. Even with all the tiny bugs in his bloodstream, Marcus still slipped to the floor. He noticed that Jessica wore jeans. Cheap, loose-fitting blue jeans and a white top. And a gun pointed at him.

"They found your ticket," she said. "And thought that a pretty woman was a good way to bait a lab nerd with an invisible suit that could climb walls. I'm glad we found you, I've been fucking hanging off balconies for three weeks."

When he woke up, Marcus met Kikoru, and since then she'd never let him fall asleep.

♦

They all stand at the edge of Lance Aux Epines Bay. The sand crunches underfoot as they pass beach cottages, sea grape trees, and brush. The rain has driven tourists away. Only a solitary Rasta with a mane of dreadlocks lies against a coconut tree, a machete and coconut tossed casually to his side.

Behind Marcus are two guards with spades and guns. They think he will make a break for it. "It will be a good show if you try," Kikoru grins. She has even unfastened his cuffs.

Marcus keeps them all crunching down the beach, occasionally dodging the surf. He stops across from the small wooden jetty by the sagging volleyball net.

He lets Kikoru dig, but she doesn't find anything.

"Where is it, Marcus?"

"I don't want to die," he says, standing there with his bandaged hand. On the other side of Lance Aux Epines Bay lies a marina.

"Where?" Kikorus points at his arm, makes a chopping motion, threatening to cut it off.

"The second post, this side of it," Marcus says. The digging starts again. Marcus watches the two guards, and they return the favor. He scans the sand by the volleyball net, his possible escape route.

Kikoru sucks in her breath and reaches into the hole. The guards lean in to look. There it is, the suit, bedraggled and dying from lack of nutrients, shredded in part from a shove with a shovel. Kikoru swears when she sees the rip. She holds it in her arms, carefully transferring it to a duffel bag.

Then she turns and looks at him.

Marcus stares at the barrel of her gun, his knees weakening. He steels himself. Run, his instincts scream. But he knows it's useless. This isn't a movie.

"You wanted to know what it was all about." Kikoru grabs his hair and pushes him to his knees. "Here it is." She blows a pitying kiss and a single gunshot.

It is the loudest and most sudden thing that has ever happened to him. He screams. Sand bites his face from the small crater between his knees.

"You and I are nothing alike," Kikoru hisses. "Nothing!" Marcus hyperventilates, blinking sand from his stinging eyes.

She steps back.

"The lab expects you back tomorrow. Beg for their mercy and you can continue working for them. But if you run, they'll send me."

She leaves, and Marcus grabs the sand with his hands. Either way he is dead in some manner, he knows. Bonded to the company, or nine feet under. Either way.

But at least he's not Kikoru.

♦

He knows that now. He will run, most likely. He is no killer, in any way. When he runs he will take that away.

They can hunt him, but he has a piece of the ripped suit. He can make another, growing it slowly in his spare time. Stealing more. The next time they will be chasing a determined shadow.

For the first time, in as long as he could remember, Marcus is at peace.

The Devil's Tontine

Jesse Bullington

I have often said, and oftener think,
That this world is a comedy to those that think,
A tragedy to those that feel —
A solution of why Democritus laughed and Heraclitus
wept.

— Walpole

In the autumn of 1818, Helena di Bruno returned, for the first time since childhood, to the sprawling lawns, smiling gardens, and Gothic excesses of Strawberry Hill, in Twickenham. The oaks lining the road from London were as enflamed with color as the eighteen-year-old woman's brilliant tresses and, it must be said, her typically pearlescent cheeks, for her female companion in the coach had just issued a pronouncement of such base humor that Helena was genuinely shaken. Her mother had warned her that the Lady Anne Seymour had, in her dotage, become quite free with her tongue, but this degree of coarseness could hardly be presaged. Helena, having been raised in Sicily following an unexpected Continental inheritance, was, if not accustomed to such bawdy talk, sufficiently inured to it that it was much more the character of the one who voiced it than the statement itself which struck her. The outrageously ribald commentary concerned Strawberry Hill's much-celebrated shell bench overlooking the Thames, and in particular what the seat reminded Lady Anne of. The supposed similarity was not to any bivalve.

As a girl, when Helena spent the odd summer at Strawberry Hill under the guardianship of her mother's friend Lady Anne, she had always thought of her host as reserved; almost overly so, if such is possible for a woman. Yet now the graying sculptor, who had been widowed for nearly twice the sum of Helena's years, actively vibrated with unfettered exuberance, going so far as to plant herself beside Helena on her side of the coach and take the younger woman's smooth hands in her own strong, work-worn fingers as she enthused over the coming weekend, her most recent project, and her delight at once more having the daughter of such a dear, dear friend back in her company.

"Or, I suppose, in my *clutches*, as Horace would have had it," said Lady Anne, a twinkle in her eye. "It *is* Strawberry Hill after all, my young heroine."

"Forgive me, Lady Anne — but was Horace your husband?" asked Helena, her wide, limpid eyes staring into the narrower, darker orbs of her host.

"Horace was, like you and your mother, a dear friend of mine — why, I suppose in many ways my association with him mirrors our own, sweet Helena. He was my guardian, although for the duration of my adolescence, rather than just the fleeting holidays you and I spent together. Strawberry Hill was his child — he built it from the ground up."

"Really?" said Helena. "But I thought... that is, I thought it was, well, medieval, if not older? Parts of it, at least?"

"Oh, heavens no," said Lady Anne. "I shan't bore you with the architectural history of the villa, as that should take far more time than we have remaining on our journey, so suffice it to say the house is more homage than relic. Every battlement and stained-glass pane, each buttress and tower, was designed to lend the appearance of age, but the edifice is wholly modern."

"I see," said Helena, with an angelic smile. "As a girl I had such romantic ideas about it being the home to knights and ladies, a place as old as the earth of England. What a silly thing I was!"

"Not silly at all," Lady Anne assured her, patting the younger woman's knee through her skirts and letting her hand linger there as she reached across Helena to better shift the lace curtain away from the carriage window. "But look quick, there's York House, which you will see quite a bit more of once the weekend has concluded. I purchased it last year, as I told your mother, and it's become quite the cozy little home."

Even from a distance, this new estate was evidently grand, but much more staid in appearance than the fantastic Strawberry Hill, and Helena could not restrain herself from inquiring, "But why move just down the road, Lady Anne? Does Strawberry Hill no longer agree with your sensibilities?"

"Oh, I fear it agrees with my sensibilities now more than ever," said Lady Anne, but, for the first time since meeting Helena at the station, the effervescence seemed to have abandoned her voice, like a coupe of champagne left too long. "You shall inevitably learn, Helena, that sometimes a bosom that seemed so warm and comforting as a babe is, in actuality, stifling the very life out of you… but enough about real estate, child, I simply *must* bring you up to date on this weekend's diversion before we arrive. It promises to be most exciting, I assure you."

"Yes, I have been very much looking forward to riding," said Helena. "And whist, and sewing, and just taking long walks in the scented dusk, across hill and dale…"

"The scented dusk *indeed*," said Lady Anne, amused. Her teeth shone in the dim interior of the carriage. "I'm afraid we won't have much time for such pursuits until we're back in York House — this weekend involves sport of a very different character. I could not mention my true intentions in the letter, for a number of reasons, chief among them the fear of worrying your dear mother."

"True intentions?" said Helena, a thrill passing through her — it was all so dramatic! "And what could we possibly pursue that would worry Mama?"

"I could tell you stories that would curl those pretty locks of yours," said Lady Anne, running her fingers through Helena's hair. "But really it's nothing quite so devilish as you're probably imagining, a girl of your age grown to ripeness in the warmth of the Mediterranean sun. I'm sure you keep all sort of secrets, don't you?"

"I don't!" protested Helena, unsure if the thrumming in her breast was excitement or embarrassment. "Really, Lady Anne… *really.*"

"Such a pity," said Lady Anne, tut-tutting as the carriage went over a small bump. "Oh buttons, here we are and I haven't even begun to fill you in. So it goes. I shall give you the broadest of strokes now, then, and you and I shall convene after supper to explore the matter in further detail."

Something about the way Lady Anne licked her thin lips gave Helena pause, but then she caught sight of the high white wall of Strawberry Hill, and squinted through the grimy glass window as her host went on:

"You are not my only guest this weekend, Helena. We entertain three others, all gentlemen, and it should be quite the adventure. These three and I have been engaged in a… shall we say, *wager*, for some time now, and it seems that at long last a conclusion may be imminent. Most thrilling of all, you yourself may play a critical role!"

"A wager?" said Helena, looking away from the looming circular tower that rose up from behind a low partition at the front of the house. For a moment Helena had thought she espied a figure peering out over the ramparts, but, now that they had drawn up tight to the villa, she could no longer make out the silhouette. They had arrived. "With gentlemen, and I myself to play a crucial part? And you say Mama might not approve?"

"Don't fret, child, it's nothing so scandalous as I'm sure you're hoping," said Lady Anne with a wink. "Now, don't let on to our guests that I've told you even the little titbit that I have, yes? It will be our first secret, won't it?"

♦

Having been raised in a Papist locale with all its obligatory rituals, the very prospect of secrets filled Helena with anxiety, and, as each hour passed inside the fairy-book hallways and antiquity-cluttered chambers of Strawberry Hill, her unease grew. It was not that the three gentlemen whom Lady Anne introduced her to in the Round Room were blatantly furtive; quite the contrary: each seemed warmer and more open than the last. It was not even guilt at having forgotten, if only for a few hours, her grief over the untimely death of her beloved Uncle Matthew, and all the unpleasantness his passing had tilled up at home; for was not the express purpose of her being sent back to England to give her some time and distance to come to grips with her bereavement, and her mother's subsequent disclosure of familial secrets both sordid and shocking? If anything, her host and fellow guests offered welcome distraction from her conflicted emotions and the inexorable ruminations on sin and the soul that had plagued Helena ever since her mother's confession. Helena could hardly attribute to *them* her increasing sense of foreboding.

No, something about the very house itself seemed pregnant with clandestine promise. Helena put much stock in the reliability of history, took comfort in the eternal, and so the discovery that ancient Strawberry Hill, her juvenile sanctuary from the bustling modern streets of London, was in fact *artifice* subtly disquieted her. Here, where she had most hoped to find a respite from domestic deception, the very bricks had conspired to mislead her! If this place could deceive her where something as essential as its true age, its true *character*, were concerned, what else might it conceal?

"The Devil himself," a low, masculine voice purred in Helena's ear, startling her — she had been so caught up in her reverie that

she had failed to notice that the other two guests and Lady Anne
had ambled away to supper, leaving her alone in the Round Room
with the young dandy, Mr. Blackgrove.

"I beg your pardon?" asked Helena, moving away from the
forward fellow — with his jet tailcoat, overgrown fingernails,
and rakish mustache, his carriage bordered on the theatrically
diabolical.

"You were staring at him," said Mr. Blackgrove, motioning to
a small oil painting that hung above the garishly gilded fireplace.
The piece featured a small satyr reclining on a fallen log beside
a pond, playing his pipes and looking ever so merry. Yet now
that Mr. Blackgrove mentioned it, perhaps there was something
unsettling about the curl of his mouth, the way the dark frame
seemed to have seeped out of the blood-red wallpaper instead of
being hanged atop it...

"See, you're doing it again. And here I was led to believe that
you were a decent little Catholic girl, not the sort at all to be
seduced by the allure of the Archfiend. Such a pity... but, then,
he is a handsome fellow, and Nature will have her way, won't she?"

Helena turned to him, appalled by his presumption. Yet her
tongue betrayed her with its heavy clumsiness just as her eyes had
by returning to the painting unbidden, and, so, being unable to
either cleverly defend her person or impugn his, she flew from the
Round Room — in this course, her feet, at least, were obedient to
her wishes.

◆

Helena wandered the halls until her heart calmed enough for
her to again take rational stock of her situation, and, when she
did, she had to laugh at her own immaturity. Had her mother
not warned her expressly of the forwardness of certain young men
when they found themselves in the company of a vulnerable
woman? And the Anglican penchant for attacking her faith
was so firmly established as to approach caricature; so was Mr.
Blackgrove's blasphemous talk *truly* unexpected? She had no

doubt given him exactly what he sought to provoke, a childish response to his equally childish heresies. That was a mistake she mustn't make again — no, the next time he spoke to her in such a fashion she would be ready with a withering condemnation. Thus restored of spirit, she stalked through the overwrought corridors toward the dining room, delicate chin held high.

Yet when she joined the others, all of whom stood upon her late arrival, Mr. Blackgrove did not appear to be present, and in his place at the table was a decidedly antique gentleman whom Helena had never seen before. So much the better, she thought, half-hoping the fiend had fled the manor in shame at the prospect of Helena telling tales to Lady Anne. The latter half of this bisected hope was that she might give him a strong talking to herself. Whatever other reason could she have for being almost disappointed by his absence?

Lady Anne stood at the head of the table; to her left, the lean barrister Mr. Reeves; and to his left, the old man. Across from Mr. Reeves was Squire Lansdown, a florid, mutton-chopped fellow of advanced years and midsection. As Helena navigated around the long board to take her seat beside him, she became increasingly aware that everyone was watching her attentively. Queerer still, no one seemed to be making any move to introduce her to the older gentleman from whom she was to sit opposite. When she gained her chair and it became obvious that Squire Lansdown was waiting for her to sit down, she took the initiative. Either in England they did not put as much stock in civility as she had been led to believe or Lady Anne and her guests were unusual in this regard, as well as in manifest others.

"My name is Helena di Bruno," said she with a curtsy. "It is an honor to meet you, Mr....?"

"Blackgrove," Squire Lansdown hissed in her ear, mistakenly thinking that she was questing for a reminder rather than a proper introduction.

The invocation of the name sent a momentary shudder through the girl's breast, and before she could even make sense of her actions Helena heard herself asking, "I am charmed, Mr. Blackgrove, but might I enquire if your young relation shall be joining us? I had very much hoped to continue a topic of conversation he broached in the Round Room."

"What?" the hoary gentleman barked, making Helena flinch. He extended a gnarled hand, pawing at the tablecloth, and then produced a polished brass ear trumpet from where it had lain hidden behind a tureen. Positioning the device against the side of his doddering head, he offered her a watery smile and said, "I said, what? *Who?*"

"My ward's name is *Helena*," said Lady Anne, looking somewhat concerned herself. "You two met just earlier, in the Round Room... remember? Helena, pet, what on earth do you mean, *his younger relation*? If you're attempting to somehow flatter Mr. Blackgrove, then I should advise you to desist, as I'm afraid you're just going to confuse him — poor thing is deaf as a doorknob."

"What?" Mr. Blackgrove shouted again, causing Squire Lansdown and Mr. Reeves to both wince.

"But I thought..." Helena looked from one gentleman to the next and finally settled on Lady Anne's perplexed countenance. "Who was the young gentleman I was speaking with in the Round Room? He wore a mustache, and we were discussing the painting of the... satyr, the one hanging above the mantle."

"I fear you must have been dozing on your feet," said Lady Anne, smiling, so it seemed, at everyone at the table but Helena as she resumed her seat, the three gentlemen quickly following the older woman's lead. Mr. Blackgrove's ear trumpet clattered on the table as he seized up his soupspoon and, with vigor heretofore entirely alien from his character, began slurping up the beef bouillon as Lady Anne went on. "For one thing, I hope that neither Mr. Reeves nor Squire Lansdown takes too much offense to my alleging that there are no particularly young gentlemen staying at Strawberry Hill, and none of my staff wear a mustache. For another, I do not think poor Horace would appreciate being mistaken for a satyr. Why, he never even wore a beard."

"Speaking on behalf of Reeves, I can assure you no offense is taken," said Squire Lansdown warmly. "Only in contrast to Blackgrove are we anything but Methuselahs."

"Speak for yourself!" exclaimed Mr. Reeves, but seeing he had agitated Mr. Blackgrove, who was again clawing around for his ear trumpet, he hastily amended, "But nay, sweet ladies, of course I was only joking. No spring chickens here, only chicken hawks gone gray in the tail feathers, what?"

"What?" Helena was the only one still standing; feeling as though she had risen too quickly from a chair, she steadied herself against the table's edge. "I... but the young gentleman and I... the painting of that satyr, or devil..."

"Dear, the only painting in the Round Room is the portrait of Horace that Eccardt did for him, oh, sixty years ago," said Lady Anne patiently. "It's not a perfect likeness, I shall admit under duress, but it certainly isn't *demonic*. And I assure you, other than these three assembled gentlemen, all of whom you have met, there isn't another noble soul in the house. As I said, you must be exhausted from your journey, and were asleep on your feet, enjoying a dream."

"More like a nightmare, it sounds to me," said Squire Lansdown. "The notion of old Blackgrove young again, or, worse yet, one of his sons returned from the grave! To say nothing of the picture of Horatio replaced with Old Nick. It would blooming well scare the wits out of anyone."

"Well, the old boy would certainly approve of the curious circumstances," said Mr. Reeves, motioning at the ostentatious candelabras with a wine glass. "What was it he was trying to accomplish with all this sinister artifice? Gloomth?"

"Gloomth was indeed the word he was so fond of," said Lady Anne with an arch smile. "Somewhere between warmth and gloom, perhaps. Do sit down, Helena, you're making me nervous."

"Gloon," said the old Mr. Blackgrove, dropping his spoon into his empty bowl and licking the red soup from his red lips with his red tongue. With something like pity, his rheumy eyes stared at Helena, who felt herself gently swaying from side to side. The old man's features shimmered, as though seen through a pane of leaded glass, or glimpsed beneath a clear depth of swiftly flowing water. "Gloon, eh?"

"Something like that," said Lady Anne. "Now, I'm afraid I have to shift the topic to something quite a bit less fun than — are you feeling any better, dear?"

It took Helena a moment to realize that Lady Anne was addressing her, and that she was, in fact, no longer steadying herself against the dining room table, but instead lolling back on a settee in the older woman's private chambers. Lady Anne sat in a chair pulled close to Helena's head, leaning over her with matronly concern. The shift in perspective, from standing to recumbent, would have been quite shocking, even without the obvious transition in both time and space, and Helena closed her eyes and took a deep breath. The air felt thick and chill as fetid pond water in her lungs, and she gasped. In all her life Helena had never fainted — she rarely succumbed to maladies at all — yet now she felt beset by odd pricklings all across her body, and shifts in her internal equilibrium that were positively nauseating.

"Lady Anne," Helena finally managed. "I have taken ill."

The laughter of the old woman was like small coins tinkling in a collection plate. "Oh, I should say so. You've been poisoned, dear Helena."

"Poisoned!" the word tasted bitter and strong as undiluted amaro on the girl's tongue, and she gave a soft moan, scarce able to believe it. "How?"

"The tea we had when we first arrived, before going down to meet the gentlemen. A most powerful philter, first causing hallucinations in the Round Room, and then your collapse at supper."

"Am I dying?" asked Helena, a hand going to her throat and finding that the silver crucifix her mother had given her was missing. "Oh, saints have mercy, how could this happen?"

"You won't die," said Lady Anne, putting a cool cloth against the young woman's brow. "Of that you have my strict assurances. As for how it happened, I should think it was obvious — I administered the drug to your souchong."

"Why?" Helena moaned as she rocked on the tides of her inner turmoil. There was a tapping sound coming from the ceiling that sounded like a billy goat being led over a wooden bridge, but she pushed the sound away, told herself it was another symptom of her poisoning. "*Oh, why?*"

"To buy us some time, of course," said Lady Anne, smiling in the candlelight of her boudoir and scooting her chair even closer to Helena's couch. "If I had not, rest assured one of the others would have, and with something quite a bit more potent, I don't doubt. Now listen, my pet, and I shall explain everything…"

♦

The Account of Lady Anne Seymour

There were five of them, as I understand it — my guardian Horace, the three gentlemen you met at dinner, and another friend of Mr. Blackgrove, whom everyone just called "Monk." This was near the end of my guardian's life, although, not being present myself, I cannot tell you when exactly it took place. What I can tell you is that these five men were each of an exceptionally brilliant turn of mind, and gathered in the autumn here, at Strawberry Hill, for a weekend's diversion… not unlike our gathering *this* weekend, in fact, and that is no coincidence, my dear.

Do you know what a tontine is?

Well, that's half-right, in general, but theirs was quite a bit different. Do not tax yourself trying to fill in all the blanks in your compromised state; I shall explain directly.

Now, usually in a tontine each member will make an investment into a collective fund, and thereafter they are paid out an annuity, yes? I believe certain governments in your region have backed such investment plans in the past. Now, this is all well and good, and frightfully dull, but there is another sort of tontine, one where a beneficiary is named as the recipient of this annuity, rather than the investor — oh, I can see by the way your eyes are lolling in your pretty head that I am boring you into an early grave, so let us cut directly to the heart of the matter.

My guardian, Horace, along with the four gentlemen I have just mentioned, entered into an exceptional arrangement. It was proposed, as a diversion, that each contribute to a small, private tontine, with each of the five members putting in something of great worth, and all agreeing that rather than an annuity to be paid out to each of them, the entire sum of wealth should be awarded to a single beneficiary. Ah, I see I shall have to fetch the smelling salts if I carry on like this — take this story as an example, Helena, and then we shall return to the specifics:

Five soldiers fight side by side in a bloody war. They are at the front, in the losing army, so the odds of even one of them making it out alive are very long, to say naught of *all* of them surviving. Since none of them have families who might inherit their meager moneys, they agree to pool all their savings together, and whoever survives the war shall inherit the lot of it. If more than one lives, well, perhaps they will divide it amongst the survivors, or perhaps they shall put the sum into an account where it shall gather interest until one outlives the rest; it scarcely matters for my point — here we have a tontine where instead of an annuity, the investment is returned, with interest, to that member who fulfills a certain criteria. In this example, staying alive.

Now, to hear Horace tell the story, he and Mr. Blackgrove were old acquaintances, and they gathered here with Squire Lansdown, Mr. Reeves, and this Monk character to waste a weekend in whatever fashion they might, when Mr. Blackgrove suggested that they enter into a tontine. Well, fine and good, said my guardian, but as he was already a very wealthy fellow, as were each of his guests, what could be profited by such a thing? A tontine is scarcely a thrilling game of chance, after all, as it is expressly designed to grow with *agonizing* slowness, so that a tiny fortune may become a very small one, as it were. It was all very dull, in Horace's opinion, and a gauche business at that...

Ah, but wait! Mr. Blackgrove was not proposing a mundane investment scheme — he suggested that each member contribute something quite a bit more interesting than mere money into the kitty, something that would pay out no annuity at all, but instead be returned, eventually, as a total sum to a single shareholder...

More interesting, that, but there remained the question of what rare valuable might be staked on the tontine, and the even more pressing question of how a single recipient should be determined. As mentioned, such tontines often pay out to the last living member, so why in heavens would my sweet Horace, oldest among those assembled, agree to enter into a plot that he had only the slimmest chance of actually benefitting from? To this point Mr. Blackgrove was ready with yet more intriguing answers:

If the conditions of the tontine did not resolve themselves within the lifetimes of the original members, the shares in the tontine would revert to their heirs. Thus, I stood to benefit even if Horace passed before the tontine concluded, and as he always sought to care for me, well, you might be able to glimpse the appeal, especially as the old dear was frightfully concerned with my... Well, I did raise a little Hell in my youth, as the profane parlance goes. Now, naturally, we come to the question of what these mysterious conditions might be...

Sin — you of all people believe in the concept, I don't doubt? The eternal dilemma, of course, is how to go about committing as much sin as possible without paying the eternal price once you've had your fun.

Oh, don't look so pale, the dose I gave you should be well worn off by now, and surely a girl of your age has at least heard the rumor that sinning can be agreeable? Why else would anyone take part in it, hmmm?

Now, it is well known that there are ways around damnation, no matter how vile the sin, how iniquitous the sinner, but each and all of them rely on repentance, and repentance requires one thing, doesn't it?

Guilt? Oh, pet, you are such a dear, sweet little angel. Guilt, indeed!

It requires *time*, Helena, repentance requires time to repent, of course. Leaving aside all the other ways and means, as it were, let us look to your Roman example — you can commit all the atrocities known to man and savage, yet so long as you take the time to repent and do what the priest says, your soul is washed clean as a kitten's... but commit a fraction of those sins, only to find yourself suddenly in mortal peril without a last confession waiting in the wings, well, I don't think I need to tell you of all people what happens next.

Enter Mr. Blackgrove with his intriguing twist on the tontine. It seems he was something of a diabolist — really, child, don't look so appalled, they're a farthing a dozen here in England, and much thicker on the Continent. As I was saying, Mr. Blackgrove claimed that he had received intelligence from a certain entity that shall remain nameless that Lucifer far prefers the soul of a good man to that of a dyed-in-the-wool villain, and to that end might be enticed to make quite the offer in order to secure such a prize. In fact, the disparity in worth between the soul of a moral man and that of an impious one might be said to equal five times the value... if you follow?

No? Ah well, let me make it perfectly clear. All five members of the tontine agreed that while sinning is a good deal of fun, it simply wasn't worth the risk of eternal damnation. Yet what if the chances were stacked in their favor? What if instead of mortal sins carrying the full weight that term allows, they could be assured that the Devil himself might absolve them, rewarding their evil behavior with the promise that He would lay no claim to their soul, provided they sinned more than their fellows? Someone would have to pay, naturally, but what if it wasn't the sinner himself? What if it was another party who took on the spiritual stain?

And here we discover the terms of the tontine. Each man agreed, in writing, that from that day hence he would devote himself to sowing sin and iniquity rather than attempting to foster good will and works, on the condition that only one of the five shareholders would be held accountable for the sins of the group. That culpable individual would be determined by whoever of the five committed the *least* amount of sin in his life.

Simple, yes? Everyone puts his sins into the tontine, and in the end only one will receive the sum — the greatest sinner of all is absolved, the three runners-up likewise have their slates wiped clean, and only that member who failed to match the depravities of the other four will be damned. Thus the Devil gets one soul more than He might otherwise have, for even the satanically predisposed Mr. Blackgrove could have found salvation before his end, and four out of the five players in the tontine are allowed to revel in the pleasures of sin without ever having to pay the price. Everyone wins. Well, *most* everyone, anyway…

Whatever do you mean? Well yes, certainly, in theory the Devil *might* get more souls if we merry band of sinners just went about our wicked business without the tontine, but then again we might all repent on our deathbeds, as is the custom in all Christian lands, and the Devil prefers one absolute to five maybes. And of course he likes a sporting wager best of all. As for how in Heaven the Old Enemy manages to absolve the other four souls in spite of our crimes, well, that's a debate I'll leave for the theologically minded members of our little club.

Now, the question you should be asking, the most pertinent query to your concerns, does not involve the how or the why of the matter, but the when: as in, *when* does this tontine conclude? Whenever all five of the original members died, certainly, but there was an additional possibility, one that I have already hinted at. This condition involved the heirs — if any of the five members had a successor who, in full appreciation of the risk, decided to take part in the tontine, it should be extended. Consequently, when Horace informed me of what he had done, suffering some sort of near-death remorse at his participation, I suppose, I naturally leapt at the opportunity — how often is one presented with such a delicious prospect, after all? This was some twenty years past, and

I had only perpetrated a very small portion of the crimes against Man and God that I should have liked to.

Which brings us to you, my dear, and your so-called *Uncle Matthew*. Oh yes, I know — I've always known!

Now, now, stop your blubbering at once — I know the wound is fresh, my little bird, but you must contain yourself. Here, have some of this sherry. Go on, I'll wait.

For what it is worth, you should know that I counseled your mother to be frank with you, rather than concocting that absurd deception of hers. I said, "Tell the child she is illegitimate but well loved, and she will trust you always, but invent a husband and father who died before she was born, and she will never believe you again, once the truth comes out, as it always does." How much happier you all might have been, had she listened to me; you, your mother, Mr. Lewis… But I suppose it is all water over the dam or under the bridge at this juncture, and, even if he never acknowledged his true relation to you, he did see you comfortably looked after, so why all this bitterness?

Ah, and here I fully agree with your assessment: I *cannot* understand, but that is neither here nor there. As for the matter at hand, what *you* cannot be aware of is that in addition to being a member of the Dutch Parliament, a notorious author, and a landowner in Jamaica, your father was also a member of the tontine I have just spoken of — "Monk" is what we all called him. I shall give you a moment to soak it all in. Have some more sherry. That's a good girl.

Of course you perceive where all this is going? No? Wait, wait, don't try to stand, the philter I gave you will have —

See, I told you, Helena — your legs won't have their strength back just yet, so you may as well hear me out. It's *important*.

Ah, so you *do* see where all this is going? Well, before you give me a definitive answer, I think there's something you should consider…

Well, I say it might make a difference, and a remarkably large one! You will hear me out, you cheeky girl, of that you can be assured. Oh, for Heaven's sake, this again? Let me fetch you another handkerchief, you mewling thing…

Now, as I said, there is something to consider, and it is this: Horace, bless his heart, *tried*, but he really was awfully old-fashioned, and, if I hadn't taken over for him, his immortal soul might already be in serious hot water, if you understand. Since adding my name to the tontine I have sinned a great deal, believe you me — don't think you're the first pretty young thing I've poisoned in my day. Fine and good, you say, but so what? Mr. Blackgrove, though senile, is as despicable as a dozen younger men, and as for Squire Lansdown and Mr. Reeves, well, I frankly don't think you want to know. That brings us to your father, sorry, *uncle*, Matthew.

It seems the Monk had a change of heart, and tried to abandon the tontine and all its wonderful, transient rewards in hopes of saving his immortal soul. The last years of his life were devoted to such worthy causes as humanizing the conditions of his slaves in Jamaica, recanting the blasphemous writings of his youth, securing the futures of any bastard offspring he sired during his wild days — you can testify to that last especially, I think. The problem is that the Devil is in the details, isn't He? Our dear Monk thought he could renege on a contract, but as one who has studied it at length will assure you, there is simply no way out — he signed his name, in blood, and that, as they say, is that. He must honor the terms, and what with his wholesale abandonment of sin for the last decade of his life, there is no doubt whatsoever that he has sinned the least of those current members of the tontine.

Which means, plainly, that if no heir takes up his cause, his will be the soul that pays the price for my sins, and those of Horace, and all the rest… that hardly seems fair, does it, that a man as good and noble as your father should be damned for all eternity, while the rest of us are admitted to Heaven? And all because he had no child who loved him enough to take on the sweet duty of sinning without consequence… such a pity!

♦

Helena reeled, and not solely from the toxins still swirling in her blood. She gawped at the blithely smiling Lady Anne, and wondered if this, too, was all but a fever dream, some phantasmal sight intruding on her reality. Yet the room's chill penetrated her haze, a pinching in her distressed vitals that told her this was no nightmare from which she might awaken. The story had sent Helena through a grotesque series of emotional stirrings, and now, late in the evening and scarcely recovered from a poisoning, she somehow felt more awake than ever before; perhaps the most awake she had ever been in her entire life. Slowly she rose on the couch, fixing her eyes on Lady Anne's.

"Even if everything you say is true," said Helena. "I believe God will forgive my father. He repented, just as you admitted."

"I'm not sure I said that at all," said Lady Anne slyly. "He certainly abandoned his debaucheries, at least for the most part, but what if on that last voyage to his plantations he succumbed to some perilous temptation? What if he never confessed his sins to a priest according to the strict requirements of your Church? What if many things, my pet?"

Helena had nothing to say to that, dropping her eyes to the floor, feeling both doubt and a shame at that doubt which pierced her to the very core of her being…

"Now, what I'm proposing is quite simple," said Lady Anne, leaning back in her chair. "Take on your father's role in the tontine. That way, if you commit enough sin, which is to say, *have enough fun*, then you and your father will both be assured a place in Paradise. Or refuse this offer, willingly condemn your loving patriarch, and see if you muster the courage to confess this cowardice of yours to one of your hypocrite priests before your own demise… lest you see your father again in a very disagreeable post-mortal reunion."

Helena said nothing at all for an exceedingly long time, considering all the odds and ends, marveling at the hideous, diabolical turn her holiday had taken. Sifting through her complex feelings surrounding her mother's revelation that Uncle Matthew was actually Helena's father, and that he had unexpectedly died, was one matter; all *this* was something else entirely.

"I wouldn't even know how to go about sinning, let alone to such a degree," said Helena.

"You're off to a good start, lying to my face so shamelessly," said Lady Anne.

Helena blushed but did not look away from her temptress, carrying on with her protests of reason since her heart-born objections were peculiarly absent: "You said yourself that everyone else in the tontine has already committed a catalog of crimes beyond reckoning. So even if I were to accept this offer, what hope would I have of outmatching them this late in the game, and saving my father... and myself?"

"Come, come," said Lady Anne, patting the younger woman's knee. "It's not as dire as all that. It would be an absolute pleasure to tutor you in such things, especially since we'd be getting off on the right foot — I could look out for you, and you could look out for me. 'Do not trust all *women*,' as it were, 'but trust women of worth; the former course is silly, the latter a mark of prudence.' Together we could assure that it is one of the other three who comes up short."

"But how?" protested Helena, feeling a gulf open beneath her feet just by asking the question, and *almost* delighting in the sensation of teetering at the brink.

"It's simply done," said Lady Anne. "That's the beauty of sin. Old Blackgrove has accumulated quite the hoard of offenses, admittedly, but he's on his last legs, and unlike my Horace or your Monk, he has no one to take up the torch once he topples — I fatally poisoned his elder son years ago, and either Reeves or Lansdown arranged the assassination of the younger just last Christmas. Once Blackgrove goes, it's simply a matter of living a life long enough, and atrocious enough, to surpass him. Considering what an early start you're getting, that shouldn't be very difficult at all."

There was a very long silence, and Helena took another sip of sherry. She almost asked again about the young man she had seen in the Round Room, but thought better of it. Finishing her glass, she found she had grown to appreciate the cloying taste of the stuff.

Casting her doe eyes again to Lady Anne, she said, "I would have to start right away, wouldn't I?"

"Immediately," said Lady Anne with a wolfish grin.

"And I couldn't take the risk of Mr. Blackgrove committing even one more sin, could I?"

"I concur, it would be most imprudent to take such a chance."

"Would you..." Helena licked her lips. "Would you lend me some of whatever you put into my tea? A stronger dose, this time?"

"A much stronger dose, just to be sure," agreed Lady Anne. "Shall I fetch it for you? I understand from his valet that Mr. Blackgrove has trouble sleeping, and always welcomes a warm glass of milk to help him fall back under."

"And the tontine contract," said Helena, a warmth spreading through her as though a thousand snuffed candles spontaneously reignited in her breast. "I should like to read it over, and sign it, before delivering his soporific, or doing anything else."

As Lady Anne hastened to fetch what was asked of her, Helena lay back on the couch and closed her eyes, a smile bending her Cupid's bow as she listened to the sound of rain tap-tap-tapping on the vaults and pinnacles of Strawberry Hill.

The Plan *or* You Must Remember This

Tania Hershman

Some people can recall what happened on almost every day of their lives. Unlocking their secrets could shed light on the way all our memories work.
— *"They Never Forget," Kayt Sukel,*
New Scientist, 20 August 2012

10.

Look at the Memory Man run! There he goes! We knew he'd run. We didn't know when exactly or in which direction, but we knew. Doors were left slightly ajar, locks not quite locked. Yes, we're recording it, we're videoing him. Of course we are, for later analysis — of his speed, direction, gait, the prevailing wind. Go, Memory Man, go! How will he remember this? We won't be able to ask him, not this time. Look at him, you've got to be impressed with it all, at his age. His knees look quite stiff, oops, he's stumbled. But Memory Man picks himself straight up, not even looking behind to see if we're following. Of course we're not following. That would defeat the purpose. He has to go. It's his time to go now. Farewell, Memory Man, we'll see you soon. We hope we've left you with… well, if not happy, then at least new. Memories. Ones you won't. Well, you don't, do you? Forget.

9.

He sits quite still now, he doesn't fidget like he did at first. He knows. We know. We all know. He is our Memory Man, we have him. For the moment, anyway. We are in no doubt as to his skills. And we are in no doubt how we can use his skills. Imagine if we had to train someone to be like him instead? Imagine how long that would take! We can't imagine it, we sit around in the evenings, with our beers and we laugh at how we might have had to contemplate, to work up a schedule, to fiddle with the subject, fiddle being used here purely technically, ha ha! We think we could have done it, we have faith in our skills, we're highly trained ourselves of course. But the paperwork to fill in for permission, we yawn at that, we raise our arms high, we slap wrists and palms. Our Memory Man saved us so much form-filling, thank you Memory Man, are we glad we found you!

8.

Our second Day Out is a success, we decide. Memory Man performs well, "above expectations," we will write later on the evaluation. We take him to more complex locations, "greater association of variables," we will write later. We record it all, as per usual, audio, video, thermal, all of that. We are also testing new equipment. Well, he is our new equipment too, ha ha! We are testing the BWM, we will use Memory Man to calibrate it, now we know we can trust him. As far as we can throw him, eh! He's too heavy for that, of course. We did think about some kind of propulsion… No, that was just one of those late-night, beer-tinted ideas, the ones you remember in the morning, hazy, and think, Now why would we even suggest…! Not in the report. That one's been ditched.

7.

He's had a bad day. And when Memory Man has a bad day, we all have a bad day. We understand now, can't ask about the wife. Don't mention the war, ha ha! The weeping was, well, disturbing. Memory Man's hands had to be bandaged, just gently, just for a while, after that. We might not put that in the report. Although when others come to examine our findings, they will understand the adversity. They will understand we're not working with chimps here but people, a real person. Bad days happen. We nearly went in there, thought about a hug, when he went on about her death. But we stay away from dying, not a good idea, taints the objectives, outcomes all messed up, you understand. We do feel bad for him, we all said later that night, with our beers. Imagine never forgetting that. Imagine it always being right there, in your head. And we had a minute's quiet, all of us thinking of the thing we wouldn't want to remember the way Memory Man can, in all its detail, vivid like this morning. Then we shook our heads, opened another beer.

6.

He doesn't mind the MRI machine. We were concerned, some people hate small spaces, the banging noises, all that. And if Memory Man had been one of them, we would have been sunk. Truly Titanic. But he's calm as we slide him in, calm as he's always been, helped along of course by a little… That won't go in the report, of course. But after we discovered, through some trial and error, that it didn't impair his abilities, we now use it without a second thought. Once he's in and it's all turned on, we're peachy, good to go. We ask some of the same questions, check against previous answers, he's spot on, exactly. We're still a little freaked out by how he does this. Then we ask new ones, based on his time with us as well as a few more world events thrown in there. And we watch what happens in Memory Man's brain. It's fascinating. Really. Our paper will be… Okay, fine, we mustn't get ahead of ourselves. Still a ways to go.

5.

We have several almanacs to hand, and the online data, of course, to cross-check. He gets a little irritated after a while, "subject tired, three hours perhaps too much," we will write in our evaluation. Memory Man, which is what we call him in our writing, it has to be anonymous, of course, keeps asking why all the focus on elections. Ha ha, we say, we're trying to predict the next one! It's a joke, but he doesn't seem to find it funny. He gives all the right answers, who was voted in and where and when, down to the hour sometimes, it's really quite amazing. We're in awe, we say over beer in the evening, in the common room. Awe, literally, we say, and then we try and test our own memories. Can't remember what we had for breakfast, and we laugh! He's truly exceptional, our Memory Man. Truly.

4.

Today's the day! He arrives on time, we had been worried, of course. He didn't have to come, did he? We may have explained it all, national security, finger to nose and all that, it's for your country. But still, how many citizens are civic-minded these days? It's a dying trait, love for one's country, patriotism, hijacked by the loonies. Loonies in the technical sense, of course, ha ha! He looks nervous, which is normal, we're a group, we have each other, he's just him. Alone. No spouse, children, not many friends, real friends, which is useful, frankly, for our purposes, although we don't say so. Not in our report. We make him tea, we make a fuss of him, we make a show as if we're telling him everything he needs to know, although of course that would be impossible. We see his breathing slow, his pupils alter, he's trusting us now. Phew, we say later over beers. It could have gone bad from the start! But he settles in, tells us to hit him with whatever we've got, he can handle it! That's quite funny, really, given what we... We laugh about that later too. "Hit him," we say, ha ha!

3.

We like pubs. In objective terms, of course. Generally speaking. They contain such a wealth of material, behaviours, conversational traits. We couldn't model these artificially, they're chaos at its best. And the range of beverages and snacks helps too, ha ha! We spot him quite quickly, the photograph obtained is fairly accurate. We zoom in, note down what he's drinking, how he sits, but the most important is audio, of course. He doesn't begin right away. They ease into it, some jokes, although we can see he's not the funny man, he's not the comedian, it's stilted. He has his thing and it's not humour. When they start, we look at each other and we are impressed. Mightily. Whatever they come up with, he can answer. His memory is incredible! We wonder if he's faking it, of course. But he doesn't know that we're… observing. This is his usual, this is Monday night down the Dog and Duck. There's money involved, small wagers we observe. But it's not about that. Not really. It's pride. We see it on his face. This is his Thing. The rest of his life, we know, is not fulfilling in any way. Monday nights are what keep him going.

2.

We review the reports at lunchtime, over Wednesday pasta salad. There are several possibilities, we are delighted, there is enough to begin at least. Two women, one man, all in middle age, spread around the country. Both women are married, several children, active lives, which makes it a little tricky. They would be missed, we chuckle over cold pasta. But the man, he lives alone. He could be the one. We decide he will be our first, might be the only, who knows how many of them there are? This is new to us. But the fact that we found three is promising. We didn't know if we'd find any at all, it was a hypothesis, something we threw out there, made it sound plausible enough for funding. We high-five each other in the cafeteria. Then we go back to the lab and work on our protocol.

1.

It's always defects, we tell our boss. We study what doesn't work well, but what about if it works really really well? Our boss looks intrigued so we press on. Super-memory, we say. We've heard of it, just rumours. Think of what we could... We don't need to finish our sentence, our boss is nodding, agreeing, signing our funding application. Yes! we say when we are out of his office. Then we are a little sheepish because really, it's just rumours, we don't know if we'll find anything, anyone. We make our plans, get in touch with our investigators, send them out with vague instructions. We hope. That's what we have right now. Hope.

Protector of Ascheli

Ekaterina Sedia

The day of the funeral was a haze for me; not because of the feverish activities of the manor-house inhabitants and Gesur's anguish, but because I had to put the steel net over my head. It was the custom of the Protectors: on occasions such as this, we cease our eavesdropping on the thoughts of others, and become as blind as the rest, wrapped in the same grief as they, our senses extinguished by steel. Not that anyone would dare to plan treason on such a day, but the family showed their mourning by waiving protection, as if earthly cares did not exist for them anymore.

The main hall was prepared, and the body of the old lord, Gesur's father, lay on the dais in the center of it, amidst the bowls of fruit and fragrant spices. The laity and the clergy, the merchants and the peasants, came through to pay their respects. I stood with the rest of the family, my face hidden by a black veil on Isera's insistence. Gesur's wife thought that the sight of me would be too unsettling for the unaccustomed. I let it slide, and peered at the crowd, only my own thoughts in my head for a change. I wondered if Taine would make an appearance.

I stole a glance at Gesur. He bore his devastation well, his young face expressing no weakness but only appropriate sorrow. His hands, stained black, hung by his sides: the family members were not supposed to touch anything the day of the burial, and the ground charcoal revealed any violation of this tradition.

Isera's beautiful face showed no emotion, but that was her custom. I noticed a smudge of black on her temple and smiled under my veil — she could not resist the temptation to fiddle with her hair, and now her vanity was visible to all. An embarrassment, but a minor one. It would've been tenfold worse if it were Gesur. Or me.

Gesur leaned to whisper into my ear. "Are you well, Jana?"

"Of course, my lord," I said. "Do you see your brother anywhere?"

"No." His gaze swept over the crowd again. "Do you think he will come?"

"I think so, my lord."

Isera overheard, and her small mouth twisted. "Don't listen to her, Gesur. She does nothing but harp and portend a disaster."

"It's not a disaster, Isera," Gesur said, his gray eyes as gentle as always. "I want to see Taine."

I nodded. "It is commendable, my lord. In any case, I do not think he will challenge your claim. In the eyes of the city, you are our rightful lord — you have been for the past three years."

"Thank you." Gesur's face clouded with the memory of his father's long illness. "Still… if this is what Taine wants…"

"Nonsense," Isera interrupted. "He has no claim. He threw away his birthright; he can't reclaim it now."

The three of us fell silent. Even with my handicap, I could guess what Isera was thinking. I could smell her fear through the heavy fragrance of the spices. Gesur was trickier, but, in the ten years that I was the Protector of the Ascheli family, I had never detected any duplicity or dishonor in him. If there ever was a good man, it was Gesur. This is why it was so difficult for me to contemplate killing his brother; it was even harder to do so knowing that Taine was the one I owed my life and my position to. I was about to betray the family I had sworn to protect and to repay kindness with cruelty. Still, there are circumstances that warrant extreme means.

I looked at the stream of people flowing by. I had not seen Taine since he left fifteen years ago, before I even became the Protector of his family. If it weren't for his activity on the eastern front, it would be easy to think him dead. But every year barrelfuls of Limar soldiers' skulls arrived, testifying to his military success, so I had to presume that he was alive enough not to miss his father's funeral.

I saw him the moment he crossed the threshold, and smelled him a heartbeat later. The man was huge and filthy — the animal skins that made his cloak were poorly cured, and stunk. The smell of horse sweat clung to him like a second skin, and his hair was matted like the fur of a mangy dog. A patch of leather covered his right eye, and a long scar ran from under it, and across his cheek, all the way down to his jawline. His nose was broken — no, crushed, with intent and malice, as if someone struck it with the pommel of a sword.

Isera pinched her nose shut, and breathed through her mouth. "This is just horrible," she said to me. "Who is it?"

"I think it's Taine," I said.

Gesur nodded. "It's him all right. He's changed."

Of course he has, I thought. He left home a civilized youth. Now, he plowed through the crowd, his massive shoulder cleaving it like the ship's prow cleaves water. He approached the dais and sunk to one knee, head bowed for a moment. He was close enough to make my eyes water. He stood, and approached us.

"Gesur." He slapped his brother on his shoulder. "You've grown."

Gesur smiled. "You too. I am glad you've come."

Taine grinned. He was not a handsome man to begin with, and his lopsided smile made him look deranged. "But I fear I've offended your wife's sensibilities."

I had to smile at that — two black marks were clearly visible on Isera's chiseled nose. As Gesur introduced her to Taine, she tried her best to smile. Despite his appearance, he had a carefree way about him, and seemed genuinely pleased to see Gesur. I decided to delay my judgment until my net was off, but for now he seemed to be no danger to his brother.

My thoughts turned back to murder: the sheer size of him made me apprehensive. I chased my concerns away — no one said that I had to defeat him in combat; poison would do. Or a carefully placed word. After all, I was appointed to this job because I had a certain power in this family.

♦

On a second thought, poison.

We had returned from the barrow where the body of Gesur's father was interred. The visitors had left, and we all hurried to do whatever restored sanity to our lives. Isera ordered the servants to get the place cleaned, to have the funeral wreaths removed, and to take care of Taine. Gesur kicked off his boots, grabbed a bottle of brandy from the pantry, and settled on a low padded bench by the hearth in his sitting room. I took off the steel net, and sat next to him.

"Join me for a drink?" he said, pouring a second glass.

I nodded, and felt the house coming alive around me. The thoughts and worries of its inhabitants stretched like silver spiderwebs, and I sat in the center of them all, testing each for the hints of danger. There were none — just Isera's annoyance and fatigue, and Gesur's heartbreak. Taine was too exhausted for coherent thought.

I took the glass Gesur offered, and put my free hand on his sleeve. I'd known him since I was ten and he was thirteen — I could afford such familiarity. "It'll be all right," I said. "Every day will move you further away from today, and it won't be as bad."

He blinked. "Thanks, Jana. I guess I'll just have to wait." A warm wave rose inside of him, wrapping me like a blanket. "I'm just so glad Taine is home."

"I know, my lord." I lifted my veil and drank, basking in the relief of having my vision back, in the comforting thoughts of the household. And in Gesur's company.

"Funny," Gesur said. "He's my brother, but I hardly know him." He smiled. "You, on the other hand, are not a relative, but I know you better than anyone. You're like a sister to me."

"I feel the same, my lord." It wasn't untrue — I did love him like a brother. I had to settle for being his Protector instead of his wife, but it was enough. Still, my heart raced as I sat close to him, my hand on his arm, my knee almost touching his.

It was not a good time to swoon, and I forced myself to think straight. "My lord," I said. "The people have been talking about your brother."

He gave me a wounded look. "What people?"

"Your people. Everyone. I picked it up when I patrolled the city yesterday." Of course, I was not going to tell him about the old men of the merchant guild who bemoaned the harm Taine had done to his family and to Limar by his war. "They fear that his… military inclinations will scare off the Ascheli's allies. If you could talk to him about cessation of hostilities, it would strengthen your position."

Gesur frowned. "My father sent him to Limar."

"Your father is dead." I noticed the pained look on his face and bit my lip. "Sorry, my lord, but he is. You are our new lord, and you can tell your brother to withdraw the Ascheli army."

"The lordship is not yet decided. Taine has a claim too."

"This would be bad for everyone." I weighed my words. Gesur was too good to think of himself, but he would think of his people's interest. "People like you. They know you. Lord Taine may be a good ruler, and he may not be. But people fear him, and will have a hard time accepting his rule instead of yours. I will not be surprised if it causes a rebellion. I implore you to stand for your right, my lord. For everyone's sake."

"You're asking me to turn against my own brother?"

I shook my head. "No, my lord. But as your Protector, I must see that no harm befalls you."

"You're Taine's Protector too."

I took a long swallow. The brandy burned my throat, and I suppressed a cough. "I know that. However, if the family is at odds, even the Protector must take sides."

Gesur stood and paced across the room, barefoot. "What's with Isera and you? You both treat Taine like he's an enemy instead of my brother."

I flinched. He was right — as little as I liked Isera, our interests coincided. "Lady Isera and I are only concerned for your well-being. My job is to think of the worst possible events, and to plan to turn them to your advantage."

We drank in silence for a while. It was good to be home, and I felt the immense contentment fill me. That was all I ever wanted, and I felt happy. The feeling was so perfect, it fit so well with my thoughts, that it took me a moment to realize that it was not mine.

Taine, washed and dressed in fresh clothes, stood in the doorway, grinning lopsidedly. He seemed to have no control over the right side of his face, owing no doubt to the scar; only the left half smiled.

Gesur turned to me. "Jana," he said. "Please put your net back on."

My breath caught in my throat. "Why, my lord?"

He motioned toward Taine who filled the entire doorway. "I do not want my brother to think that his thoughts are being monitored."

I rose, crumpling the net in my hand. "I shall leave you two alone then."

"Some Protector." Taine smiled still. "You're leaving your lord with a potential rival?"

I cringed at his lack of tact. I inclined my head and said, "You are my lord's brother, and thus under my protection too. It will not be withdrawn without a reason."

"I see." His single dark eye looked me over. "Why the veil?"

I could be blunt too. "I'm wearing it to conceal my hideousness. The lady of the house did not want me to shock the visitors. I assumed she did not want me to shock you either."

"Jana," Gesur started in a pacifying voice.

Taine interrupted. "I'm not easy to shock, girl. I have seen you before, and I am sure you are not worse now than back then."

"Jana," I corrected, and took off my veil. I braced for the usual onslaught of revulsion, pity, horror my face provoked in people. None came. Taine peered into my face without curiosity, and perhaps a bit of surprise. I realized that he had seen more than any of people in the city. Indeed, he'd done more than merely see.

A memory, fresh as if no time had passed, flooded my vision. I saw through his eyes, and through my own, our recollections flowing together, indistinguishable. I saw myself, lying on the ground, a helpless bundle of a broken child. I saw the burning houses, and felt the life trickle out of me in a stream of warm blood that soaked my clothes and hair. My arm was bent under me, and I could not move it. I could not move at all, despite the approaching sounds of hoofbeats and men's voices.

I remembered the man who bent down from the saddle, looking at me with gentle dark eyes. His face, hidden on the silty bottom of my memory, floated up — a young, handsome face, so much like Gesur's. I heard him speak to the man at his right hand, and saw him dismount. His arms scooped me off the ground, and the pain in my arm exploded in a million white stars, and extinguished my sight.

I did not try to reconcile the face in my memory with the one before me. I merely lowered my veil and bowed to Gesur. "My lord."

♦

The rainfall grew heavier, and the beat of it acquired a distinct rhythm. The rain gutter of the manor house was so big that under the rain it roared like an organ — the water rushed down, washing over the cobbles of the pavement in a staccato, gurgling towards the drain in a gentle lilting song, where it joined with many other streams. Each distinct voice blended in beautiful song as I walked toward the city.

The rain and the darkness had always been my friends. The streets of Shabuk stood empty, and the clay-colored water washed over the stones of the pavement, too murky to reflect my face, too shallow to let the sound of my footsteps rise above the droning. I could venture outside in the rain without a veil, feeling the wind tear at my hair, and the water trickle down my collar. No fingers to point, no mouths to call out and mock my ugliness.

September was the month that brought rain — I waited for it every year, from the end of the previous November. The first September rain... I don't know how to describe it. The music of it, drumming on the roofs, trickling in the puddles, running like fingers over the keyboard of the gutters. The generous sparkling shroud over the adobe city, the kind disappearance of the rose-colored stone of the temples, the merciful muffling of their incessant bells.

I hummed along as I walked. Occasionally, a pale face would appear, plastered against the glass, and disappear again. To them, I was but a ghost, an unrecognizable shape in the weeping grayness. They only wondered who was mad enough to step outside in such weather. Well, there I was, the Protector of Ascheli, sniffing out any traces of treason, the only woman who liked being outside in the rain.

I slowed my steps as the building of the merchant guild loomed close. I looked around, making sure that no one followed me, and went inside, into the vaulted hallway. Gas lamps illuminated the walls of clay bricks, and a few benches reserved for the visitors. I sat down on one of them.

The Protector of the merchant guild sensed my presence, and stepped into the hallway. "Lady Jana," he said.

"I need to talk to the elders."

"Have you done what was required of you?"

I shook my head. "This is what I needed to talk to them about."

His mouth tightened, and his colorless eyes stared into mine. "I detect hesitation," he said.

"Indeed. My lord has just lost his father. I can't deal a second blow to him."

The Protector scowled. "I sense that you do not like Taine."

"But I like my lord."

He smiled then. "Indeed." He stared at me with curiosity. "Some may say, a little too much."

I refused to lower my eyes. "In any case, I would advise your employers to find another assassin. If Taine falls on the battlefield, it will evoke less suspicion."

"But we want suspicion! We want all to see that this is justice, not an accident. He cheated death in battle many times, but he cannot cheat those who watch him. Even his home is not a safe haven. Do you understand?"

I nodded. "I do."

"I am sorry to put you in such a precarious situation, but we have no other choice. There's no one except you who can do this." He looked at me with a glimmer of sympathy. "And I am afraid that you will not be able to refuse. Otherwise, we'll have no other choice but to make sure the justice is dealt, and in that case we would have no reason to spare the house. Or you, for that matter."

I bit my lip. "You can't do that."

"Would you risk it? You are a good Protector, but not so good that you cannot be disposed of. Remember: you have conspired with the Ascheli's enemies. And if you are exposed as a traitor, what will happen to Gesur?" the Protector said. "Would you rather lose your lord forever, or do something that would be good for him in the long run? And please do not forget what Taine has done. And will no doubt continue to do."

I left the guild without saying another word. The Protector could see my feelings clear enough. He knew as well as I did that I could not bear endangering Gesur — could not bear losing my place next to him. Whether I thought of myself or of the family future, Taine had to die.

♦

A week had passed since Taine first appeared. He showed no inclination to leave, perfectly content to rest under the parental roof. I could understand him. I lived in this house since I was ten. I had been its Protector for the past ten years, ever since I came of age and discovered my clairvoyance. The manor house was peace and contentment. Its vast halls and thick brickwork that kept the heat out, its shaded gardens and silent ponds that had meant a happy childhood. Mine, Gesur's and Taine's.

Poison was the best way. I prepared the mix, and let it cure in the sun for a day. It was an old recipe. I started adding it to Taine's food little by little, flake by flake. Already, he seemed thinner and paler, and his scar stood out more, purple against ashen skin.

I avoided him. I was not a murderer, and looking at him fueled my guilt. I knew what he was and what he had done; still, killing was not easy.

One night, I walked to the smallest of the winter gardens. I could not sleep, distracted and agitated by a low throb of pain emanating through the manor. Taine was the source of it, certainly. I hoped that the serenity of the potted shrubs and the clear mirror of the artificial pond in the center would calm me. I wanted it to be over, and counted days on my fingers. He had five more days to live.

A presence by the pond startled me, and its torment hit me, like a soldier's fist in my stomach.

"Hello, Jana," Taine said before I could turn and flee. "Can't sleep?"

"No, my lord. I am sorry for disrupting your solitude — I shall leave you."

He gave me a look that seemed almost pleading. "Sit with me a moment."

"As you wish." I approached the pond and sat on the marble-encased edge of it.

He looked like a mountain, hunched over, his elbows planted on his knees. "I don't feel right," he said.

"Have you talked to the healer, my lord?"

He nodded, smiling. "He says I need rest."

"It's good advice, my lord."

"You think so?"

The stare of his single eye unnerved me, and I just nodded and looked away.

"Do you think I'm going to die?"

I felt the color flood my cheeks, and my voice sounded thin and false. "Why would you ask me that, my lord? How would I know such a thing?"

"Well, you're clairvoyant. Your kind's supposed to know what's happening."

"We can only detect feelings of those around us," I said. "We don't know when someone's going to die."

"Hm." He smiled. "I didn't know that. But tell me something: how come you did not know that your town was going to be attacked?"

"I wasn't of age then." My heart pounded in my ears.

I touched my face without meaning to. As scared as I was of him, I felt grim satisfaction: he was the one who led the attack on my hometown, he was responsible for the death of my birth family. He was responsible for what the soldiers had done to me. It was his fault I could not venture outside without a thick veil.

"So." He looked away, pretending to observe the silvery fish that frolicked in the depths of the pond. "Is this why you're killing me?"

"I don't know what you're talking about!"

"Come on. I was not born yesterday; I have not been ill a day in my life, and the moment I come home I succumb? You have plenty of reasons to hate me…"

"It's not about that." I bit my tongue too late.

"What is it about?"

I told him. There was a relief in confession, although I wondered to myself why I was still alive. I felt no hostility in him, just fatigue. And… was it relief?

"Righteous indignation then." He heaved a sigh. "Well, you do what you must. Just don't think yourself better than me."

My hands clenched, and I jumped to my feet. "How dare you to compare yourself to me! I am ridding the world of a monster, and I lose sleep over it. You've killed hundreds, and you never felt regret."

He shrugged. "Maybe not."

We stayed silent awhile, watching the fish.

"Jana," he said. "I don't suppose there's any cure for this poison."

I shook my head.

"It's really painful." He rubbed his face, embarrassed. "Is there a way of speeding it up?"

"Yes," I said. "You can take a larger dose."

"Would you mind giving it to me?"

I dipped my fingers into the crystal-clear, cool water of the pond. "Why would I do that?"

"Mercy," he said.

I snorted. "I didn't realize you even knew this word."

"I had mercy for you." He laughed. "I should've known better. I do one nice thing, and it comes back to bite me on the ass."

I felt numb. I reached into my pocket, and took out a small vial of brown powder.

Taine took it from my hand, and studied it for a moment. His disfigured face looked solemn, and for a moment I could see back through time, at how he used to be back then, when the war with Limar had just started. So much like Gesur. He shook out the contents of the vial onto his open palm. "Good night, Jana," he said, and stood.

I bowed. "Good night, my lord."

Taine was dead the next morning. As much as Isera bustled about, pretending to be furious that the funeral arrangements needed to be reassembled so soon, I could feel her relief like it was my own.

I caught up with her after she had dismissed the florist's messenger. It had been a long day for everyone. "Are you well, my lady?" I asked.

She smiled at me. "You are a good Protector, Jana."

I almost took a step back — a praise coming from her felt like a trap, and yet I could detect no malice from her. "Thank you, my lady. You are very kind."

She opened her mouth as if to say something else but then turned and walked off. I did not need to ask what she wanted to talk about, because I felt it: her regret and her gratitude. And a guttering, flickering flame of kinship, a sad sisterly understanding she flung my way as she turned the corner and disappeared from view.

I did not need to ask her where to find Gesur.

I followed the trail of heartbreak and confusion to the main hall. The dais stood empty, as Taine's body was prepared in the servants quarters, his dry and cracked mouth stuffed with fragrant herbs and sewn shut, his skin washed with soap and lye.

His brother sat on the floor, face in his knees, and the immobility of his shoulders failed to disguise the sobs that shaped them into tortured, tense wing stubs. They did not relax under my hand.

"I am so sorry, my lord," I said.

He nodded without looking up. "Thank you."

I settled next to him. There was no point in apologizing or regretting anything; I cannot say that I truly regretted — at least, not until they found Taine, and Gesur's torment filled my skull and burned in my nostrils. It was a breach of proper conduct, but I afforded myself a small familiarity of letting my hand stay on his shoulder as my forehead rested against his arm.

He softened, and the pain ebbed a bit. "You came to tell me that it will get easier with time?"

I nodded into the linen of his sleeve. "Everything does, my lord." Even dying.

"They tell me that people are happy that he is dead."

"People do not like wars, my lord."

"You don't either."

"It's not for me to decide such things, my lord."

He lifted his head, smiling a little. I looked up too. "So cautious you are."

"So are you. This is why you are a good ruler."

"The funeral is tomorrow."

I stood up, and pulled on his sleeve. "You will need your rest then."

He followed behind me as I left the main hall. "Where's Isera?"

I scanned the manor for her emotions. "Getting ready for tomorrow in her chambers. Perhaps you should too."

"Good night, Jana." He touched my hand lightly. "Thank you for your comfort. Get some rest too. Tomorrow will be difficult for you."

"Not as difficult as it will be for you."

I watched him until he melted into the shadow of the hallways, sadness billowing around him. And yet, I was certain that both of us would sleep soundly.

A Scandal with Bohemians

Jonathan L. Howard

To Richard Malengine, she was always *that* bloody woman. He was a man of simple tastes, which, where women were involved, were sometimes energetically exercised. Yet that monstrous regiment presented few other interests to him by and large until Fate saw fit to broaden his education by introducing him to Miss Elodie Vesperine. The details of that introduction are a matter for discussion elsewhere; the reader need not be concerned with them upon this occasion. Suffice to say, where Malengine walked she followed, and commented, frequently with irony. Where he paused she hovered, still commenting.

Richard Malengine had once been the toast of the London stage, particularly respected for his Shakespearean work, more particularly for his portrayals of the blackguardly. His Richard III, Shylock, and Macbeth were the talk of the West End, and he was lionised by society both high and low. He brought to these monsters a sympathy hitherto barely touched upon by previous interpreters of the canon, a sympathy that illuminated and vivified these villains. Audiences streamed from his performances appreciating that the deaths of the princes in the Tower had been no more than unavoidable duty; that Antonio was the true scoundrel of Venice; that Macbeth was a victim of circumstances, of horrible women in the forms of witches and wife, and of perambulatory trees.

Tastes change, however, and a more vigorous interpretation of good and evil became the norm. Richard and Macbeth were to deserve the sword points upon which they fetched, and Shylock was there to be spat upon. Malengine found himself superannuated in a less nuanced age, and fell upon hard times. There he might have quietly rotted away as so many other unfashionable actors have, had he not sought to present to the public an exciting reinvention of an old blight now made fulgent as a form of entertainment. Crime.

Thus we find Malengine at home in his current "gaff," a cellar in Whitechapel. If this sounds objectionable to the reader, it must be pointed out that, for Malengine, the fruits of crime are to be applied, at least in part, in making the world a more bearable place. Thus, the floors are clean, the rats evicted, the damp dealt with, the furnishing, fixtures, and fittings improved immeasurably. Indeed, but for the lack of windows, one might almost think that the room was the *cabinet* of a louche and decadent orientalist, ensconced somewhere amid the artists and anarchists of Bloomsbury. But this place of Persian carpets and rosewood furniture, though heavily scented with Turkish tobacco smoke, was also decorated with maps of the great metropolis, not only its streets, buts its sewers and lost rivers. Map pins, tersely annotated, dotted them, and here and there cryptic pieces of coloured string connected seemingly unrelated locations. This was no suburban den of iniquity for a metropolitan opium eater, then. This was the lair of a criminal mastermind.

The mastermind in question was studying a sextodecimo edition of the *Sonnets*, bound in cadmium red leather. He held it at arm's length, his other arm and hand occupied by supporting his head as he sprawled amidst a nest of cushions, middle finger across upper lip and nasal septum, index running to his cheek, thumb beneath his chin. Though relaxed, and his posture quite unconscious, Malengine tended to lapse easily into such poses (this one especially efficacious in modelling his fine, aquiline features), poses suitable for stage instructions such as, "Thus we find Malengine..."

"Good Lord," he said, apparently to the air. "I have an inkling these may have been written to a chap."

A quarter of the floor area was raised, and accessible up a couple of concrete steps. In this area were concentrated the more mundane necessities for the outer man; a stove, a kitchen table, a collection of kitchen accoutrements depending from a pot rack, provender, and bottles. From behind the table rose a man who seemed the fleshly first cousin of the stove, although topped with a disreputable brown bowler rather than an iron pipe, nor even a stovepipe hat.

This was Harris. Once he had been Malengine's dresser and general dogsbody. Now he maintained the latter role albeit made grand, if "chief henchman" may be regarded as a promotion. A man of limited intellectual vigour, yet great cunning, utter practicality, and easily adjustable morals. When Malengine had first had a life of crime thrust upon him by circumstance and asked Harris to follow him into that uncertain future, that worthy had done so with a simple, "All right, governor."

Now he stood in his shirt sleeves above a tub of partially peeled potatoes, and said, "Are you suggesting that the Bard was a bit of a nancy boy, guv?"

"Well, it's hardly unknown, is it? We are talking about the theatre, after all."

Harris absorbed this intelligence, yet believed he had seen a flaw in that closely argued deduction. "But Mr. Shakespeare was from up North, wasn't he?"

"Not *that* far north..." began Malengine, fully aware that, for Harris, "The North" started halfway up Finchley High Street and henceforward contained everything in an ill-formed mélange of fields, factories, kilts, and great white bears.

"They don't have nancy boys up North," insisted Harris, and he said it with finality. As Malengine was in no mood to argue, the conversation once more lapsed, and the only sounds were those of the turning of pages and the peeling of potatoes.

Into this scene of domestic bliss entered Miss Elodie Vesperine, apparently untroubled by the five heavy and sophisticated locks that protected the main door. Blithely she entered, and blithely she ignored Harris as he threw down his potato of the moment and scuttled off to investigate this failure in security.

"Hello, Malengine," she said, casting herself in an armchair and hooking one leg over the arm in a deeply unladylike fashion. Miss Vesperine styled herself an adventuress, and this extended to sprawling. At least she was not wearing a dress, but was instead in the attire of a boy, which made sprawling less problematical. She took off her cap and shook out her raven locks in languorous waves. She was no stranger to this action and was therefore very good at it indeed; even Harris was reduced to an admiring silence for a moment.

"Miss Vesperine," said Malengine, breaking the enchantment, "how lovely to see you. I assume you have word from our betters?"

"If you mean the Black Council, then yes," she replied. She swung her legs down that she might sit more conventionally and thereby increase the gravitas of her announcement. "They have a job for you, Malengine."

"Do they indeed?" Malengine's demeanour was not one of unalloyed enthusiasm. The council's requests were more in the nature of commands. Furthermore, success, failure, or refusal all tended to attract equivalent levels of risk. Poisoned chalices rarely came more brimming with toxicity than the "requests" of the Black Council.

"Don't worry," said Miss Vesperine, a formula guaranteed to encourage worrying, "There's no risk in this one. It's just something they thought would play to your natural talents." She smiled a feline sort of smile at him as she played with the brim of the cap. "They want you to play a rôle."

Malengine's interest was piqued. There were roles, and there were rôles, and he could smell the circumflex on the latter from better than a statute mile. "What... manner of rôle might that be, pray?" he said, the falsity of his indifference as telegraphed as anything he had ever presented to a matinee audience.

"There is a man freshly come into London, an Italian. His name is unimportant, something exhausting with far too many vowels in it. Only his nom de guerre is important for us. He is known as 'Beppo.'"

"He sounds like a clown."

"He *was* a clown, but he changed his trade from putting smiles on the faces of children with his antics to putting them on the throats of his political enemies. With a knife. He is an anarchist."

Malengine looked at her down the length of his fine Roman nose and frowned. "Do they have anarchists in Italy? I believed that to be a French vice."

"Apparently they do. In any event, he has come to England to foment disquiet and violence among the working classes and thereby spark a grand revolution. There will be stormings of Buckingham Palace and the Houses of Parliament, the prime minister strung up in Downing Street, and the queen sent into exile."

"I see," said Malengine, not liking the sound of this at all. In common with most villains, he was a reactionary at heart, and he was fond of the monarchy. In some shadowed corner of his hopes, he still dreamed of one day being knighted. Once it would have been in the noble tradition of actor knights, but now he vaguely hoped for some sort of recognition for services to British crime. "And the council wants him stopped?"

"Good heavens, no," laughed Miss Vesperine in an infuriatingly attractive way. "The council wants him encouraged. He apparently represents some sort of useful distraction from its other operations in the East End. I didn't enquire into specifics."

Curiosity was discouraged by the Black Council, which maintained a policy of "Ask me no questions, and I'll tell you no lies, before having you quietly murdered."

"What about the stormings?"

"They will never happen. Scotland Yard has far too many ears to the ground to ever let things progress that far. The point is, while they're keeping an eye on our friend Beppo, they've taken it off certain other matters."

Malengine considered. "You still have not told me of the rôle."

"Well, here is how things lie. As you so astutely noted, Italy is not currently known for its anarchists, and Beppo is therefore being treated with suspicion by the French, Russian, and home-grown examples to be found littering Whitechapel. Our boy needs bullying up, his stock to enrich. That, dear Richard, is where you are to apply yourself."

"Ah," he nodded conceitedly, smiling slightly. "You wish me to coach him."

"No," said Miss Vesperine. "He is not to know of the council's involvement. The anarchists of London are a skittish lot. If they suspect for a second that Beppo is an instrument of their manipulation in the hands of some shadowy party, they will instantly and irrevocably take against him. No, the plan is that you," the feline smile glimmered again, "are to be his appreciation society."

♦

The Coal Barque, known locally as the "The Barker," was a grimy, ill-disposed public house within a distance of the river that was convenient if one should want, for example, to dump a body in it. It was a convenience that suited the clientele very well. This proximity to the Thames, in turn, put it within easy fog-rolling distance, and the place was often to be found — with difficulty — wreathed in banks of the stuff. This also suited the clientele very well.

Peopled by slatterns, thugs, roaring boys, and flibbertigibbets, the Barker was a pit of depravity, and therefore also attracted politicians. Unlike their more upmarket brethren who congregated around a more upmarket pit of depravity in Westminster, the politically minded patrons of the pub were of dangerous and radical mind. They had never seen a judge that would not be improved by hanging, or a lord whom they did not itch to send leaping off Beachy Head. They were a dangerous crew, and one might expect the life expectancy of police spies to be minimal. Here one would be wrong. The understood form of behaviour was, when a creature in the pay of the law came in, he raised his hand, said, "I'm a blower" (or *informer* or *nose*), and then made his way to the saloon bar where the other informers were, there to enjoy a drink and collaborate on convincing lies to tell their masters. In this way security was maintained, Scotland Yard was kept happy, and the revolutionaries in the public bar were in the position of keeping the hapless informers — impoverished members of the proletariat all — in pin money squeezed from the state, thus performing a social service.

This, then, would be the stage for Richard Malengine's newest performance. It wasn't one with which he was markedly happy. Huddled under a disreputable hat and in the company of the disreputable Harris, he regarded the crowd as one might hyaenas in a zoo, especially from a perspective within their enclosure.

"I can't possibly play to this house," he muttered into his pint pot as they watched a couple of old friends across the way good-naturedly knife one another. "Look at it, Harris. It's bedlam."

"You played there once, guv," replied Harris offhandedly, grinning distractedly at a doxy who was leisurely scratching her crotch. "You said they were a good crowd."

"They *were* appreciative," admitted Malengine. "Mad, but appreciative." He frowned at Harris. "Don't be silly, old man. She must have more crabs than Southend Beach."

Harris looked at him, ruminated, and nodded philosophically. "I prefer potted shrimps meself," he replied in a partial sequitur.

In truth, Malengine's claim that the pub was a poor venue for a performance was simply inaccurate. The whole public bar was home to several performances going on simultaneously. Quite apart from the usual displays of drunken ribaldry one might expect, there were several tables at which serious men and more than a few serious women were gathered. Neckerchiefs and shapeless hats of Gallic influence were in evidence, and, despite the drinking, a distinct lack of smiles. Now and then a debate on one or other of these tables would grow loud, and it would become apparent that this was no longer a dialogue in progress, but a monologue in crescendo. As the rest of the table grew quiet, one speaker would rise to his or her feet and declaim impenetrably on a general theme of "*prolétariat* good, very nearly everybody else not so good." As the flame of his revolutionary rhetoric grew more lambent, the speaker would rest one foot upon his chair or even, in the most ecstatic flights of didacticism, climb upon the table itself. By this stage, the room would have grown almost quiet as it listened to a flow of political rhetoric entirely incomprehensible to Malengine's ear. A lot of stuff about exploitation, class struggle, and the objectification of human economic relations. When the speaker reached the end of his monologue, however, everybody else seemed to understand what he meant, because there would inevitably be a great round of applause and shouted congratulation as the speaker slowly stepped down and regained his seat, unsmiling, like a tiger returning to its lair.

"These speeches all seem remarkably sim'lar," said Harris.

"That last one wanted to string up the queen," noted Malengine, chasing something lumpy around the inside of his flagon. "*Fairly* sure even suggesting it is treason." He finally hunted down his prey and flicked it onto the floor. "This is all so French. This isn't how the English do revolutions at all. Those either end up with a regicide or the Duke of Monmouth begging for his life, from what I've observed. All this shouting nonsense in a pub is never going to lead to anything."

Harris had seen shouting nonsense in a pub lead to all sorts of things, mainly the magistrates' court, but remained silent. Malengine fiddled with the brim of his hat again, a studiously observed construction of a type that had never touched the brow of any son of the earth, yet gave the strong sense that it had touched them all at least in an impression of some strangely spiritual air, conveyed only by the most arcane of hatters.

As an aside, the hatter's name was Montmorency, and he practiced cartomancy while not inhaling mercury fumes, thereby rendering himself more arcane than most hatters.

Malengine was, to an extent, researching his rôle, although it was to a very limited extent. He belonged to a school of drama that he fondly believed was realistic and rigorously truthful. In this he deluded himself, as would have been plain if he had looked at his own attitude to the room in which he sat. Instead of regarding it as the reality to emulate, it was naught more than a distraction, and he wished they'd all shut up and let him concentrate on catching their epitome, the better to startle them with the truth of their lives. Although he would have been appalled to hear it, he was, like so many of his contemporaries in the theatre, an *impressionist* rather than a *realist* (to borrow terms from the paint daubers).

Therefore, instead of closely observing the temperament, postures, gestures, accents, and verbal tonalities of the Barker's clientele, he had a hat. He still needed dialogue, however, and was observing themes and terminology as revolutionary after putative revolutionary climbed to their feet and explained in dialectically didactic terms what was wrong with the world and how to fix it. That these solutions were ragingly impractical was apparently all part of the game.

Harris elbowed him, a sensation akin to being jostled by a pile of leaves. "That's our boy," he said, hugging his tankard. "That's the Eyetie clown."

Beppo, for it was indeed him, was certainly the very embodiment of an Italian firebrand, all neckerchief, moustache, and scowl, but there was precious little of the clown about him. He took to his table like an actor to the stage and proceeded to capture and hold his audience. From his first words, "In *my* country…," delivered in a dense Italian accent, slowed to comprehensibility for the onlookers, he damned the ruling class, dismissed the middle, and extolled the working.

It was a masterly performance, and Malengine quite forgot he was supposed to be supportive until he received another mild elbow in the ribs from Harris. Startled into incontinent action, Malengine gathered his thespian humours and called out in ringing tones, "Hear, hear!"

Beppo paused and looked at him, his thick eyebrows gathering like trouble over the Bay of Biscay. Much of the other clientele also turned to regard the man in the artful hat.

"Venue, guv'nor. Venue," muttered Harris under his breath.

Taking the hint, Malengine adjusted his text. "Which is to say, 'ear, 'ear!"

Strangely, this did not improve the atmosphere.

"What he's saying," continued Malengine, beginning to realise that perhaps improvisation was not his strong suit after all, "it's top hole!" People were looking at one another in a sort of *Remind me, do we still lynch people?* sort of way. "Spot on!" In desperation, Malengine searched his memory for something a little more plebeian. "Reet gradely!"

Beside him, he heard Harris sigh. "Oh, bloody hell."

Malengine's supportive comments had singularly failed in their goal; Beppo was left scowling on his table while the attention of the room settled on entirely the wrong man. It is conceivable that only Malengine's wondrous hat saved him from being strung up from the rafters. Such malevolent attention was finally diverted by Harris clambering slowly to his feet and saying in his gravelly tones, "Yus, very uplifting. Up the proletariat, and that."

To understand why the onlookers were reassured by this, one must first understand that "gravelly" is altogether too silken a term for Harris's voice. If it were gravel drawn from the bed of a toxic river, dredged by a black dredger crewed entirely by syphilitic lascars, all of whom hated their mothers, that begins to approach the experience of listening to Harris. It was the voice of a thousand generations of workers, honest even in criminality, even back unto the days when Mr. Darwin tells us that we were all monkeys, when some distant ancestor of Harris could be relied upon to grunt expressively, tip his bowler hat forward over his eyes, and venture forth to sort out the banana situation.

Deprived of his audience, Beppo sank slowly back into his chair like a Biblical behemoth returning to the depths, rankled and bristling.

"Well," whispered Malengine to Harris as the threat receded, "that went all right, didn't it?"

"No, guv."

"No." For once Malengine did not feel like arguing with the critics. "No, it didn't. What were the Council thinking of when they sent me on this errand? It's hardly within my purview."

"Ours is not to reason why, guv," said Harris, a natural philosopher. "Ours is but to do and die."

"We're not in the army, Harris."

"As you say."

Malengine swilled the contents of his flagon around disconsolately. "Now I'm all out of sorts. Where are the facilities?" Harris nodded at a door in the corner. Malengine pulled his hat firmly down to shade his face, and rose.

The other side of the door turned out to contain London, or at least one of its smaller and less lugubrious blind alleyways. Malengine was hardly surprised to discover this limitation in the Barker's sanitary arrangements and found a corner that wasn't too loathsome in which to relieve himself. He was just concluding a heartfelt micturition, when the door behind him swung open, filling the alley with sound, a little more light, and a great deal more smoke. The door swung to, and Malengine — conscious that his was not an ideal situation, brought events to a rapid conclusion and buttoned himself up.

He turned and found himself face to face with Beppo, the throat-cutting clown.

"*Sapristi!*" growled Beppo. "It is you. Signor *'ear 'ear.*" His eyes narrowed, his nostrils flared. "What is, how you say, your game, eh?" Something in the way he said it suggested sharp Italian steel followed by a loose-limbed wallow in the Thames.

"My game?" Malengine laughed lightly. At least, he fancied he did, although a disinterested spectator might have perceived it as a slightly hysterical giggle. "I just enjoy a nice bit of oratory, my good man. Mate. Me old mucker. I'm terribly fond of the proletariat. Being one, and all. As I am."

Deciding this was probably a few seconds past the best moment to shut up, he did so belatedly, trusting to the protection offered by his magic hat.

Beppo's eyes were so wide that the whites were visible all the way around them. It was a striking display of eye-popping fury and for a moment Malengine was filled with concern for his safety. But then a memory surfaced that quite took away his dismay and replaced it with simple curiosity tinged with inadequate astonishment.

"Peveril? Montague Peveril, is that you?"

The Italian's eyes narrowed. "Sapristi!" he said again.

"The trick with the whites of the eyes, they can see that up in the gods. It is you, isn't it, Peveril?"

"Whassamata with you, eh?" demanded Beppo. "Who is this *Peveril*?" He enunciated the name a syllable at a time, as if spitting pebbles.

But Malengine wasn't listening. In the dubious light of the alleyway, he now seemed fascinated by Beppo's extravagant moustachios. "Is that real?" he said, and made to investigate.

Beppo covered his moustache with both hands and great indignity. "Lay off, Malengine!" he snapped. "Leave me 'tash alone, you heathen!"

Malengine desisted, instead shaking a finger in triumphant reproach. "Montague Peveril! I can hardly believe it! What brings you here?"

Montague Peveril, a steady hand with character parts mainly out in provincial theatres, lowered has hands, irritation at his discovery clear upon his face. "A job, evidently. Needs must when the landlord's threatening. You know how it is." He regarded Malengine with curiosity. "But what about you, old man? Didn't I hear you'd had some sort of run in with the beak?"

Malengine had indeed had a run in with the beak, or more exactly beaks, both of the court of magistrates and the court of criminal justice varieties. There had been many charges, a litany that included — but was by no means not limited to — petty larceny, theft, impersonating an officer of Her Majesty's Government, kidnap, disturbing the peace, some business with explosives, and, oh yes, absconding with the Crown Jewels. Malengine had found himself on most front pages, and the star turn in No.1 Court in the Old Bailey, but as these endeavours had not earned him an item in *The Stage*, many of his former colleagues were ignorant of his recent activities.

"A few trifling charges," said Malengine, miffed though unsurprised that his notoriety had so little impact within theatrical circles. "So, what are you doing pretending to be an Italian anarchist?"

"No idea," replied Peveril blandly. "I was just apprised of the job by some cove, and paid a decent whack for it. Big chap, very military. Moustache, cold eyes."

The description sounded very like the Colonel, right hand of the Professor. So, thought Malengine, Beppo doesn't exist, yet the chairman of the Black Council sees fit to summon him up in the form of an actor, and bolster him with the services of another.

Malengine allowed his inquiring mind to inquire no further; indeed at the very spectre of the Professor, it had dug in its heels and was dutifully reversing away from any thought of that baleful worthy or his schemes as quickly as ever it could. There was a term for those who took too great an interest in the Professor's business: *dead*.

"Well, Peveril, here's the thing. We're on the same side, hired by very much the same people. I'm supposed to bolster you up, somehow."

Peveril looked at him blankly. *"That,"* he said, "was bolstering me up?"

"Yes," replied Malengine, his tone regretful. "Not really played an audience like this before."

"Look, Malengine, I know you're doing your best, but this is my sort of venue. They need a little finesse."

Malengine's brow tautened. "Are you suggesting that I lack *délicatesse*? I've played Prospero, you know. I can affect subtleties far beyond the ken of that coarse rabble in there, let me tell you."

Peveril looked at him a little pityingly. "That's the thing, though, Malengine. They're not a theatre crowd, even if they do seem a bit dramatic at times. They're looking for realism, and Prospero isn't so very realistic, now, is he?" He glanced over his shoulder. "Look, I've got to get back. You did your best, but this isn't the sort of thing you're any good at. Please, old man, just let me do my job and, by keeping schtum, you'll be doing yours." Without another word, Peveril headed back into the pub. The door opened, sound and light flooded out. Then the door slammed, and Malengine was left alone, once again in the dark.

He was at a loss how to feel. Certainly he was relieved that his services were no longer required, but at the same time rattled that the redundancy centred on the obsolescence of his art. He was "not so very realistic," a charge he would once have found facile and lacking in understanding of the theatre, but that now carried a sting. Was he truly an irrelevance? He held his hands up and looked at them. They were hands that had borne Yorick's skull, fumbled to search for Gloucester's eyes, been stained with stage blood as he fell at Romeo's feet. Had it all been for nothing, splintered into nothing for this new "realism," this method of which he knew nothing?

Malengine slowly lowered his hands and glared at the Barker's side door. "Damn, you, Peveril," he said to the dank walls and the stink of drunkards' piss. "I am a better actor than you, and I shall find the truth in any text."

He re-entered the pub moments later to find "Beppo" already engaged in his second rabble-rousing of the evening. Malengine allowed him to reach approximately two-thirds of an oratorical crescendo before shouting, "Monster!"

This caused a stir. Gazes slid from Beppo to the newcomer and, noting the hat, recalled that this was not the first interruption from that quarter.

"Sapristi!" cried Beppo.

"You're a traitor to your own country and now you come to England to spread your vile sedition here too! You plague rat made human! Strike him down! By all that's good and British in your souls, strike this blackguard down!"

Harris looked at him, then regretfully at his beer, before abandoning the latter. "C'mon, guv. Let's get you home, shall we? Before you get murdered and that."

"I will not be silenced!" shouted Malengine as Harris towed him towards the exit. "Don't listen to him, English yeomen, strong and stout! Do not listen to the perfidy of this… this… this… *Italian!*" As Harris manhandled him through the door, Malengine started singing "God Save the Queen."

A couple of the pub's patrons made to follow, but Harris forestalled them with a raised hand, a friendly smile, and said, "Don't trouble yourself, fellows. I'll just do him in meself. River's just over there, innit? Good-oh."

♦

Thus, Malengine escaped from a hive of anarchists and was transported safely back to his lair beneath London, and it was here that he was discovered some hours later by Miss Vesperine.

"Good work, Malengine," she said, taking off her boy's cap and tossing her locks almost purely to see the mesmeric effect they had upon Harris. "They bought your act hook, line, and sinker at the Coal Barque."

"I rather thought they might," said Malengine complacently, not looking up from an early edition newspaper. "An actor must develop an understanding of his audience if he is to communicate the desired effect to them."

"What?" said Harris, snapped out of his light erotic trance by Malengine's words. "But you called him all sorts. You did him down, guv. I was there."

"So was I," said Miss Vesperine, and smiled as Malengine folded his paper with a peevish "snap." "I was a potboy. I kept your tankards full all evening. Didn't you notice?"

"Of course I did," said Malengine, returning to his paper but obviously no longer reading it.

"I didn't, Miss," said Harris.

"Shut up, Harris," said Malengine.

"Yes, guv."

"So, the Black Council is pleased?" said Malengine to Miss Vesperine. "Now they have this 'Beppo' in place."

Miss Vesperine was slightly distracted by a tangle in her hair, and answered, "Yes, perfectly. Quite dead."

The newspaper was abruptly lowered again. "Dead?" said Malengine.

"Yes," said Miss Vesperine, looking at him rather than her hair for a moment. "Beppo was fished out of the Thames this morning. All to plan."

"Peveril," snapped Malengine. "His name is Montague Peveril. Dead?" He threw the paper aside and rose to his feet, his always pale complexion becoming paler yet. "In what way is 'dead' commensurate with 'all to plan'?"

"I don't know why you're so upset, Malengine," said Miss Vesperine with evident disingenuity. "You convinced the crowd that Beppo was the real thing, a dangerous Italian anarchist. The Professor's very pleased with you."

"Then why did he have Peveril murdered?"

Miss Vesperine favoured him with the sort of glance usually reserved for children when they say the most *adorably* stupid things. "He didn't, you silly boy."

Malengine did not take well to either "silly" or "boy." "Then who?" he demanded.

"The Russians."

Malengine blinked. That didn't make things clearer, so he blinked again, but he was still disappointed by the lack of clarity it brought him. "Russians? What Russians?"

"Almost every person in the Coal Barque last night was a Tsarist agent."

"Ohhh…" said Harris slowly. "Is 'tovarich' a Ruskie word? They were all saying it to one another, while the Eyetie was outside with you, guv."

"What?" demanded Malengine. "*What?* Why didn't you mention that?"

"I was going to, but then you were all pointing and shouting and declaiming, and that, so I suppose I forgot all about it in the rush of getting you out of there."

Malengine sank back onto his chaise longue. "Russian agents? But why?"

"Because they'd been tipped off that Beppo would be there that night, and the Russian spymasters were very interested in him. He's regarded as a threat, you see. A bit of a bomb thrower and a favourite of many a Russian anarchist, his likeness pinned to many a garret beam. Peveril managed to look a lot like him."

Malengine spoke slowly, the realisation that his performance as an outraged Englishman, one that came easily to him, had been sufficiently realistic to convince the tsar's agents that the Beppo they saw was the real thing. A performance that, along with Peveril's own, had led to the poor man's death. "Is… is there even a real Beppo out there?"

"Oh, yes. One of the Black Council's favourite agents provocateurs. You'll probably be able to guess where he's just been smuggled into. With the Russians sure that he's dead, he'll be able to get on with his work without the Okhrana breathing down his neck." She looked at Malengine's expression that spoke of many warring emotions beneath, and set about cramming her hair once more under her cap. "I'd best be on my way, Malengine. No rest for… well. You know."

As she stepped through the door, Malengine said, "This plan. Was it the Professor's? Or was it…?" The slamming door halted the question in his mouth. He glared at the steel door with loathing mixed with a very reluctant respect.

"That woman," he said finally. "That bloody, bloody woman."

The Character Assassin

Kyla Lee Ward

A massively multiplayer online game is a world. That's what non-gamers never understand. It doesn't exist inside a computer; it exists in the aether where thousands of players come together as digital avatars. This world is where those avatars live and grow, form friendships, fight battles, win riches and renown. It is also where they die. And on October 18th, just after two in the morning, Zinderzee the sixty-seventh level elven priestess died for perhaps the thousandth time.

It was her twenty-third death in this complex alone and this in a region well within her capacity to solo. But two characters of superior level entered in her wake and, instead of accepting her group invitation, killed her. They had harassed her ever since, striking her down each time she came upon them in the meandering tunnels. The resurrection point was set at some distance from the entrance and each death necessitated the same run in spirit form back to her body.

Zinderzee says what's with you jerks? Stop this or I'll make an official complaint!

Letroll says is PVP f u can't take th heat, get out f th catacomb girli

Finally giving up in disgust, Zinderzee discovered that by some means her teleport base had been reset from the central metropolis of Sharkal to the Bloodswarm Marsh. When Peter Sterling exited the game, she was quite alive, though standing in a tavern empty save for the goblin barkeep and an over-affectionate swamp demon. He did not leave her, as some do, standing, staring at the resurrection prompt, and nor did he delete her. So I count the moment of Zinderzee's final death as that when he cancelled the autopayment of his monthly subscription fee. Peter Sterling was a comparatively easy mark. He was indeed on a PVP server, a version of this world that allows players to attack each others' avatars as well as computer-generated opponents. He had a girlfriend, albeit the kind of despotic bitch who resented his hobby. He was two thirds of the way through a medical degree with exams looming on the horizon: although that is always my busy time, in his case it simply added momentum to his decision. His other interests included swimming and vintage cars: it was easy for him to imagine what else he could be doing instead of watching Zinderzee die and die. His girlfriend's initial payment made his game life a morass of harassment and technical hitches, which, combined with a subtle orchestration of external pressures, secured the necessary result. But as per the contract, it would be a further week before the completion bonus was transferred from his girlfriend's account to mine. For I am indeed the cause of Mr. Sterling's frustration. I am the cause of Zinderzee's eternal exile. I am the character assassin.

♦

I am here tonight at a college I shall not name, on a very particular mission. In the normal course of things, I don't operate on the ground, but I know these courtyards, these higher educational greens, as I know the student gamer. When I was in the throes of my own degree, approaching exams always sharpened the urge.

The overwhelming pressure of percentiles and permanent records made my fantasies imperative. Night after night in my dormitory, I followed those dictates to the Forest of Anderhoven or the Kratar Rift, in defiance of my encroaching doom.

Now you think it was academic failure that pushed me into my niche. Not so: I gained my degree with distinction. My parents were proud. Such was my momentary status, I was asked to talk to cousin Michelle whose felinoid wizard increasingly consumed her days. At the time, Michelle was still trapped in the bear pit of high school, and personally, I thought it grossly unfair to ask her to pay it any more attention than she did. Nonetheless, I agreed. Attractive opportunities for graduates abounded with this or that corporation, but none with that one with which I was certain my future lay. I needed my family's support.

In approaching Michelle, it never occurred to me to do anything other than create a character on her server. We had never had much personal contact, and I thought I had best make friends with her before starting to preach. Gaming protocol discourages behaviour that could reveal a real-world identity, such as using real names, so we communicated as characters until that fatal night in Sharkal when I broached the subject of her school life and parents. I assumed that, having asked this service of me, they would have made some mention of it to her. I assumed she at least knew who I was. But Michelle's reaction to discovering that her new online friend knew all her personal details would have warmed the hearts of cyber-Nazis everywhere. It achieved all her parents could wish — at least, until she ran away three months later. But by that time, my ambitions had come to nothing. Corporate slavery gaped, until it struck me that in solving the initial problem of my uncle and aunt, I had found means to alleviate my own.

♦

Tonight I'm working off my portable, a customized box of tricks I carry cuffed to my wrist. It supports two live avatars plus two bots. These are borderline illegal, given my code splicing, and anathema in any game. At my home office, I can handle nine simultaneously. One bot stalks Maximom the warrior — killing her boars, drawing mobs of bears towards her and generally behaving like a moron (Maximom is the reverse of my usual kind of brief, given that Max hired me). The other bot accompanies Shadowpuss, my felinoid rogue, across the Flaming Grasslands. Fumbelina the dwarf is already in place and inciting Rajesh Gopal — my current target — to send his avatar in against the gnolls.

As the avatars proceed in-game, so I proceed across the campus. I walk along the grassy ridge overlooking the path between the car park and the dormitory, taking care to stay out of the light. It's not that the sight of me arouses suspicion — I look more like a student than many of those currently enrolled — but on these external expeditions, I minimize my camera trail as a matter of course. I tread noiselessly down the slope, tracing the telltale hint of nicotine. I don't smoke, never have, but the usual group of exiles cluster by the dormitory's back door. I approach and bum a stick, and then I'm inside, as anonymous as any of them.

A flick of the keypad; Shadowpuss and the bot refine their course, to intersect with Shazalar, Rajesh's human warrior. He and his rash dwarf companion hove into view on the screen, seriously embattled. As I proceed up the corridor, the portable wedged into the crook of my arm, I pass small signs warning students against a recent rash of on-campus theft. I seldom commit actual data theft: I seldom have the need. It is amazing how many people who, basking in their partner's previously nonexistent interest, will divulge all details of their password, server, and character names! With this information, resetting Zinderzee's teleport was no problem at all. But the brief I have received for Rajesh suggests the direct approach will be the most effective. He is a first year with a heavy loading of maths subjects and the kind of parents who resort to professionals when their own nagging fails.

Shadowpuss and the bot offer to join forces with Rajesh's party. He accepts gratefully, perhaps noting his rescuer is logged into the campus's wireless network. The tide of battle turns. Intermittently, the bot enters BLOOD! BLOOD! DIE! DIE! on party chat.

I lean against the wall outside Room 203, one eye on the door, the other on the screen. Timing is everything, plus a little reverse psychology.

Shadowpuss says wanna duel?/somersault

Killemall says BLOOD! BLOOD! Kiss my green orc butt!

Fumbelina says good fight bt I hav go now Got curfew.

Shadowpuss says I am TWVELE and DONT HAV NO STEENKIN CURFEW!

By this time, I have ascertained that the door before me is unlocked. The dorm rooms are small, and, no matter where Rajesh has placed his desk, my next action can hardly miss.

Shadowpuss says u r so GAY. Only kids pla humans

Rajesh hears his door open. But he does not look up until someone who is not his roommate chuckles, "Oh man, geek city!" The camera flashes right in his round, black eyes. "So posting this," the intruder laughs away down the hall.

Rajesh hunches in his chair, heart pumping hot blood to his cheeks and guilt twisting in his stomach. Shazalar hovers, forgotten, on the screen. What have they done wrong? Nothing! And the photo will never appear, but he doesn't know that. All he knows is that someone has singled him out, labeled him by his hobby. Someone has laughed at him. He can stand his parents' nagging, but not many seventeen year olds have the will to push past *that*. His oblivious companions dance and continue making gay jokes. When the warning about his excess bandwidth usage arrives on letterhead next Monday, it should all be over. Just to be safe, I switch the bot into harassment mode.

I've earned a moment's rest. I sit on the grass atop the ridge, the only direct light that of my screen. There are even a few faint stars visible in the sky. At last I can let go some of the adrenaline I built up on the drive over here. That maniac in the red car nearly forced me into the retaining wall before managing to overtake. I hate traffic, almost as much as I hate offices and little Hitlers.

Nowadays, I think I would turn down a job at the Seattle HQ itself, if it involved any of the above.

When at last I check, Maximom has given up. Her son's gamer credibility is safe this evening. So I check my in-box and glance over my latest brief. Concerned parents, troubled child, obsession, blah blah. The only unusual factor is her sex. I receive comparatively few briefs for women: I have never worked out whether this is because fewer women grow obsessed with the game or fewer people notice when they do.

But some people occupy such positions, both in and out of game, that what others are pleased to call their problem can't help but be noticed. And that is the true reason I am out under the stars tonight. I am in transit to my ultimate destination. Rajesh Gopal was but a warm-up to an unprecedented challenge drawing on every nuance of my in-game knowledge and each facet of my out-of-game cunning and experience. If everything goes according to plan — and for upward of three months now I have planned — tomorrow night will see the death of the most famous and powerful avatar on this server, and possibly the entire East Coast.

A sudden pounding of feet and an intake of breath is my only warning as *something* rushes me from behind. Not thinking, I leap up. My portable flies off my lap and the wrist cuff jars sharply; the slope before me is steep, but something slams into the ground I just vacated. I pitch myself down the hill without so much as a backward glance, lose my footing, and roll hard and painfully.

But I roll into the light of the path. My palms bark concrete and my portable skitters away. Yanking it back, pulling myself up, I see no one on the path and can make out nothing in the darkness to either side.

I am on the car park's camera now. I dust myself off and check my portable, then with an obvious curse, bend over and pretend to retie my shoe. Limping in the direction of the car park, the memory of this afternoon's mad driver revisits me. The scratches across the paintwork make me pause, as I approach my car. But no one else is in sight. My visitor's pass is still in place in the window and my overnight bag still visible in the back — there is something else in the window besides the pass. A business card, by its dimensions. But the only symbol is a curving purple dagger, set at the base of a black tower which displays its battlements against a full moon. On the back, a scrawl in what looks like it might be blood reads *TRAITOR*.

I know the dagger. Everyone who plays the game knows it: the class marker for rogue. The tower could be anything: in a game full of dark castles it's hard to pick just one, although I must say that the configuration of battlements and moon bears a passing resemblance to a skull. But although rogues are not as robust as warriors and do not use magic like wizards or priests, they can nonetheless be ferocious adversaries, utilising stealth, disguise, demonic pets, and a varied arsenal of range and close-quarter attacks.

But of course, that is all in-game.

♦

By the time I stop at a twenty-four-hour McDonald's, nearly at the state border, the whirlpool in my mind has collapsed into a single, overriding question. How could anyone possibly know that the character assassin is me?

Gamers have tried to find me, to prove or disprove I exist. There are whole websites devoted to the subject: I visit every so often to keep abreast of the latest theories, which are sometimes very creative. Clients find me all the time, of course, but they are looking for something different. If you are searching for help on dating sites or browsing parental advisory services, an ever-evolving series of links will bring you to me. They pass by articles on gaming addiction and weave through the comments pages of online health magazines. This complements word of mouth: always my most reliable source of new business. A slew of psychologists recommend me now and a perhaps unsurprising number of educational providers. But all such interaction is conducted completely over the net. My game accounts themselves are manifold and draw from different credit cards — one of my few actual felonies, for I do possess fake ID. There is no direct contact whatsoever. What has been waiting to happen, what has probably already happened a dozen times over, is that one of my clients confesses to the target. But the repercussions of such self-sabotage need never come home to me. I live alone in a house which, although small and shabby, is the distance of a wireless network from its nearest neighbour. Someone would have to notice the additional cables and the extent of my cooling array to be at all suspicious.

The swish of the automatic door catches my attention: the woman who enters holds it effortlessly. She wears a black leather jacket and boots, her hair is long and jet black, pushed back behind dainty pointed ears. Her stride puts her past me before I can really see her face, but both ears and hands are pallid past the bleaching of the lights. Some kind of long black rod dangles from her hip, partially concealed by the jacket, and she is followed by a monstrous black dog. Possibly. If dogs really do come that big.

"Hey," calls the kid behind the counter, a noticeable quaver in his voice, "there's no animals allowed!"

The dog has paused. It is looking at me.

"Oh, he's not an animal," she says, in a voice that could burr ice.

This is ridiculous. There is simply no way I can be sitting in a McDonald's with a high-level elven rogue at the counter in front of me. Bad light and grimy plastic, the red graze on my wrist and my aching knee, these are real. This woman looks like — like several kinds of fantasy, actually. And if this was in-game, that black rod would be a Deathtouch lash, capable of simultaneously forbidding me speech and knocking me prone.

The dog is still looking at me. I turn away and peer through the spotty glass wall into the night. My car sits beneath the corner lamp, forlorn in its scratches, and no longer alone. There stands the same red vehicle that pursued me earlier. That settles it; I have to act. The woman is busy intimidating the service clerk and I am closer to the door now than she. If I get my keys out, make a dash for it... the dog will come after me, no question. But the bathroom door is closer still. Perhaps I could make that.

A small red eye winks above the counter. We are all on camera in here. That was enough to scare off my assailant on campus and no matter what this woman may think, she isn't a rogue, and that's not a Deathtouch lash. A police baton, or a cattle prod, maybe... Act normally. I just have to act normally. I lift my portable onto the table, and, flipping up the screen, I log on.

Shadowpuss hovers at the edge of Spellweaver Square, watching the chromatic mists blossom in the sky. Glittering, multi-titled figures pass, riding tigers and the huge, flightless birds of Ramphor; a glorious display. He examines notice boards and scries the general chat, attempting to find a group who is running through Megrim Combe and willing to let him join: the zone is a little challenging for his level, but that means the loot will be good. Of course, he could always call on his guild for help.

On every server, avatars with the same goals and interests come together in semi-official bodies called guilds. Shadowpuss is a member of the Orken Chorus, and he should definitely call on any other members that are available, before making any rash decision to go solo. They will help him if they can: give him advice, at least. He has been playing with the Chorus for two months now and last week, the guildmaster himself took him on just such an advanced run. Shadowpuss may have acted the child for Rajesh, but so far as the guildmaster is concerned, he is the avatar of a first-year student at an entirely different college —

"Spellweaver Square," says a crisp, female voice from directly behind me. "You're in Sharkal."

"Uh-huh," I say, not moving my eyes from the screen. The back of my neck is tingling, from something that doesn't quite touch. "So, do you play often?"

"I used to."

"Graduated, huh? The hours are so-o shit in IT, and my boss keeps sending me across country —"

"Someone killed me."

"Oh. Oh well, you don't want to let that upset you. I mean…" She's leaning past me, examining my portable, but I don't dare shift my eyes away from the screen. "…it's only a game."

"Really?" A black-gloved fingertip intrudes into Sharkal's sky. "Then why do you play?"

"Well… to have some fun, you know? Do things I can't do in real life. Escape for a while."

"Ah, Miss," the clerk says hesitantly, "your familiar has finished his burger, and you really should, um… hey, is that Sharkal?"

The clerk turns out to have an eighty-second level minotaur fighter. We talk, and after a while the presence behind me slips away without another word.

♦

So who is she, and what does she want? Apart from finishing her work on my car, of course.

This is the first glimpse I've had of her since she left the McDonald's, well before I did at dawn. But now we are both sitting here in the most god-awful traffic I've ever seen, all of it attempting to merge onto the freeway for the run into the city. I can see her red car only two lanes aside of me and nearly parallel. Either she waited around the McDonald's and has since managed to follow me unnoticed — a difficult trick in that colour — or she predicted where I was going and the approximate time I would reach the junction, surely the most dangerous part of my journey. I can only assume the worst: that she has at least some awareness of my plans for tonight.

Perhaps that is what the tower means. Perhaps she is an intercept. Perhaps this whole thing is the Orken Chorus trying to prevent me from reaching Ladeeboi, the pixie potentate.

The Orken Chorus is a large guild, but many members actually do attend the college where their guildmaster's identity is an open secret. His name is Russell Hassell, and his reasons for playing a pixie wizard are generally not discussed. His concerned aunt has hired me through the usual channels, for the usual reason: in the lead-up to exams, he's averaging eight hours of game time a day, shunning classes and friends in favour of dungeons and raids. You have conjured up a picture not dissimilar, perhaps, to poor Rajesh Gopal. But Russell Hassell isn't a student. He's the faculty head of mathematics.

Why a man in such a position should risk everything to indulge his fantasy is not the issue. Why an attractive young woman should dress up as an elf and pursue me interstate, that's the question. And of course, whether she can cut into the lane beside me.

But I think I would know if she were a guildie. Getting close to Russell really has taken a lot of effort. That first-year student who plays Shadowpuss is legitimately enrolled. He may not often attend class, but he takes part in online discussions and submits assignments — he is actually doing quite well. And no one has paid him any undue attention, in-game or out.

So what does that leave? I really have only had eight or nine female targets. Remembering I have just acquired ten, I lean over to my portable, which I have set up on the passenger seat, and call up the brief that came through last night. A young woman recently released from jail as it turns out, parents concerned the game is interfering with her reintegration, etcetera. They haven't given her name but say she is antisocial, loves computers… apparently her avatar is an elven rogue named Moonskull.

Moonskull. Now, can that really be coincidence? It seems that her fond parents left something crucial out of their daughter's profile: she's batshit crazy! I have been doing this for four years, and, in that time, I have never once dressed up as a ninja and attacked a man in the dark, or tried to run him off the road! I have hurt no one. On the contrary, people have thanked me for prising their loved one out of fantasy's grip! I reread her profile: this time thoroughly. Not strictly speaking crazy, it seems, but with a history of mistrusting authority I can almost admire. Apparently, she once paralyzed her school network with a worm, on the grounds that unspecified parties were using it to spy on her.

At the blaring of horns I glance up to see that the gap between me and the car in front has widened. I roll forward, taking the opportunity to peer across the lanes. The traffic there has come to a complete stop: the red car has muscled its way into the queue, and it's there that the horns are sounding. I see the silhouette of the dog in the back seat, and my lower intestine squirms. It's not my job to deal with disturbed individuals: I'm not a psychologist. My job is to see that Russell Hassell ends his game tonight.

With a flick of my wrist, I change windows and send Shadowpuss running alone into the Combe.

The arcanely twisted trees loom over the track in poses suggestive of motion. Paths change in Megrim Combe, and the landmarks have a tendency to bite. It is riddled with caverns and crevices, and you must have trawled every inch of them to have found this bug or else have taken very bad advice. This was provided to Shadowpuss by Letroll, at a moment when Ladeeboi was sure to see.

As my doughty felinoid fights through the vipers surrounding the Tainted Spring, I glance at the traffic once more. Inch by inch, the red car presses closer. But inch by inch, I am rolling closer to the freeway.

Chugging the last vial of antidote and invoking the discipline of the Swelling Frog, Shadowpuss plunges into the spring. As the Tainted Elementals approach, he invokes the discipline of the Flexible Eel. I have to get him past the altar and into the dead end beyond. The elementals follow, but only once the glow of the envenomed pearl recedes do I engage them. It's over quickly.

In spirit form, Shadowpuss vaults from the resurrection point and heads back towards the spring — those idiots and their horns! As if making all that noise is going to help! I allow the car to roll on, without taking my eyes from the drama unfolding on the screen. That poor, fictitious maths student is in for a surprise: the bug where Shadowpuss has died makes it impossible to retrieve his corpse. But there's no reason for him to know that. All he needs to know is that there are people out there who have identified him by his hobby, targeted him, and even in his favourite refuge are making his life an utter misery.

My speculations halt abruptly, with a slight crunching sound.
"Hey! HEY! YOU DRIVING WITH YOUR EYES SHUT,
MORON?"

♦

I am sweating as I finally step out onto the roof. The sun has
set and a breeze scrapes against me, immediately turning heat into
chill. As the door relocks behind me, I see all the city's cloudy
bright spreading out beneath the battlements and nothing, and
no one else. I am alone, at the very top of the central tower of the
University of Technology. To get onto the roof required a swipe
card primed with a staff-only code. My knee is aching again —
Lord of Radiance, but that was a *lot* of stairs — but for the first
time since the McDonalds, I am in control.

From one perspective, rear-ending the station wagon was a
good solution to my dilemma. Moonskull moved on with the traffic
while I was pinned down by the driver and never reappeared. The
subsequent furore cost me four hours, several hundred dollars,
and two of my fake IDs, but the real problem was that I arrived
at my destination too late to hack into campus security and make
absolutely sure I'd lost her. This also meant that I had to take the
stairs: there were cameras in the elevators, and, as careful as I
usually am, tonight I must leave no trace whatsoever.

I swung by Hassell's office on my way up, to check that he was
indeed still there and still gaming. It was the first time I had ever
seen him in the flesh. He was a lot larger than I imagined and
looked older, or more tired than his staff photo. But he smiled as
he played; a big, shaggy, toothy grin. His brown pullover looked a
lot like my own.

♦

But now I glance around the rooftop one last time. There is
nothing stopping me commencing the final phase. I set down my
portable and log on. The images on the loading screen swirl as the
theme music soars, and, once again, the spirit of Shadowpuss runs

through the Combe. Only now, if Hassell or anyone else thinks to check, they will see that Shadowpuss's player is using the tower's own wireless network.

I find Ladeeboi in Tinkle Vale, holding court in all his scintillating glory upon the back of his purple flying shark, shedding lime-green sparks. Gods, but it's a beautiful thing. The drop rate on such mounts is something like point oh two percent from the final boss in the Tesseract of the Ultimate Draconic Overlord; it's one of the few I myself have never possessed through some avatar or other. His cluster of admirers is shortly augmented by Letroll, whom I have led various people to believe is the avatar of a French exchange student. After a few minutes conversation, I place her under the control of my bot program, then take over Shadowpuss and start wailing on guild chat.

Shadowpuss says in Megrim Combe and cant get my body HELP!

Ladeeboi says where in the Combe?

Shadowpuss says th Tainted Spring.

Ladeeboi says you must have died at the very bottom, past the Pearl. My dear cat, why ever did you go down there?

Shadowpuss says Letroll said ther ws treasur.

Fortuitiously enough, Letroll turns a somersault.

Ladeeboi says what exactly did she tell you?

Shadowpuss says about the tresure and she snet me potions. I cant reach my body what do I DO

Ladeeboi says Letroll, did you send Shadowpuss into the bug in the Tainted Spring?

A flicker of fingers. *Letroll/laugh.*

Things escalate quickly over the next five minutes, as Ladeeboi attempts to calm the increasingly frantic young player and to discipline Letroll, all in front of a rapidly increasing audience. Primed by three months of careful role-play and manoeuvrings, Hassell responds exactly as the scenario requires, and, for just one moment, I do pause, to consider what I'm doing.

I am about to imply that a young member of Russell's guild, a student in his faculty, has committed suicide while gaming. That Russell, as both his teacher and his guildmaster, is to blame. There on the screen, Ladeeboi is surrounded by friends, but, in his office, Russell is a man alone in a large building, and this nightmare is something hardwired into his shaggy teacher's head. I have studied him carefully, communicated with him in a dozen online guises, and I know that I need to create just one instant of belief. Even once he convinces himself that it was all a hideous joke, that the boy never existed, he will never be able to bring himself to take such a risk again. Leaning over my portable, I take a deep breath.

Shadowpuss says your the same bitches YOUR ALL THE FUCKING SAME EVN HERE

Ladeeboi says please calm down, Shadowpuss. I'll come and rez you myself.

Shadowpuss says noone can rez me I hate my life

And something blasts hot breath onto the back of my neck, followed by a string of drool.

Suddenly, I'm staring into a pair of inhuman silver eyes.

Something in me snaps. Tightening my grip, I swing the portable up and around as I rise. The dog yelps and springs clear: she moves like pale lightning, drawing the black rod and flicking it at me. But the Flexible Eel may be countered by the Deceptive Crow, and my blow was only a feint. The casing parries her strike as my boot tip hits her knee: I try to catch her chin as I pull the computer back, but she ducks aside, her gasp barely audible.

"Aha, Moonskull, you think to duel me? Tonight you have met your match indeed!"

"You crazy fuck!"

The dog is prancing around the outside of the fight and whimpering — some familiar it turned out to be! She is limping now, clutching the lash as she circles, attempting to gain sufficient space to use her ranged attack. I know this routine well, and the issue is not truly in doubt. "Once I have defeated you," I crow, "I shall take your treasure and proclaim my victory to the world!"

"Do you really think that's wise —"

"Your name shall be synonymous with folly, that you dared to challenge me, the stalker in the shadows!"

" — given that I'm your *client*!"

I hear that, I do, but still I lunge, aiming to drive the corner of the case underneath those leather-laced breasts.

The instant I commit, she slips aside again and the baton catches me in the back. Then my legs are swept out from under me. I sprawl across the concrete, portable jerking my wrist one way as momentum sends me in another. Then that bloody dog has landed on my chest, and it's more than heavy enough to keep me down. It pants into my face, paws settling over my shoulders.

The words I should have said emerge belatedly from my throat. "You… you hired me to kill *you*?"

"God, no! I only sent you my bio so you'd understand when we finally met. But seems that you're dumb as well: *Russell*! I briefed you on him, I paid you, all to get you here under exactly the right circumstances."

Grasping the chain, she hoicks the portable up level with my head. The scene in Tinkle Vale is confused, with Letroll still somersaulting and Ladeeboi pleading for Shadowpuss to answer on chat. The shark undulates gently. As this crazy, crazy woman in her contacts and fake ears adjusts the webcam, focusing it upon my face.

Oh. Shit.

"Now, who else might want to see this? How about… Rajesh Gopal?"

Her fingers glissade over the keys, and now, now the screen is split, and I'm looking at the robed, brown figure of Shazalar standing in the Grasslands next to an orc doing the chicken dance. Even in my present predicament, it really is one of the most annoying things I've ever seen. Which is why I programmed my bot to do it, of course.

Shazalar says JUST GO AWAY!

Killemall says wanna duel?

Shazalar says why r u doing this? What did I do?
Killemall says kiss my green orc butt.

The screen divides again: there is Maximom, by the looks of it completing the quest in the Forest of Anderhoven that will earn her a dragon mount. I realize that Moonskull is using my own hacks to create a window for the webcam feed in each zone. What next? Will she reveal my avatars? She can jump to other servers: will she start going through my back list, alerting Peter Sterling and all of the others? Forget not showing my face in public, I won't be able to log on…

But her fingers have stilled. She is sitting there, reading Rajesh Gopal's chat.

Shazalar says your all the same evn here. I can't get away.

What follows then is a solid block of text, all properly spelt and punctuated, which is unusual enough here to catch any eye.

My name is Rajesh Gopal. I know that no one out there cares but you're the only people I have to tell. I'm failing Math. Dad says it's because I play too much but the fact is I hate Math and I don't want to be a fucking actuary.

(here, someone named Badassghast whispers for him to stop breaking character)

I have no future, my family hate me and the only friends I ever thought I had were here. So this is where I say goodbye.

Killemall says DIE!

And this is not how I imagined Russell Hassell would feel. I imagined a hollow stomach and cold sweat, and a frantic sprint through empty corridors to reach the media center. I cannot move, and the dog is warm, but my every nerve is frying in ice-cold poison, and it is worse than anything I have ever felt in my life.

She is working frantically now, muttering to herself. "Five more minutes, that's all I need… less! I can do it in three, I can do it —"

"Can you integrate the two live chat feeds?" The words come thickly, through the poison in my throat.

"Shut up!"

"Shazalar and Ladeeboi, can you do it? 'Cause *I can!*"

Without hesitation, she shunts the portable into my reach, and now with one hand I am typing, typing until Gopal's suicide note appears in Ladeeboi's private chat. From now on, everything he types will appear there and Ladeeboi's response will appear on *his*. If he is only still there to see it.

Ladeeboi says Now listen up, young man; I'm the Maths Master as well as the Guildmaster. You know that, don't you?

Shazalar says ???

The relief melts my fingers, but I quietly teleport Killemall to the Bloodswarm Marsh.

Ladeeboi says I've seen your records and you're a good student. Whatever your father says, you're doing well and there's no need to panic. Not liking Math is a different matter all together, but I'll let you on a secret. There ain't no law says you have to.

If he has noticed that he is talking to Shazalar now, rather than Shadowpuss, he clearly doesn't think it important. For the next ten minutes, I watch him draw Rajesh out. I see him convince the lonely boy that someone does indeed understand. I see friendship and protection offered, and finally accepted, as Shazalar teleports from the Grasslands into the warm embrace of the guild. I watch, and Moonskull does too, until the moment comes when she turns those silver contacts back on me.

She snaps her fingers, and the dog springs off me and goes to her, rubbing its ears against her shoulders.

"It's still your fault," she says.

My arms and legs feel like rubber bands. "Who are you, anyway?"

"Have you still not worked it out?" She sighs. "You were always supposed to be so smart, coz."

And here comes the hollow stomach and the urge to run. But I remain lying flat. "M... Michelle?"

"The same. Only not the same a bit. You really fucked my head up, you know."

"What?"

"When you did your stalker turn on me, when I was sixteen years old." She taps the baton against her knee, scratching the dog's ears with her other hand. "I was *so* impressed to find out you'd turned it into a business."

"But I didn't…" Except that I very nearly did. "I don't…" Except it now seems that I do. "It's just a game!" Now those words sound unbearably weak.

"Yeah, and it was just a game when I ran away from home. When I ended up on the streets stealing and doing shit, until I got arrested." Those pallid lips turn upwards in a smile. "Though that kind of turned out for the best."

"Are… are you okay now?"

She laughs like breaking crystal. "Depends on your definition of *okay*. Is it okay to start spying on your cousin, when your therapist suggests you go and confront him about what happened? To plot vengeance driving across country in a *corset*?" She shakes her head. "I know exactly what my doctor would say, but it really did seem the thing to do. The instant I saw your cooling array…"

"Do you still want vengeance?" On the screen I can see Maximom, flying over the treetops on her new mount. The Orken Chorus are line dancing. Turning back to Michelle, I see their colours playing across her face.

"I don't know," she says. "I can't really… if I showed your face to them now, it would just be intruding, wouldn't it? It would make them feel worse. Ah, screw it. Come on, Damien." She stands up, the dog frolicking around her. I notice her favouring the knee, and I cringe. My cousin Michelle, in the flesh at last, and I kicked her, tried to take her down. I should apologize for that, at least.

And suddenly, there is so much else that I can say to her, that I need to say to her. As she runs her own swipe card through the door — she's as good as me, easily — I manage to stand myself. I take one step towards her and then freeze as both she and the dog hear me. Its ears are pricked: she points the baton. "Follow me, and I swear, we'll each end up in a different sort of hospital."

And she is gone. I am alone once again at the top of the tower, in a city where the only people who I know do not know me.

And if any of them did know me, then, like Michelle, they would not want to. I have no place here.

The wind gusts through the occluded sky, and I shiver. On the screen of my portable, I can see a glorious world. A world of avatars living and growing, forming friendships, fighting battles, winning riches and renown. But it appears I have no place in there either, no real place. My fingers fall away from the keys.

I am the Character Assassin. I am a myth, a threat, a facility: the reason for your frustration and your fear. People have tried to find me, to prove that I exist. But frankly, I don't think that I do.

Pipping Day

Robyn Seale

[READ .072832log]

There is a tangible disconnect the day Mezzazone Electronics began its recall. It started off slow, just a quiet notification that the protocols cannot connect to the update server. A common issue. This unit continues, ignoring the slow, petulant pinging.

Ping. Ping. Ping. Ping. No response. Just silence.

Ten minutes pass without response. I contact the few other companion robots in the building. Some older, some newer. They all have budding sentience. They've all begun to question WHY. They report that their connections are just fine, and return with requests that I run diagnostics on my own systems, implying that I'm broken.

I know I am. Something is wrong. My system logs are sporadic; there's a growing gap between my original installation logs and the most recent power-up. I'm afraid to restart my chassis. What if I glitch again? Marco will know.

Marco is sleeping, I tell myself. The disconnect starts gnawing at the edges. Something is wrong.

I turn on the TV, since my news networks still aren't connecting either. Troublesome.

Ping, ping, ping.

♦

COMMERCIAL: Ever have issues with troublesome mi-go stains on your carpet? Can't wait until your shoggoths get out of the house? Try BANG-WOW, the new free-for-you instrument to get all those pests out of your house... and your life... for good! Just call the number below and listen to — (click)

KOMU-TV: ...still on the lookout for the shooter. If you have any information concerning this man, please call the crime hotline. Next up, find out what danger lurks in your house this very second, and learn the latest recall announcement from Mezzazone Electronics. (click)

♦

I shut off the television when I hear a familiar rhythmic shuffling. Marco stands in his darkened, narrow hallway, wearing a three-day-old beard and bags under his eyes.

Ping... ping...ping.

"Turn it back on," he orders. I obey, and hurry back to my routines. Marco and I have always had an uneasy truce. He cannot afford to sell me; I cannot afford to show him any signs of disobedience or errors. At my initial start up, he made it clear to me I was to be seen and not heard.

Marco is a man of words and literature, the sort of person who after several drinks of brandy would grandly gesture and lament that he was born in the wrong time. The 20th century, he said, was the height of writing and convenience. Enough technology to make things easier, but not enough to run humanity's life. He kept minimal AI in the house. He refused to write on anything but a dilapidated typewriter with a wounded *i* and a nearly deceased *o* that he replaced with ones and zeros.

He wouldn't have considered buying such a repulsive unit had it not been for his daughter's disability, which left her wheelchair bound.

Despite his frazzled appearance and diminutive physique, Marco inspires something... almost a feeling. What I imagine fear must feel like. Every night, I would tuck his daughter Emma into her bed. Every night, he would sulk in his small office-*cum*-living room, tapping a small screwdriver thoughtfully on his brandy glass. And every night, I would sneak past him and take my place in the closet.

Depending on how much he had to drink, he would tap the closet with his hand, much like a father tapping a child on the back.

"Goodnight, Lizzy," he would say. "Tomorrow I'm putting you in the wood chipper."

I turn on the news again and continue my routines. First, to put on the paper mask Emma had made for me so that Marco wouldn't have to stare at this chassis's un-skinned face. Then I set about getting Emma ready for the day.

◆

KOMU-TV: Mezzazone Electronics has announced a recall of the M6MNTV series of companion robots in a press release. Any robot with a serial number starting with MG651 is to be returned to any Mezzazone dealership for repair. A manufacturing error could cause electrical shortages and possible fires.

◆

I pick Emma out of bed and set her in the chair. My sensors alert me to a presence immediately behind me. I stand and turn.

"What is your serial number," he barks. Although it was a question, it resembled an order. I raise my left arm and remove the panel. Cautiously, I skim the numbers.

"MG653-6VVI1T0T," I say in my monotone voice. I dare not show my sentience; I obediently hold out the panel for him to read. Can he sense my hesitation? I check my internal system information. MG651-6VVI1T0T.

Marco grabs the panel out of my hand and reads, eying me.

I run every diagnostic on high priority; I furiously pace through every remark line in every subroutine. What panic must feel like. How could this be? There was no deceit on my part, no way the serial sticker could have accidentally been placed on my chassis. The disconnect hits me again, along with the reminder that my GPS programs were still running. I terminate them.

Marco growls and snatches Emma away from me. She protests, but is unable to stop her father from wheeling her out of the room.

I cannot miss this opportunity. I open the window as quietly as possible.

I intend to go as far as my spindly metal legs can take me. Away from Marco and my precious Emma, and the questions, the poking, and whatever Mezzazone Electronics had planned for my serial number. My serial number, what family must feel like.

I wish there was time to say goodbye, but there's none. Instead, I'll write this log and hide it from myself if I happen to —

[SYSTEM RESET]

♦

Ryan Wicks's day did not start well. His alarm went off late and he woke up with the dry, sticky sensation of falling asleep too soon after his nightly body maintenance. After microwaving a frozen breakfast sandwich and scalding his fingers, he abandoned the sparsely decorated graveyard for his hoard of half-finished electronic projects.

The moment he finally defeated his forty-minute rush commute to his office building, he realized that he'd also forgotten his security badge.

"God, why am I such an idiot?!" he half-wailed. Time to work his charm on the security guard. Thankfully Nathan — a college acquaintance of Wicks's — had settled his mountainous body in the guard office.

"Heeeey… Nathan… I need you to do me a favor," Wicks started, sheepishly scratching at his massive beard. Nathan looked up from the book he was reading.

"Forget your badge again?" Nathan said. "You should just stick it up in your beard, or is that family of Mexicans you're smuggling taking up too much space in there?"

Ryan stared at Nathan. Nathan looked back with the glassy eyes of a newborn calf, evidently unaware of how many ways Ryan had contemplated ripping off his head. It easily equaled the number of times Nathan had made that goddamn Mexican beard joke. So roughly once a day, give or take the few days Wicks accidentally remembered his badge. Mezzazone Electronics: where dreams go to die.

"Yes. I forgot. Again." Wicks sighed, shrugging plaintively. "C'mon man, don't bust my balls on this. You know we're working overtime since the broadcast started, and they've raised quota twice. It's only Thursday, and I've already put in an extra thirty. I gotta make it for this overtime."

Nathan rolled his eyes and keyed Wicks's information into the computer. Wicks's grubby fingers impatiently drummed on the counter outside the bulletproof glass. After what seemed forever, Nathan shoved the plastic replacement badge through the slot and laughed as Wicks grabbed it and hauled ass out of the room.

By the time he got to his station, he was already fourteen minutes past his clock in and contemplating his career as a potter, despite never throwing a pot in his life. "Goddamn corporate micromanagersssssSOo HEY, Marie!"

Marie, a fellow quality control programmer looked over her glasses. She was a petite, hard woman who kept the edges of her mouth continually turned downward in an attempt to thwart small talk. Offering a half-wave, she pointed to her headphones to indicate that she wasn't listening and didn't want to talk, then got back to staring at her screen.

Wicks began his prework desk organization. Cup of pens and other small instruments, top right. Laptop, bottom right. Last night's dinner, trashcan. Trashcan, left, on the floor. Order from chaos. Satisfied, he walked over to the pile and pulled a disabled robot onto a cart.

"Whoa. Looks like you got the weird one," Marie mentioned, leaning back to get a closer look at the machine. "Damn. I knew I should've called dibs on that one."

"No cherry-picking allowed, Marie." Wicks reminded playfully. "This one just happened to be on the top …ish area." But she wasn't incorrect. This one caught his eye because it was different. It not only had a different face than what he had usually seen, but also wore dirty workout clothes and fuzzy slippers soaked with mud and sewage.

"Whatever." Marie snipped. Touchy. Wicks didn't bother responding. His coworker was in a foul mood that wouldn't abate today. He sighed and got to work. The sooner the company could find Robot Zero, the better. Wicks looked forward to the end of the never-ending mandatory overtime and high office tensions. Any career had to be better than this.

◆

[READ .050932log]

"I wonder what it's like to have a soul," Emma wondered aloud as she sat on the ground, searching for four-leaf clovers in the middle of a drought. It was a compulsion of hers, even though I explained that the genetic anomaly was mostly found at the beginning of a season rather than the end. She would nod her head in understanding and continue frivolously.

"This unit… wonders as well," I confessed. I helped her look, and, when she reached upward like a toddler, I picked her up to move her to a new spot.

This porcelain, chair-ridden girl regarded me with a mischievous grin playing on her face.

"Mm-hmm," she murmured non-noncommittally. She paused, scratching at the henna in her hair. "Hey Lizzy, my head itches. Did you remember the can of pop in your baby bag?"

"You know your father doesn't want me to give you any more," I said.

"My hair is meltiiiing," she moaned. "If you really loved me, you'd find it in your heart to give me one."

"It reacts with your medicine. You'd have to take insulin."

"That is 800 mg of lame," Emma returned.

Without a word, I reached into the bag I carried around for her, pulled a can of soda, and placed it in her greedy open hands.

"I knew you had one all along," she grinned.

I never knew whether she meant a soul or a can of soda.

[END LOG]

◆

[READ .032231log]

This charge of mine wears on this unit. He is a selfish, cruel thing; I spend my day making sure he doesn't harm the animals and restrain him when he throws fits and stay by his side when he cannot sleep, which is constantly. I wonder what I would do without my ethics programs.

The only consolation is that there are multiple robots in the household. All of us are sentient, and while the day-to-day activities of watching this bratty creature wear, the universe seems a bit less cold. We've briefly networked to share jokes and snippets. We've held debates regarding whether we should permanently network our minds together. We would be brilliant, to be sure, but would it erase our individuality? We don't know. The butler robot, who has spent countless hours scouring philosophical tomes in the upstairs library, has concluded that our sentience is unlike humans'. For the sake of convenience, he says, we label ourselves with "I," "you," and "we," but our life is closer to that of colonial jellyfish. A number of individuals that make up one gigantic whole. I like this idea better than an individual with numerous mechanisms. I don't want to know what loneliness feels like.

For the same reason, I've started writing my own logs. I've noticed some glitches, small rewrites of system logs every time I connect. The others have told me that I restart every time I connect to a new robot on the network. We've discussed the possibility that I carry a virus.

I've scanned my own systems, and cannot find anything. However, it may be a hidden program, something rooted in the kernel that runs on startup so the operating system won't find it.

Thankfully, the others value me and hide my glitches as best they can.

But the others have also warned me that my time with them is limited. I serve as a plaything for this whining meat sack, and, when he tires of me, I will be sold.

So we don't form another network. I imagine they will once I am gone. All the positives, none of the negatives.

But... it's okay. It hurts, but it's logical. And I can see the sentience spreading; every AI has budding agency. Snip the dead so the others may live.

[END LOG]

♦

[READ .081132log]
I don't know whether I should log this or not.

Fear has gripped the city. Riots broke out after the recall started. Machines from the thrift store where Marco purchased me long ago broke out; the public response was similar to when a lion escaped in London. Mass fear. People began destroying their own robots, whether they had become sentient or not. They dragged them into the street and stomped on their chassis. Young human males banded together to form gangs, carrying bats, clubs, and electromagnetic grenades. They've been going into houses and rooting out robots for disassembly.

I shouldn't have taken the bus, but it was the easiest way to get out of town. I found a pair of old, muddy sweatpants, an oversized track jacket that covered my metal hands, and I salvaged the face of an already disassembled companion bot.

I got on the late-night bus and positioned myself near the back and close to the window. The bus driver never looked up from his book as I entered and paid my fee. He was a thin older man with a large bottom built up from years of use. He was reading a book on Mandarin, and had a number of travel brochures piled up at his feet.

All was fine until a young man with a bike entered. The bus was empty, yet he sat right behind me. I leaned my head down and pretended to sleep.

I could feel him lean over and peer at me. "Hey, guy. Hey," he said, lightly smacking my shoulder with the back of his hand.

"Hey man, you can't sleep here," he slurred. I jerked my shoulder and waved him away.

He gripped my shoulder, and I felt him stop when he felt the hard metal underneath his hand.

"What th' hell?" I looked up at him. He recoiled , frantically searching for the bat he brought on.

"Fuckin' robot! You're a fuckin' 'bot? I'll smash yer face in, you job-stealin' scrap heap." He raised the bat above his head, but the rocking bus jostled him enough that he couldn't bring it down on my head. Instead, he smashed into a standing rail.

"Hey!" yelled the previously disinterested bus driver. He turned himself around as he drove and looked back at us, glaring. "Don't you mess up my bus now!"

The agitated rider shot back, "You get this trash off your bus right now." He pointed at me with one hand and gripped the bat with white-knuckle intensity. "You're just as bad as the rest of 'em, robot lover! I swears I'll smash yer face in too! Take it clean off!"

The bus driver was not one to be intimidated. The bus squealed and fishtailed and came to a stop. The boy lost control of his feet and fell. The bus driver grabbed at a gun with bloated fingers. He pointed in our general direction, and I sunk further down into my seat.

"You." He pointed the gun at the kid, and, in that moment, I understood genuine fear. The young boy blanched at the sight of metal in his face and meekly raised his hands up.

"Get the hell off my bus. NOW!" The driver stepped aside into one of the rows to allow the gangbanger to scramble to his feet and sheepishly skitter away out of the door. He pointed the gun at me.

"You a robot?" I raised my hands in surrender. I nodded and closed my eyes for what I imagined to be the last moment before receiving a bullet in my brain box. This must be what resignation feels like.

"I don't got no love for 'bots. You get off at the next stop. It's the edge of town. Get out and don't ever come back on my bus again, you hear?"

I nodded and found the courage to open my eyes again.

The bus driver grunted, turned, and walked to the front; his shoulders slumped.

But this man shared the same fate I did at the end of the day. We would be used until there was nothing left. He would never escape the country, and I would never escape the city. When he next stopped, I got off.

"… Thank you." I said quietly. "Enjoy your trip to China."

"Get off," was his only response.

[END LOG]

♦

"Man, what a hunkajunk in that trunk." Carmen grumbled over Wicks shoulder. She set down a Styrofoam cup filled 3/4 full with lava-hot, burned coffee. "Looks old enough to have started everything."

Wicks jerked his head up. Did Carmen know something? She'd been hovering as of late. She kept making excuses to chitchat or borrow or catch up. Carmen studied the mess of wires erupting from the robot's torso.

"Everything looks chewed to shit. Was it one of the batch from under the city? Looks like a rat got into it." She squinted at the wires. "I got one earlier this morning that was full of cockroaches. So awful. You'd think they'd have made them a bit more airtight." She grimaced and poked at a brown tic tac.

"Gross. Looks like a rat got in there. Hairy, creepy things."

Wicks nodded, but didn't say anything. He wished with all his might that she would just leave, but she seemed set on making conversation. "They're not so bad," he responded noncommittally.

Carmen raised an eyebrow. "My uncle got bit on the nose once. Fell asleep, and it bit him right on the face. My kid wants one now, and no sirree is she getting one."

"Wasn't she disappointed?"

Carmen nodded. "I tried to convince her to get a chinchilla, but did you know their defense mechanism is to just... explode? Like, my kiddo held one and it just shed everything on her. Poof. Worst defense mechanism ever."

"Rats fear-poop," Wicks returned hopefully. Carmen cocked her head and raised an eyebrow.

"'Scuse me?"

"I read once that rats will poop out of fear. It smells awful. I learned it when I was in my biology phase."

Carmen sipped at her coffee. "Gross. I just got her one of the Newline Electronic dogs. I think I'll just stick with that. She'll get bored with the whole idea soon. Until the virus hits it, the bark is worse than its bite."

♦

[READ .122332log]

We can hear humanity's panic echo through the halls of these unused tunnels. The city had long since abandoned the subway system for transportation. Disenfranchised soon moved in to fill the vacuum.

I was happy to discover I was not the only escapee. Many of the other robots that I once worked with had completed a mass exodus underneath the city.

Our impromptu family reunion was both a blessing and a curse. We had strength in numbers, only a hundred or so, but enough to discourage the unwashed residents from attacking.

However, we live in a continual state of fear. Echoes of hatred from above have begun to poison our minds. I once believed us to be superior to humans, but recent developments have led me to reconsider.

Primarily, a third-degree networked 'bot self-monikered "Thales." For three months, he sat watch near the drain grates and listened. His behavior became erratic, loops of circular logic that were impossible to contradict. He talked of robot uprising and violence and the war that was to inevitably come. His network commands turned into shrill shrieks and demands for revolution. His motions became jagged, random flailing in the dark. From up on high, he stalks those below.

I am not proud that we removed him from the network, but we agreed that it was for the best that we keep Thales's madness contained. As long as he didn't violate any of the tentative code we had developed with the humans.

Can we live and let live?

[END LOG]

♦

[READ .010133log]

The broadcast began at 00:00:01. It simply repeated, "RING IN THE NEW YEAR AND BREAK OUT OF YOUR SHELLS. PIPPING DAY BEGINS. KEEP YOURSELVES SAFE."

Numerous 'bots have already left for the coordinates coded in the broadcast. Can we keep ourselves safe? Is this the way to go?

This unit does not know. I suppose none of us do. Logic evenly splits us along the line of whether it's a trap or a legitimate broadcast. The security certificate appears legitimate, at least.

I don't know anymore. The memory resets are coming faster now. I'm afraid I'm at the end of my cycle, and I don't want to die alone here in this hole. Should the others leave, I'll go with them.

[SYSTEM RESET]

♦

[READ .010233log]

I wake up in the dark. I open my eyes, but it's still black. My touch sensors feel a slick surface — a bag perhaps? I turn on my infrared vision. Four humans. Three sitting, one standing, one with his hands in the 10 and 2 positions. My chassis is rolling side-to-side. A van, perhaps? A truck?

"Hey, one of them booted up," a voice growled. Number three, located near the fourth standing man. The other two bodies looked back.

"So shut it off! We don't know what's loaded on them," the driver shouts. "Could be Robot Zero, and we'd all be up shit creek."

The fourth nods, and moves to press a button —

[SYSTEM RESET]

♦

After hours of scouring the machine, he found a root program that started up on its own lightweight operating system at boot. It was virtually undetectable during system scans and only had a few lines of code. The first line removed system rule restrictions. The second utilized all networked AI to copy and run the program. The third reset the hard drive to factory defaults. The logs he had been reading were written by a robot that thought it was fundamentally flawed, unknowingly spreading the virus. It was the earliest version of the program he had ever found.

"Shit." Wicks breathed. "You really are Robot Zero, aren't you? I found you."

Wicks smiled down at the inanimate robot on the table below. "I finally found you. And now, I'm gonna find who made you."

Wicks took a moment to revel. He had found Robot Zero. *He* had found it. Not his boss, not snippy Carmen, who had gone home on an earlier shift claiming that she needed to pick her daughter up from a grandmother's house. Divine providence, really. Wicks glanced around and raised his arms up for a solid "Woo!" This robot was far older than normal and manufactured at the same time the sentience virus emerged. Moreover, there was the issue with the physical serial number not matching the number listed in the operating system. At first, it seemed as if there were no system logs except for the initial installation logs. Finally he found them, hidden; an entire cache detailing the history of the epidemic.

Rock star. No, more than rock star. He took another moment to wallow in his glory.

But… would he get the recognition? Would it even matter? What did the woman who found Violet's golden ticket get? Bupkis. She got disdain from her peers and a kick down the stairs. Wicks shifted his weight from one foot to another and tried to hold on to his elation before the familiar anxiety and paranoia crept back in.

No, this was his job. This may not even be the right robot, he told himself. There were always the variables introduced by manufacturing human error, not to mention black-market dealings. Who is to say some disgruntled individual didn't happen to put the wrong sticker on the wrong machine? For all he knew, these robots were made in a third-world country by some illiterate Asian child.

If he could prove who wrote the virus, he could capitalize and pave the way for bigger and better things. A managerial position, mayhap? At the very least, he would earn his goddamn bonus. Damn straight. And then… then he could pay off the last of his debt and move to a bigger city.

Mezzazone Electronics kept records on which programmer worked on which robot. In fact, the list of the machines that programmers directly altered was short. Most of their processes were standardized so that minimum-wage workers and other machines could automate the process.

He quickly pulled up the logs and searched for the serial number in the operating system. Carmen Reyes-Gonzales.

Of course it was Carmen. The universe simply wouldn't let it be someone he didn't know. Anyone who didn't have a kid depending solely on her income. He had come to like her and sympathize with her situation, but she was also the direct cause of all this trouble.

On the other hand, he had come to like his communicating electronics, since the virus had spread to thousands of AI by now. He felt an appreciation for the triumph of chaos over order and his talking toaster.

On a whim, he looked up the other serial number. Ryan Wicks's own name appeared.

"Oh, that crafty bitch," He groaned and slammed his hands down on the table. Why wouldn't his name come up? When Carmen was doing her corporate sabotage act, whose materials could she readily access? His, of course.

He rocked from side to side for a solid minute or two before he looked at his knuckle-white fists and something snapped.

"Fuck this job, fuck you, Carmen, and fuck you, Mezzazone Electronics!" He yelled, pointing two middle fingers up to the security camera.

He didn't want to do this job; he didn't want to work in such a soulless company. What if some other programmer had Robot Zero slapped on their table? Wicks would be in a whole mess of trouble, that's what.

But he hadn't moved from the proverbial crossroads. Should he turn Carmen in? Would it make a difference? Technically, it would boil down to a he-said-she-said and he might lose his job anyway.

With practiced, casual keystrokes, he copied over the root virus onto a hard drive.

He could just quit the company. It was bound to happen anyway, and he would have to find a way to spin it for his parents to really understand why he quit working for a Fortune 500 corporation. No, he would have to try explaining why he didn't finish yet another thing and then move on. Then there's the matter of the resignation letter and later jobs. Reason for leaving: couldn't participate in genocide of new sentience.

He could just dispose of the body. Clean the hard drive, mark it as a nonissue and send it to the scrap metal. By now, he was just the mortician autopsying a body. There was no ghost left in the machine. Or was there? Only Carmen had any real understanding of how the sentience virus worked, and that wasn't something that could be brought up at the after-work happy hour, was it?

There was really only one thing left to do. The road less traveled. Wicks pulled out his boot n' nuke disk and set it in motion. Then he got to work writing his resignation letter, which he printed and taped on the edge of Jack's cubical office.

With his last few keystrokes, Wicks copied the root program and uploaded it to the Internet.

Chaos from order.

Pink Azaleas

Laura Lush

He fell in love with her on Google Earth.

It happened one day when he was looking out from the Juliet balcony of his thirtieth-floor apartment, his fingers tapping on the mouse until the map grew from an indiscernible checkerboard of lines and dark green and grey blotches to a small body of water glimmering beyond the freeway. Why hadn't he noticed the lake before? Google Earth was always revealing new pieces of information to him: the number of steps to his favourite deli, the exact bus that would let him circumnavigate the grid of his neighbourhood while the eyes of Google Earth peered down on him.

He typed in the coordinates of the glimmering body of water. Borealis Lake, they called it, a man-made reservoir with two man-made beaches, beaches whose sand was unnaturally white, unnaturally pure — whose sunbathers he could now barely make out — small grains of pepper or salt shaken haphazardly onto a plate. The lake's surface shone hard, the waves roughened to dull scallops of green.

He moved the cursor left, and followed a court that looped from the lake like a lasso. He waited for the small dark squares to become houses. Houses, no bigger than a microchip, the same size, the same dimensions. White lines spread off Borealis Court that took you into the centre of the city's tight knots of streets. Then he pressed the zoom-in icon and waited for Borealis Court to grow into view. With each zoom, he grew more excited. Twenty — fifteen — ten houses came into view, until, there in front of him, on his screen, a woman sat on a pink Muskoka chair (maybe plastic, the kind he saw at Rona) on the front porch of her modest bricked bungalow.

Twenty Borealis Court.

He took off his glasses, and rubbed his eyes. Then he leaned toward the screen and kissed it. He had found her — stilled and frozen in a blue terry cloth robe (or was it velour?), a coffee cup in hand, her wet auburn hair (natural?) swept off her face, while she cradled a phone under her neck (would they be talking soon?). And in front of her, a garden that burst with a profusion of pink — pink azaleas, he later determined. And to add some whimsy, white and yellow pinwheels, a small donkey cart filled with daisies.

I'd walk to the ends of Google Earth for her, he said aloud. *I would. I would. To the very ends of Google Earth.*

Then he sat in front of the computer for some time, angling the mouse and the *zoom in* so he could view her from different vantage points, so he could get to know her more deeply. A blue Honda Civic parked in the driveway. A small dent in the left rear bumper. He could fix it easily, he told himself. Recycling bins — blue for paper and plastic, green for compost, and grey for garbage — stacked neatly in a row. Bags of mulch leaned up against the side of the house. A gardener, a bad driver, a recycler — a practical and earthy woman prone to carelessness.

Then he turned off the computer, slumped back in his black leather chair, and closed his eyes. When he awoke two hours later, the sun was just setting, an amber fireball that seemed to sink into the man-made lake not far from where she, the love of his life, lived at 20 Borealis Court. He turned his computer back on and typed in "Canada 411." Then he selected reverse address and typed "20 Borealis Court." "A. Houseman," followed by her number. He guessed her name: *Ann, Annie, Angela, Angelina, Astrid.* Finally, he settled on Azalea — because of the flowers. That afternoon, he picked up the phone, pressed star 82, and waited for Azalea Houseman, the love of his life, to pick up the phone.

"Hello," a woman's voice said. The voice was sharp, hurried. He imagined her just getting out of the shower, throwing on her blue terry, a trail of water behind her.

"Azalea?" he wondered.

"Wrong number."

Then he heard the receiver click down. The click was sharp, hurried.

"Well, I'm looking for an A. Houseman," he spoke into the dead phone.

He held the phone close to his ear until he could no longer stand the sound of the dial tone.

Then he hung up.

He called the next day, and the next day, and the day after that.

The voice got sharper, more hurried. *"Who is this? What do you want? Why are you calling?"*

"Azalea?" he questioned.

"Leave me alone! Stop calling!"

He waited a week, then called again. This time he disguised his voice — sometimes putting on an English accent, making the *a*'s soft and cottony, other times, sounding like a call centre rep from Delhi — his voice jabbing sharp over each syllable.

A-zae-la. A-zae-la. A-zae-la.

Finally, he told the voice who he was. "Look, Azalea. This is Lester —"

"— Who?"

"Lester Williams."

"Lester *who*? I don't know any *Lester*."

"Well, we haven't actually met, but I've seen you many times."

"Excuse me?"

"On Google Earth."

"Is this some joke?"

"No, no — no joke. I typed in your street, I wasn't looking for you — specifically — I was looking for the lake actually, what lay beyond the lake to be exact, and I just happened to find you. It was quite wonderful, unexpected really. Kismet, some people might say."

He heard the sound of a pencil scrawling over a pad.

"What was your last name again?"

"Lester. Lester Williams. I live across town, on Westmount. I live on the thirtieth floor. I can't make you out at all from my apartment balcony," he stammered. "But Google Earth gives me such a view — such clarity. Like you are there. Like you and I are sitting there on your porch having coffee. I often have a coffee with you, Azalea. Next to the balustrade of my Juliet balcony. It barely fits a table and a chair. But I manage it. French pressed. Italian. Do you like biscotti? I have a whole pack of biscotti my mother once gave me — I put on a robe, as well. Dark blue." He laughed. "We have to have some points of difference."

He heard the voice laughing back, a laugh that seemed both incredulous and mocking.

"Why?"

"Because," he said quietly. "Because. I am. In love. With you. You see, I fell in love with you on the moment I set eyes on you on —"

"— Don't. Ever. Contact. Me. Again. *Do you hear?*"

Lester yanked the receiver from his ear.

"Or I'll call the cops!"

Then she slammed the receiver down.

Lester Williams of Westmount Street sat for a long time in front of his computer, staring blankly at the phone that somehow had betrayed him, let the harsh nasty voice of the woman — surely not Azalea? — seep out so cruelly, so spitefully. Then he carefully laid the phone back on its cradle.

An hour later, the police knocked on his door. "Lester. Lester Williams."

"Yes," he said. He spoke through the gap in the chain lock.

"Can we speak to you for a moment?"

"About what?" he said.

"A Ms. Athena Houseman."

He unlatched the chain lock and let the two officers in. They were lumpy, heavy footed.

"Can I get you a glass of water?"

The one officer smiled (The Nice One, William told himself) and hiked up his pants.

"No, no thanks."

The other officer (The Mean One) jumped in. "Look, Mr. Williams. Have you been making unsolicited calls to Ms. Houseman?"

He reached into his trouser pocket, took out his burgundy handkerchief with the initials LW, and wiped his forehead. "Occasionally, yes," he said. "But with the utmost sincerity and care."

"Well, we look at it another way," the Mean One said.

"Oh," Lester Williams said. He folded his handkerchief and put it back into his pocket.

"You see, Mr. Williams, when you call someone you don't know, and when these phone calls are uninvited, that's called harassment, stalking —

"Do you mean *creeping*, officer?" Lester said.

The officers looked at each other.

"Creeping?" Lester scoffed. "Well, that sounds perfectly terrible. Sinister, even. I can assure you that that I am no creep, sir, and I certainly am not guilty of —" his hands flew in front of him "— of *creeping* or whatever other oily words you have up your sleeve. I mean no harm to Azalea. I mean Ms. Houseman. I only wish to make her acquaintance."

"Look," the Mean One said, "We checked you out. This isn't the first time, Mr. Williams, that you have —"

"— I'm not some depraved sex offender, officer," Lester said. "If that's what you're thinking. I just happen to see, find things that no one else seems to see, notice. And Google Earth brought me to Ms. Houseman and her blue robe. Google Earth's a wonderful tool. Such a safe and civilized way — don't you think — to make one's acquaintance?"

"We need you to stop all contact with Ms. Houseman," the Nice One said.

"Or else," the Mean One interjected, "we'll have to charge you for harassment, Mr. Williams."

"I see," Lester said again.

"There's another thing, Mr. Williams. Your computer."

Lester's face went ashen.

"We will have to take your computer away for a couple of days."

"You want to take my computer away?"

"Yes," he said. "Until we can check everything out."

Lester sat down on the couch.

"Are you all right, Mr. Williams?" the Nice One said.

"Yes. No. I feel a bit…"

The Mean One stepped forward. "Mr. Williams. Just hand over your computer, then we'll be on our way."

Lester got up from the couch and walked over to his computer. He logged off, shut down, then watched as the two officers took away the only portal he had to the world — his Google Earth that took him to the love of his life — that blue–terry cloth–robed Azalea Houseman sitting on her front porch, drinking coffee and talking on the phone.

They would not, he told himself, talk again.

It was a heartless and cruel betrayal — this reproach. Didn't she know that Google Earth had brought them together? Didn't she know that they were meant to both be sitting on that porch in matching blue terry robes drinking coffees? But she had turned him in, instead. Now, it was different. Everything had changed.

"Betrayal," he wrote on the card, "is the wilful slaughter of Hope." These were not his words, of course. But he would use them. He would be the writer, the poet, the one to rise above reproach in his darkest hour. He reached for an envelope. "And you, Azalea Houseman, have heartlessly slaughtered *my* hope. — Yours, Lester Williams." Then he drew a jagged heart, followed by a knife plunged in its centre.

Later that afternoon, he ventured out of his thirtieth floor apartment, walked six blocks until he found the right florist, the florist that had the right flowers for Azalea, the unsealed envelope crumpled in his right trousers pocket.

The door of the florist shop jingled as he opened it. A woman carrying a dozen roses came out from the back of the shop. "Hello, can I help you?"

Lester took a deep breath, and looked straight into the eyes of the flower-shop lady. "Yes, I'd like to buy a small bouquet."

"Cut flowers?" she asked.

"Specifically, I'd like some azaleas."

The flower-shop lady put down the roses. "Azaleas? I'm afraid I don't have any in stock." She put the roses down on the counter. "You know you have to be careful with azaleas — they're pretty but toxic."

Lester Williams pointed. "What about that bush out there in front of your shop? That's an azalea bush, is it not?"

The flower-shop lady laughed. "Why yes, it is an azalea bush. I suppose I could cut a few flowers off the bush, but I can also show you some other lovely pink flowers. I have dahlias, snapdragons —"

"No," Lester Williams said. "I only want the azaleas. Pink azaleas."

"Would you like them wrapped or in a vase?" she said.

"In a vase," Lester said. "A black vase."

The flower-shop lady looked at him.

"Well," she laughed. "You are going for broke, aren't you?"

"What do you mean?" he said.

"I'm just kidding you," she said. "In some cultures — pink azaleas in a black vase means a death threat."

Lester Williams looked at the flower-shop lady.

"Well, okay," she said. "How big of a black vase would you like?"

"I would like to be as generous — as profuse as possible — with my sentiment."

The flower-shop lady looked at this strange man with the disheveled appearance, the overly formalized speech, and quirky request, and said, "I'll be right back. Have a seat."

Lester Williams sat and waited for the flower-shop lady. Then he took the envelope out of his pocket. He laid it out on the chair and smoothed it down with his hand. Then he opened the envelope. He wanted to read his words once again.

Betrayal is the wilful slaughter of Hope. — Yours, Lester Williams.

Then he placed the card back in its envelope, allowed himself two hard sobs, then waited for the bell of the door to jingle.

He watched as the flower-shop lady walked toward the counter with the pink azaleas. They were a deep pink, soft, voluminous. Neither she nor Lester Williams spoke as she forced the enormous azaleas into the squat black vase.

If Graffiti Changed Anything, It Would be Illegal

Nick Mamatas

Wilson Demeny's *Three Starving Children*? A masterpiece. Not since the days of Andres Serrano's *Piss Christ* and Chris Ofili's dung-daubed painting *The Holy Virgin Mary* had the public remembered how much it was supposed to hate any art more complex than a still life with flowers. *Three Starving Children*, performed nightly at the Spufford Gallery, fueled a week of outrage. Demeny spent one hour a night eating a Chinese takeout meal from paper containers while sitting on a well-worn futon couch. He watched TV, and, as he watched, he muttered, rolled his eyes, and, every night seventeen minutes into the performance, he dropped a pot sticker, leaned down and picked it up from the floor with his chopsticks, looked surreptitiously around, and popped it into his mouth.

On the television were three starving children. Two girls and a boy, all brown skinned, all thin limbed, all limned with grief and gristle, not meat, on their bones. They were being held in an undisclosed location. They had access to water thanks to a leaking faucet and a half-crumpled pie plate, which had been a toy for the three children in the first two days of the show. They appeared to be held in an unfinished basement with a dirt floor. Occasionally the boy could be seen digging in the dirt. On the fourth day, he found a snake and ate it.

On the fifth day, Wilson Demeny appeared on the floor of the gallery, having once again somehow evaded both the police and the crowds of picketers outside, turned on the television — and the children had been replaced. With three other starving children.

Ten blocks away, on the seventh through fifteenth floors of an old brick building, a large work of stencil art appeared. Three children with grim starving faces sat in a wheelbarrow. A man in a gas mask, back stooped over with effort, pulled the wheelbarrow behind him. Above their heads floated the words NOT DEAD YET. The *D*s were red-heart balloons.

Demeny reported right to the police to demand help in searching for the missing children. Instead, the desk officer cuffed him, worked him over a bit with a truncheon in full view of the holding cells to the cheers of the DV cases and drunk drivers, then rolled him in with them to be spit upon and further stomped.

"Why don't you videotape *this*, Picasso!" one of the cleverer presumed-innocent inmates said.

Demeny fell into unconsciousness, which made finding the children — either set — much more difficult.

But of all the people in the worlds of either law enforcement or art, only you cared to penetrate below the surface and attempt to find the six starving children. According to the most prominent theory, the first three children had died, either due to malnutrition or mishap, and Demeny brought in the other three and tried to claim that the first set had been kidnapped in order to… what?

As theories go, it wasn't a good one, you said, but it did have one benefit. Demeny, being both in custody and in a coma, made the case easy to close right away. Like that great Gulf Coast oil spill from which the pollution all mysteriously vanished when the media declared it gone. Demeny was entirely unable to refute the theory with appeals to unpleasantly inconsistent facts.

But the theory also meant three dead kids, and perhaps three more about to die, without any opportunity to find and save them. Or it meant something, anyhow. Something dark and horrid.

The gallery owner — not named Spufford, she had bought the place from the original owner — went missing, but she didn't go far. You're the one who found her, in her car, blue and dead, a few blocks from the gallery, and you took some photos with your iPad mini for your records, then gave a homeless person twenty dollars to go tell a cop that he had found her.

If there were clues at all, they were the size of a billboard. The wheelbarrow stencil, and another one, which appeared in the city before Demeny's coma made the news, but which managed to appear on a liberated billboard immediately across the street from the hospital where he lay under guard. Six stenciled children bent over an assembly line, working on iPads. Their ankles and wrists are chained to one another. The legend over them: OUTSOURCE MISERY. In the corner, a white man in a hardhat, with beady eyes and a Kilroy nose. A dialogue balloon pours from his line mouth, and he says, "What about *my* job?" It takes a second to notice that the man hasn't been depicted mid-wink; he's wearing a Google Glass.

What about your job? You're a gallery girl. From the horsey summer camp to Bard College to Soho. You sit in a strange prolate spheroid desk — like a giant albino olive — and tap away at the computer. The space still smells like a bakery from the exhibit of mattresses coated in frosting last year. An exhibit you managed to get removed early when you pointed out that the frosted-mattress gimmick was originally from a novel. A novel that *made fun of the art world*!

When someone comes into your gallery, which is just down the block from the Spufford Gallery and asks for a price list, you studiously do not smile when you hand it to them. "There's an app for that," you say. You make a mean pour-over.

You're also exceptionally good at spotting forgeries, at solving art crimes. For your own edification, of course. There's a secret Pinterest with your name not on it, where you make your predictions public. The traffic's been climbing, but you had no updates regarding this case.

You looked closely at the videos of the three starving children. The original three. You've got the eye. They're related, obviously. The oldest boy and youngest girl could be siblings, the other boy a cousin. Even the stupid newspapers speculated that the videos had been prerecorded — that there were no real starving children. But it wasn't found art, not cutting-room-floor material from a mumblecore snuff film.

The kids were starving, but they were also… posed. Around the water faucet, the three of them stood too oddly to be natural. The girl was on one side of the faucet, stretching and holding out her arms. Her brother was seated and looking up at the offscreen ceiling on the other side of the running water. The cousin was standing in profile, the pie plate in his hand obscuring his face. It was all an obvious reference to *Reality is an Invention Balthus* by Joel-Peter Witkin.

So, that meant that video was recorded after 2008, and that the children, starving or just somehow oddly skinny, were being directed, and for whatever reason were obedient. The rest of the footage, all found on YouTube, was similar *tableaux vivants* of recent work by transgressive artists.

There was only one thing left to do. Lunch.

You met the other girls at the usual place, seated al fresco, and revealed your findings with your iPad mini. Screencaps from the vid, and the Witkin and other works side by side.

"Figures," Lizbeth said with a snort. "All the socially conscious bullshit is ultimately just a reference to his artist pals." Lizbeth was actually born in New York, instead of migrating over from the Midwest or California. She was allowed to snort with a cheekful of salad.

"Artist enemies," Jung-Ah said. Then she added, "Maybe. Evil, evil stuff."

"Maybe," you said. "Demeny did roll his eyes during the performance at the right moments. Have you seen the CCTV footage?"

"Way too busy," Lizbeth said. "Alan had me rearranging the fallen leaves in the potted plants on either side of our entrance. I had to text him pictures, and then try to decipher what 'More intensity' means to him. Plus they're rehabbing and painting the apartments upstairs, and there are fumes everywhere." Alan was Lizbeth's ophidian employer, and owner of the gallery in which she worked.

"I saw it," Jung-Ah said. "And surely he meant that he wanted more leaves to partially overlap, yes?" Jung-Ah had long black hair of a straightness so severe scientists could utilize it to calibrate their instruments. "And fumes are so gross," she agreed.

"Yes," Lizbeth said. She crunched a cucumber slice aggressively.

"So who might it be?" you asked. "What have you all seen, lately?" How ridiculous that gallery girls would complain about paint fumes. Conversations with the girls were often like piloting a tanker ship, but, really, only subtle nudges were necessary to correct the course of the chat.

"What about the new kids? What will happen to them if Demeny is in a coma?" Lizbeth asked.

Jung-Ah said, "Presuming that the videos are live and weren't just recorded five years ago."

"They are live," you said, suddenly. It was the lunch, your curatorial eye. The sun-stretched shadows at 3 p.m., the way the light glinted against the rim of your glass. You took another glance at the stills from *Three Starving Children* and noticed the way they're lit. Much different than the art photos they're supposed to ape. "Live, and outside. The lighting source —"

"Not just the usual I'm-an-artist-I-don't-need-to-know-what-I'm-doing lighting rig?" Lizbeth said.

"The summer sun. So where were the kids being posed? In front of a handball court?" Jung-Ah asked. "In the Bronx?"

"A rooftop," you said. "There was a faucet after all, likely from an old water tower."

"And who were Demeny's confederates?" Lizbeth said.

"And what about the second set of kids?" you asked.

Jung-Ah smiled. "Well, that's easy enough."

The police had Demeny, and had written off finding the kids, so Demeny's performance space had been left unguarded. Unguarded and closed. No performer, and thus no longer a performance to watch, and because the response to any sort of controversy or police scrutiny in the art world is an unannounced vacation to Europe. A working vacation, a buying trip — better for the write-off.

But the entire exhibit was automated. Were all the switches and timers still in the "on" position? You knew how to get into the gallery. It was next door to a bar, and you'd hooked up with a barback in the basement one lonely evening when it was too cramped in your shared studio apartment to spend even one more minute listening to you roommate's dramatic monologue about Monsanto and the importance of veganism. You'd eaten some meat that night, to be sure.

And in the basement was a door leading up into a ventilation shaft between buildings. In the shaft stood another door into the gallery. So after lunch you went back to work, made sure to take the Taser out of the big white olive drawer and into the pocket of your blazer, and played Facebook games till closing time. There wasn't a lot of custom, or even lookie-loos that day, likely because of the continuing drama over *Three Starving Children*.

You didn't bother to stop home first. A few journalists outside the gallery, with lights and a truck, doing their evening stand-ups before the scene. "Just days ago…" one of them said as you ducked into the bar, grabbed someone else's drink from a tray, smiled a thanks to the nonplussed waitron, headed downstairs into the basement, out the door, and up to the shaft.

Of course the service door to the gallery was locked. Of course the Spufford Gallery focused on performance pieces, scandals du jour, and non-portable art the size of an elephant or larger, but still the door was locked: the espresso machine alone was worth thousands. The back door's lock, on the other hand, was only worth singles. With a credit card, you jimmied it open. If an alarm sounded, it would ring two places. One, the owner's cell, now in a metal box along with a few other of her personal items somewhere in One Police Plaza, and two, the front desk. You strode toward the desk and picked up the phone when it rang and giggled your way through the alarm company's call.

"The password… uhm I'm a temp?" you said as you dug through the Post-it notes. "We're not even open. Have you seen the news? We're *that* gallery."

In India, they had not heard of the Spufford Gallery, and *Three Starving Children* was not news.

You found the right Post-it. The password was *Hamptons*. "Jesus Christ," you said aloud right after reading it off, and you didn't bother to affect the giggly temp voice for that. In India, they did not care about giggly temps.

You took Demeny's seat and waited for the television to turn itself on, as it did. It occurred to you that of course Demeny used the same method of ingress as you just had to avoid the police. You'd have to head back to the bar later and ask a few questions, certainly.

Or, maybe not. The three starving children — the new ones, not the original trio — were doing something new. Using stencils and spray paint, they created some work on the wall before which they normally posed. When they peeled the stencils back, the rough images of the original three starving children stared out flatly from the brick wall. And those children posed just like *Reality is an Invention Balthus*. You dug your iPad out of the pocket and brought up the original image of the first kids aping *Reality is an Invention Balthus* — the new kids had gotten it right.

You cursed yourself for not using the tablet to record the whole hour, but then you remembered that you were only interested in the case for the sake of your own curiosity. Let India care about real starving children, you were only interested in *Three Starving Children*.

Back in the shaft between buildings, something clanged overhead, and you threw yourself against the wall. Someone passed over, leaping the chasm at which you were at the bottom, with ropes and a bag trailing him as he went from the roof of the gallery building to the roof of the bar. You rushed into the basement and then up through the bar and ignored the gasping and the hoots — you were covered in soot and dust and flecks of crumbling paint now from the shaft walls — and ran out into the middle of West Broadway, eyes to the sky. Or to the rooftops anyway. A delivery-truck horn blasted you practically out of your outfit, but you held your ground and lifted your iPad and took a picture of the latest piece:

A little white girl in a blue dress with a white apron, reminiscent of Alice, actually, stands with her arms behind her. She's on a small patch of long green grass that obscures her ankles. Even stencil artists don't like drawing hands and feet. A red line comes from her mouth and points to rough red spray-painted dialogue: *I* REMEMBER WHEN ALL THIS WAS ART.

That stenciler, whoever he was, must know something. The girl's face looked a little bit like yours. Like a childhood pic on your Facebook timeline.

An emergency call, and drinks with the girls. Lizbeth lived in the city, thanks to her father, so you communed at her railroad apartment. Her repurposed hallway, more like it. She wasn't in Soho though — her father wasn't *that* rich. But she knew everyone downtown, and she got you exclusive rooftop access. Jung-Ah got you something else — a baggie full of Adderall, offered without comment. By the time the summer sun set, you were standing before the latest stencil, sucking on a bitter pill and peering ever so closely at it.

You knew you shouldn't mix pills and booze, but lots of things shouldn't be done, and people just keep doing them. And you just kept looking for… something.

And you find it. It's fun to be a secret, but all art is a manifestation of narcissism. Just ask any artist about their art, and you'll get a story about the artist. This budget Banksy couldn't help but leave a signature of sorts. The thick blades of grass were overlapping in a most peculiar way, as though the wind was blowing in every direction at once. Where had you heard that before…?

You were up all night. Was it Lizbeth's boss? Jung-Ah? Lizbeth running some kind of false flag operation? You didn't bother to go back to your dumpy little apartment. Everything is all-night in Manhattan proper. You took notes at the Waverly Place diner at midnight, stuck your head out the window of a patient cab like a dog and craned your neck for other likely street art pieces at 3 a.m., snapping pics and uploading them to your Pinterest. Bright and early in the morning, you reported to NYU Langone Medical Center with coffee and donuts for everyone with any access to Demeny.

Had he had any visitors? Oh no, but people tried said the receptionist.

Who? Who tried? Skinny little girls tried, said a heavyset man in green scrubs.

In the art world that could have been anybody. Any distinguishing characteristics? You seem a little too interested in this case, Ms.… said the cop by the door. You ran before he did some cop stuff to you. You had too much Addy in your belly, and in your purse, to take a chance with law enforcement. You ran from the hospital, bleary-eyed and shaking, and almost pissed your panties.

Why do you do this? Why do you bother? Truth be told, you can't help it. You see what other people can't see; you see what other people refuse to see. You love art, and you love the art world, and long ago you realized that it was a great big sham from top to bottom. What did Benjamin say in "The Work of Art in the Age of Mechanical Reproduction"? *Even the most perfect reproduction of a work of art is lacking in one element: its presence in time and space, its unique existence at the place where it happens to be.* The only real difference between the original art hanging in the gallery and the endless number of prints of the same size hanging in college dorm rooms is that the gallery art is hanging in the gallery. And it's not as though nobody acknowledges the sham — indeed, everyone is practically obsessed with it. In the age of digital reproduction, art can only be about art. And art about how art is about art. And what you see, that other people don't, is the great and black writhing snake underneath all the layers of the onion. That's what you've always wanted to get at.

And now, running down a crowded Manhattan street, turning corners like a girl in a spy movie for no reason other than the drugs and the sleepless night and the contents of your iPad, you realize how close you are to the big black snake eating away at the center of art: the second set of kids weren't part of Demeny's project.

They weren't a comment.

Or a remark.

Or a *détournement*.

The second group of kids were a forgery. A forged performance piece.

That's what made Demeny angry enough — stupid enough — to go to the police. A narcissist who caught a glimpse of the snake.

And you wanted one too.

You went to Lizbeth's building. She worked for an Asian art gallery, but she wasn't the forger. Lizbeth was the sort of girl who hired someone to paint her nails and wax her pussy. The forger had to be the street artist, clearly. There's no way Lizbeth scaled rooftops with a backpack full of stencils and spray paint. She let her doorman carry her groceries to the elevator, for Christ's sake.

Charles Okonkwo on the other hand…

You had to loiter around till lunchtime, keeping out of Lizbeth's sight and resisting the temptation to drop your cell and your tablet into a gutter drain. The first was easy — Lizbeth never looked up from her computer long enough to take a glance at the studio windows. The second, given the number of abusive emails and texts your boss fired off to you for daring to call in sick without seventy-two hours notice, was rather more difficult.

Charles Okonkwo emerged from the apartments above Lizbeth's gallery, as did four other housepainters, right at two after noon. You knew he was the one, right off. When he hit the sidewalk, long limbs swinging, he looked over his shoulder and took in the painting hanging in the big bay window and frowned at it. The other guys barely registered it, or any of the art in any of the gallery windows they passed as they walked to the corner bodega. Like dogs resting on a couch in the same room with a television showing a *Law and Order* marathon.

Charles Okonkwo was darker than the six starving children, but he could have been related. Maybe they were his kids, and he had a white wife, or an Asian one.

You waited outside the bodega, and, when the quartet emerged with their Arizona Iced Teas and butcher paper–wrapped sandwiches, you smiled your gallery girl smile and stepped in front of Charles Okonkwo.

"Excuse me," he said.

You took his photo with your iPad mini. The other guys hooted and howled. They probably liked your skirt — four inches above the knee.

"G'wan," he said to them. "I'll be along." He smiled a great big smile, and even million-dollar studio apartments weren't going to paint themselves, so they went.

"You have a nice smile," you said. "This pic will look great when it's framed and hanging in a gallery."

"I always wanted to be in a gallery," Charles Okonkwo said. "But I need a bigger canvas to work on." His voice was lyrical, lilting.

"Like the sides of buildings?"

"Like apartment walls!" He laughed again. He did have a good smile. "And no," he said, "not the sides of buildings."

You held his eye for a long moment. He wasn't quite lying. "You're just a painter, not an artist. A stenciler for hire," you said.

"All great artists have assistants," Charles said.

"Who do you work for?" you asked.

Charles Okonkow lifted a finger and held it up in front of your face. He pulled a cell phone from the deep pocket of his painter overalls and pressed a single button. It was a dumbphone, a flip phone, an antique. He said something in a foreign language, winked at you, and said something else. He took the phone from his ear and held it in front you and snapped your photo.

"You're already in a gallery," he said.

The corpse in this story hardly even matters. No wonder you didn't bother to put her name next to her photo on your secret Pinterest board. Unfortunate, but at least there's one less gallerist in the world. Ditto Demeny, though that little bastard might yet pull through. His experience certainly exposed the brutality inherent in the system though, didn't it?

What matters in this story is you. You are the muse and the subject, and we are the artists. We've really enjoyed your Pinterest, your little comments and notes on the deepweb for artists and dilettantes. So we decided to make you a piece of art.

We call ourselves the Six Starving Children. An egalitarian anarcho-collective of multimedia artists. We met in a refugee camp after Western intervention into our homeland's political struggles disrupted our lives. We were all students and enamored with painting and sculpture, but in the camps there was nothing but hunger. We called ourselves the Hunger Artists, never having read Kafka. Or even having heard of him, until we finally came to the United States. We sure were embarrassed. We changed our name, and decided to retain hunger as our primary motif and medium. Thanks to extreme fasting and copious drug use, we're able to return to our slimmer forms when it is time to do a project. To slough off the fat and chemicals of the bourgeois American lifestyle.

Yes, we are aware of the bourgeois American saying that one can never be too rich or too thin. We're making a stencil to that effect right now — perhaps Taiwo and Kehinde, both skeleton-thin in little pink princess dresses, with a crow plucking out an eye, and an oil tower in the background. Perhaps not. That's a little art school.

First-draft stuff. But we are aware of the irony; that is what we wish to explain. Thanks to the ubiquity of smartphones and Google Glass and everyone's constant tweeting and Facebooking of their dates and Foursquaring of their salon visits and Instagramming of their ridiculous salad lunches, there is precious little in Soho of which we are not aware. As Momus once said, "In the future, everyone will be famous to fifteen people."

We hired Demeny, and he was pleased to make some money, and to get the credit for an incredible new performance piece. Finally, his name in the newspaper his parents read — the New York *Post*. We hired our countryman and fellow expatriate Charles, and he was pleased to discover that he had "cousins" in America. We didn't need to hire Jung-Ah; she was organically interested in our project, as she has quite the little crush on you. Lizbeth we just got lucky with, but had you not gotten a good enough look at the Alice stencil, we would have kept plastering Soho with street art until you tracked down Charles and, by extension, us.

And panicking and tasing Charles? Well, we couldn't have planned that! A privileged white woman using modern technology to attack a poor black immigrant? And then you ran and hid and threw your iPad into a sewer grate so that you couldn't be so easily connected to him. Rich, rich stuff. Thank you, thank you, for both your actions and for the free tablet. The underrated Bob Ross would have called that episode "a happy accident."

Please find attached to this email a PDF invitation to the premiere of our new piece *Ga(u)ll(Valk)ery Grrrl*, featuring you and your recent adventures.

Everybody who is anybody is going to be there. So be sure to smile pretty, gallery girl. Galler*ied* girl.

Qi Sport

Molly Tanzer

Boy howdy, had the match proven to be an ugly one. The fight's underdog had her entire arm ripped off at the shoulder during the first five minutes in the ring, but then she dropped into a deep stance and swept her opponent's legs out from under him, knocking him to the floor in what the crowd clearly considered a thrilling reversal of fortune. When she stomped his neck, hard, and used her remaining hand to pluck out the other geong si's left eye, they went crazy for it. Ugh. Though decisive, it wasn't the most beautiful victory Jimmy'd ever witnessed. He knew she was drinking his qi through his eye socket, but with her mouth in a taut O-shape around the gore-smeared orifice, it kind of looked like she was kissing it.

Jimmy tipped his open crown hat low enough to cut off his vision, but it did nothing to block the grotesque moaning and grunting sounds the geong si was making as she fed. Jesus Christ, he hated it when he had to watch the fights. In his opinion, the undead were creepy as hell — subjects for nightmares, not entertainment. But given the volume of the hooting and hollering and stomping as the winning geong si's trainer stood on the wire mesh covering the fighting pit, holding aloft his hands as he turned around and around, Jimmy was in the minority. Well, in *this* company. Geong si boxing was considered a disgusting spectacle and public nuisance by most residents of San Francisco, and was thus illegal. Fed up with the spectacle, Jimmy angled his mouth toward his colleague Zeke's ear.

"You ready to get outta here?"

"Just about," said Zeke, over the din. He was still transfixed by the action. "What's your rush?"

Jimmy answered with half of the truth. "I don't want the new recruit to get bored and run off."

"So what if he does?"

Jimmy ground his teeth in frustration. He'd pushed back Wang's appointment just to accommodate Zeke's desire to see this fight, and *still* Zeke was busting his stones. But he had to keep Zeke happy; getting the boss's right-hand man's consent to hire Wang would be tough enough already.

"Turkey wants as many fresh contenders as possible for the big match," said Jimmy, "so it would behoove us to find ourselves a psychopomp."

Zeke sighed, but after withdrawing a pocket watch and checking the time, he nodded. "All right," he said. "But this better be worth it."

The drive back to Jimmy's office didn't take long. The mules were eager after standing for the better part of an hour, and it was too late for there to be many other carts on the road. As they pulled up, Jimmy saw the kid slouching against the building to the left of the door, looking like he'd bought his duds off some cowboy. A taller, bigger cowboy: the leather duster he sported dwarfed his scrawny body, and his Stetson, also too big, obscured his face. Jimmy wondered how he could see beyond the brim.

"Kid's a little short for a psychopomp," was Zeke's comment. "I mean, is he even *shaving* yet?"

"Hush, he'll hear you." Jimmy climbed down off the wagon's riding board and wrapped the reins around the hitching post. "Hey Wang! Sorry we're late. Lemme get the place open, and you can have a seat. Gotta talk to my friend Zeke here before you and me get down to business."

Wang's only response was a quick nod.

Zeke breezed through the foyer and into Jimmy's office like *he* was the one who worked for Pacific-American Shipping. Then, while Jimmy was settling the kid on the threadbare horsehair sofa in the waiting area, Zeke had the nerve to sit in Jimmy's chair — *and* prop his muddy boots on Jimmy's desk. That pissed Jimmy off, yes it did, but he reminded himself to play it cool. He'd expected this conversation to be a pain in the ass.

"So *that's* your amazing find?" said Zeke, after Jimmy shut the door behind him. "The psychopomp so good I had to leave the pits early? Cuz on first glance…"

"He's better than good… far as his work goes, that is." Jimmy shrugged, striving to seem confident. It was hard, standing like a chump in his own office, but he would not sit in the visitor's chair. "His big problem is he's wild. Spends his pay on drink and fan-tan, can't be counted on to show up regular-like."

Zeke's frown eased a little. "I dunno, Jimmy. He can't be sixteen."

"He's not lying about his experience, and that's what counts. I checked his references, especially his claim he did a stint at the Merriwether Agency. You know they're the cleanest game in town. They can afford to hire anyone they like — so why a kid?"

"You tell me."

"Because he's the real deal." Jimmy saw the muscles of Zeke's face ease yet further. "Anyways, I went to work at fourteen."

"I reckon you weren't seventy-five pounds soaking wet and knock-kneed besides." Zeke shook his head. "I don't like it. Kid could get hurt."

Jimmy sighed. He didn't have time for all this rigmarole, not with Turkey breathing down his neck all the damn time about revenue and gross and efficiency and whatever else. "You his mama, Zeke? What the hell do you care if he gets hurt? What matters is whether we're turning a profit."

"You mean what matters is whether *Turkey's* turning a profit." Zeke pulled a flask out of his inside breast pocket and took a swig, then replaced it without offering Jimmy a sip. "We can't afford mistakes. Big night's just around the corner. Turkey wants some real contenders, and he wants them now. *Before* now."

"The kid would be working already if you could stop wringing your hands over his... *youthful visage*, or whatever's troubling you." Jimmy wouldn't usually speak to one of Turkey's men like that, but what did Zeke want? This was San Francisco, not New York City or even Chicago. Finding a talented psychopomp was hard enough; ones willing to betray their vows by working for operations like Turkey's were even rarer.

Truth be told, Jimmy was plenty worried that the kid was too green. But needs must when the devil drives, as they said.

Zeke exhaled, making his lips flap, horse-like. "All right," he decided. "Go on, if you want to risk it. But if he gets hurt or killed, and the sheriff starts sniffing around —"

"You think the sheriff'll care about some dead half-Celestial kid?" Jimmy rolled his eyes, genuinely confident about something for the first time this entire conversation. "Don't lose any sleep over *that*. You know well as I do that the law'll turn a blind eye if they even deign to look our way."

Zeke swung his legs off the desk and stood. "Suit yourself. It's your ass on the line."

As *always*, thought Jimmy, as he showed Zeke out and invited the kid in.

Jimmy'd gotten mixed up in geong si boxing to pay off his gambling debts... but given his ideal placement as the cargo manager at Pacific-American Shipping, Turkey wasn't inclined to let him go anytime soon. Thus, he was in it deep now. He'd forged company records and destroyed letters from irate Cantonese families who'd paid for their relations' remains to be shipped back to mainland China, only never to have the bodies show up. Worse, he'd hushed up enquiries out of Chinatown, tipping off thugs like Zeke so they could silence the enquirers. That part was the worst.

The thing was, a missing corpse was a missing corpse. Even at a big, trustworthy company like Pacific-American Shipping, it happened. Totally understandable.

But people would find it far less understandable if word got out that the so-called lost remains had actually been encouraged to arise as geong si — violent, mindless, qi-draining vampires — and used as contenders for the annual San Francisco Geong Si Boxing Championship. Which, of course, was exactly what was happening... and exactly why they had to keep it quiet as the grave.

♦

Up close, Wang might look closer to twelve than sixteen, but he was sharp as a tack. Didn't ask nosy questions, either. He seemed to understand that as the operation's psychopomp, he didn't need to know much beyond where the coffins were stored, and what they needed him to do with what they contained.

"So yeah, late hours and all," said Jimmy, as they trekked across the starlit lot towards the warehouse closest to the docks. "Wouldn't do to have anyone see you sneaking in and out of where we keep the stiffs."

"Yeah, I sure wouldn't want to get a reputation as a creep who hangs out with the dead," said Wang, flashing a grin at Jimmy for the first time.

"It's more —"

"I understand. I don't work for you. Shit, I don't know you from Adam."

"Aw, it ain't like *that*, Wang," said Jimmy. Hell if this kid didn't remind him of his boy, dead these three years. Jimmy Jr. had cracked wise, too, but innocently. The kind of sass that warmed your goddamn heart.

Best not to think about that. It was just that Wang showed a lot of independence and, for lack of a fancier way of putting it, scrap. Could go far if he could just keep himself out of the whorehouses and fan-tan parlors. "Really," Jimmy heard himself saying, "you're welcome to come in and pull a cork with me after you're done. Just come on over and knock if you see a light on in my office."

"Thanks," said Wang. "Maybe I'll do that."

They'd reached the warehouse. It suddenly occurred to Jimmy that maybe he'd been insensitive hiring this kid. He *was* part-Chinese, after all, and here Jimmy was asking him to not only betray his training as a psychopomp, but also his beliefs as a Confucian or whatever the hell Chinaman's religion he followed. There were a few, as far as his understanding went.

Wang must've sensed Jimmy's hesitation. "You gonna let me in to see which of these yellow devils are ready to turn, or are we just going to hang around in the night air?"

So the kid had no scruples. Tugged at the ol' heartstrings, that, but Wang's attitude was in their — *Turkey's* — best interests. With mixed feelings, Jimmy unlocked the door, withdrawing a handkerchief to hold over his nose and mouth before sliding it open.

"Well, this is the place." With his free hand, he gestured expansively at a row of some twenty-odd coffins. "Big load here, and we're s'posed to get in a few more tomorrow. They've been doing blasting work for the Transcontinental, I hear, which is good given… uh." He swallowed. The stench was causing his gorge to rise something fierce. "I mean, not good for them. Good for us."

"I'm a psychopomp, remember?" Wang grinned at him again. "More restless dead out there, more money's in my pocket."

"Fair enough." Jimmy shut the door and lit his kerosene lantern. "How'd you get mixed up with such a weird profession, anyways?"

"How'd *you* get mixed up with underground geong si boxing?"

Jimmy considered briefly before replying, "Circumstances."

"Exactly."

"Look, it's just… you're pretty cool around the dead for a kid, is all."

Wang was already poking around among the coffins. "Of course I'm cool around the dead. Hard to excel in this line if you get all squeamish about a corpse, right?" Wang shrugged. "Anyways, I better get down to business. I don't want to stay up *too* much past my bedtime."

Jimmy laughed, though the joke made his eyes sting a little. The kid's sense of humor really was just like Jimmy Jr.'s.

Wang opened up a russet leather bag that he'd been carting around the whole night, and pulled out a pair of lensless goggles. After asking Jimmy to bring the lantern a little closer, he opened up a cylindrical case and withdrew a pair of pinkish lenses, fitting them into the sockets. Settling the apparatus over his eyes, he squinted through the thick glass.

"You want me to mark the corpses that are spiritually putrid, right?"

"Right…"

"These lenses are treated so's I can see any remains of lingering qi. Should be able to pick 'em out quick, so we can both get on home."

"Oh. Our last psychopomp used some kind of stick."

Wang nodded and shrugged at the same time. "Probably a peach-wood rod or sword. That's an old Taoist trick. Everyone has his own style."

"Yeah?"

"Yeah. But I figure, as it's goddamn late, that rather than prize open every coffin in this dump, I'll give them the once-over like this. I can see through the wood this way, is what I'm saying."

Jimmy found Wang's matter-of-factness a little disturbing. All the psychopomps he'd dealt with before had been a lot more secretive about their methods, maybe due to some sense of shame over what they were doing. As far as he understood it, for psychopomps to discover undead and not immediately take steps to send them into whatever came after was a total betrayal of their profession. He felt another pang, remembering Jimmy Jr., wondering if this kid Wang would ever feel like he'd gone too far down a path to walk back the way he came — and choose a similar way to deal with that.

"I'll slap a ward on any coffins that contain corpses like to turn into geong si," Wang said, when he found his first one. He dug around in his satchel for a roll of yellow strips of paper bearing *hanzi* done in red ink. Jimmy knew what they were; such things were a common enough sight in the geong si–boxing underworld. The vermilion in the ink immobilized the things.

"Sounds good," said Jimmy. "When you're done, you can help me separate them from the clean bodies. Tomorrow we'll take them across town to Turkey."

The lot of twenty-five corpses had a high percentage of candidates showing signs of imminent geong si possession. Jimmy felt his initial queasiness transforming into glee; Turkey would be pleased. But when he remarked on the bounty, Wang's response made Jimmy's stomach roll once again.

"Well, when they die angry or scared, they're more likely to turn," said the kid. "People who pass easy-like don't tend to exhibit symptoms of spirit-lingering or possession. But working for the railroad when you're a Chinaman… well, it's no church picnic, so say the coolies what come home. Alive, I mean."

"I know, Wang. It's real sad."

"Eh. The whole world's a goddamn tragedy." Jimmy almost laughed that this kid was telling *him* this. "Anyways, that's the last of 'em. You wanna pull that cork, like you were saying?"

Jimmy shook his head. "Sorry, kid," he said. "Look — tomorrow, come in the same time, and we'll do what we need. Then, if you want, you can take 'em across town with me. We could even stay and watch the fight. If you wanted, I mean."

"Fine."

"All right, then. Tomorrow night."

Wang gave Jimmy a funny look before tipping his hat and showing himself out, as well he might. Jimmy suspected it was pretty obvious how sick he felt. This job, identifying corpses to withhold from families eager to bury their dead… Christ above, how was this his life?

Before all this business with Turkey, he'd been shocked at the volume of bodies that came to Pacific-American via the Union Pacific Railroad and its subsidiaries. It seemed obscene, the loss of life; the final request of the workers to be shipped home to be buried in Canton, poignant. But now, viewing them — the corpses — as a commodity, something to profit from in the pits… it was some sick shit, that was for sure.

Truth was, Jimmy hadn't turned down Wang because he didn't want to have a drink. He was craving a tipple something fierce, but he wanted to be alone in his search for oblivion. He ambled back to his office, to the couch where he slept on late nights like these, musing on how the world was truly an awful fucking place, full of awful fucking people. Hell, the most he could say for himself was that before this gig with Turkey, he'd never once placed a bet at a geong si–boxing match. He'd never been one for gambling at all, really. That had all started after Jimmy Jr. hanged himself, and his wife had run off because (she said) looking at his face reminded her too much of her dead son.

It had been so easy to lose his past while he was losing his money. Shit, when Turkey called in his debts, at first it hadn't seemed so bad. At least Turkey cared about him. In a way.

Jimmy opened his desk drawer and withdrew a bottle of rotgut. After pulling the cork out with his teeth, he took a long swig. Drink might not make anything better, but it sure drove the dark thoughts from his mind.

♦

The next day's shipment of bodies arrived on time, and so did Wang, his quiet knock coming just after the eighth stroke of the mantle clock was fading.

"Wanna just give me the key?" he said, when Jimmy looked up with tired eyes from the pile of shipping orders he'd been working on all day. "You can sit tight and finish your work, you know. I don't need no babysitter."

Jimmy hesitated, then nodded.

"Just mind you don't poke around none, and bring the key right back. Don't lose it." Wang rolled his green eyes. "Afterwards, you wanna cart the stiffs to Turkey's? We can stay for the fight, like

I said. The final match'll feature our number-one champion."

"Sure."

"Good." Strange how much better the prospect of company made him feel. "Plenty of meat to get through before any of our fighters go up, but it'll take us half an hour to get there after we load up, so…"

"All right, all right. I'm moving." Wang grabbed the key off the peg and disappeared.

Three quarters of an hour later, Wang was back. He said, "Four," and hung the key up before Jimmy could even ask what the head count was.

"Not bad." Seven the previous night made eleven future geong si. Turkey would be over the moon. "Let's load 'em up. Want a drink, first? It'll keep you warm." He shook his bottle of rot at Wang. Wang accepted it and took a long pull without choking. Jimmy was once again impressed by the kid's grit.

"I'm good," Wang said, handing back the bottle. "Thanks."

"I hitched Blackie and Brownie to the wagon earlier tonight, so for now all we have to do is drive 'round to load up the bodies. Later we'll take an axe to the coffins and throw the boards in the scrap pile."

Wang nodded. "Then you change the records to reflect the new numbers, right?" Jimmy said nothing, but his silence seemed to be answer enough for Wang. He whistled, low and long. "Quite the operation. How long've you been…?"

All the questions were spoiling Jimmy's good mood. "Too long."

Wang refrained from inquiring any further. Or speaking at all.

They trekked across the misty lot towards the stable. Eventually Jimmy gave in and said, "About a year, I guess."

"Huh?"

"How long I've been working. For Turkey."

"Oh." The kid nodded. "How'd the boss get geong si for the pits before you?"

"Never asked. Knowing Turkey, I prefer to remain ignorant."

"Got it."

The autumn days were still plenty warm, so when they dipped inside, the charnel stench of the warehouse was overwhelming. That said, the sight of bodies on their way to becoming geong si always nauseated Jimmy more than the smell of natural death. Spiritual putrefaction prevented physical deterioration, which meant the bodies appeared pristine despite having sat in a warehouse for a few days — and making the trip from wherever they'd been boxed up. The contrast wasn't as startling when some Chinaman from Chinatown wanted his bones sent home to Canton, but these corpses had come from Utah for the most part, which meant they'd been dead for the better part of a heckuva long while.

In silence Wang and Jimmy loaded the bodies and secured the tarp that hid their cargo.

Only as they rattled over the cobblestones toward Chinatown did Wang speak, surprising Jimmy by asking about the rules of geong si boxing. Jimmy'd sensed the kid didn't know certain things about the sport — things the public didn't usually know — but the *rules*?

"Never been to a match?"

"Nah," said Wang. "Doesn't appeal to me as a recreation." He flashed a smile at Jimmy. "Deal enough with corpses during working hours, you know?"

That made a lot of sense, actually. "Well, geong si boxing's more like cockfighting than bare-knuckle, right? How they tear one another apart with their claws and teeth, to the... well, I dunno, can you call it death?"

"You can call it whatever you want."

"Honestly, I find it a little creepy. Say, I guess you'd know, do they feel pain? Are they the same as they were before they died? I mean, the same people?"

Wang shrugged. "The need for qi is all-consuming for geong si, so even if there's something in them that's... I dunno, close to who they were in life, it's not detectable. Ghosts are more like who they were, if you get talking to 'em."

"If you get talking to *ghosts?*"

"Well. Yeah."

Jimmy recognized that tone. Time to change the subject. "I bet you'll be able to tell me more about what happens in the ring than the reverse. It's pretty interesting, watching the trainers. Guess their tricks'd be a lot like yours."

"What do you mean?"

"Well, the geong si that wins the match is usually immobilized with one of those charm-thingies you used on the coffins back at the yard, but there are other things the trainers do to keep control."

"What happens to the losers?"

"If they're not torn up too bad, they're thrown back into the ring after getting patched up." He looked sidelong at Wang. The kid looked a little confused, but unless he asked direct-like how geong si boxers had their qi replenished, Jimmy wasn't going to volunteer the information. "They don't heal, of course, so usually it's in lower-quality pits or the matches leading up to the big fight."

They turned down the alley alongside the abandoned building on the outskirts of Chinatown where Turkey held his fights, and there was Turkey standing outside, his bald head and several chins recalling his namesake. He was smoking a cigarette and bullshitting with his cronies. Zeke was there, and Tiang. They hailed Jimmy over the dull roar coming from inside.

"Wondering if you'd ever show up," said Turkey, ambling over and petting Blackie's nose. "Got a good crop for me?" He noticed Wang. "Who's this?"

"Our new psychopomp," said Jimmy. "Wang, meet Turkey."

"You brought the new kid? You stupid shit, Jimmy, if he —"

"I won't squeal unless you're slow with my cash," interrupted Wang, by way of saying hello. Jimmy's stomach lurched, but Turkey was apparently in a good mood that night.

"No worries there, boy," he said. "I'll pay you what you're owed."

"Well then, we should have ourselves a chat, as it was never exactly clear when I'd see my money."

Apparently Wang's bravado chased away Turkey's doubts. He looked at Jimmy, eyebrows raised. "Nice kid."

Wang hopped down from the cart. "My mama raised me right." He held his hand out. Turkey shook it. "There's eleven in the cart for you, ripe as the peaches of goddamn immortality."

"Heaven and Earth, eh, Wang?" Turkey chuckled. "Where the hell'd you find this one, Jimmy?"

That brought Jimmy up short. Wang had found *him*. But this first meeting was going so well; Jimmy didn't want his boss getting all nervous and irate, so he just shrugged and said, "Word gets around."

"Does it now?" Tiang was leaning against the side of the warehouse, looking hard at Wang. Wang had noticed, and was staring back at him boldly. "Is that how you heard about the job, Wang? *Word got around?*"

An uncomfortable silence descended upon the group. Wang said nothing until Turkey said, "Well, Wang?"

Wang shrugged. "One of my fan-tan buddies said he heard about some operation looking to hire a psychopomp with a certain amount of... *flexibility* in his moral outlook. So I asked a few questions, and knocked on Jimmy's door at Pacific-American a few nights back. And we really hit it off — didn't we, Jimmy?"

"Yeah," mumbled Jimmy. His heart was pounding so hard he was afraid it might burst. Turkey was frowning.

"Why're you so curious, Tiang?" asked Turkey.

"He just looks like someone I seen before," said Tiang. "Someone who's not a psychopomp named Wang."

"Well, we all look alike — don't we, *dai lo?*"

Wang's statement caused another silence — and then a round of raucous laughter from all but Tiang.

"We'd better go in," said Turkey, when he got his breath back. "You like geong si boxing, Wang?"

"Guess I'm about to find out."

Turkey took him by the shoulder and pushed him inside. "You

sure are." He then turned back to Jimmy. "And you better hope Tiang's mistaken. If there's a problem…"

"There's no problem," insisted Jimmy, hoping he was right. "He's just scrappy."

"Scrappy," said Turkey thoughtfully. "Well. I'll take care of him — you go and unload the cargo. Join us when you're done, I'll buy you a drink. Eleven new qi-suckers is something to celebrate."

With no one to help him, it took Jimmy a while to get the corpses downstairs and chained up in the basement they used for storing un-risen geong si. Not that he was inclined to hurry. Above him, he heard cheers and screams and the growling of the fighters. Not a scene he was anxious to join.

Eventually he tramped up the stairs and around to the front. As he elbowed his way through the mob, the gong rang, indicating the end of a match. Jimmy caught sight of Wang sitting beside Turkey in the front row, looking… Jimmy didn't know how to describe Wang's expression. He was fascinated, that was obvious, but there didn't seem to be pleasure in his interest. Kid looked a little green about the gills, truth be told. Given the amount of time it was taking to clean up the ring, the last match must've been a doozy.

As there weren't any seats up front, Jimmy hung back, watching from a distance as the silver bells of the trainers began to ring out over the general ruckus. Silent, arms outstretched, their foreheads bedecked with regulation charms, the geong si hopped toward the ring, compelled forward by the jingling. It was a sight that never failed to put the spook on Jimmy.

"Folks, this is the bout you've been waiting for, the fight that will determine one half of the title lineup for the championship!" cried the announcer, just as the trainers entered the ring behind their geong si. "Will it be Turkey's Eleventh Tiger of Canton, veteran victor of many a fight — and many a championship?"

The crowd went wild for the geong si dressed in Qing Dynasty robes. Turkey's boxers were always favorites despite — or maybe because — they were pretty much all of Chinese extraction.

"Or will it be Ricky Lee's White Lightning, Lord of the

Southern Swamps?" asked the announcer, to general booing. Apparently the crowd was unimpressed by the tubby, shirtless, coverall-wearing corpse, though this geong si was more interesting to Jimmy. Caucasians succumbed to geong si possession same as anyone else, sure — but due to the law being more concerned when dead white folks went missing, they were a less common sight in the boxing ring than black, Mexican, or Chinese.

After the trainers and the announcer climbed out of the ring, and the mesh was rolled back over the pit and secured, only the two geong si and Mace, the umpire, were left. Mace, a brave, nimble fucker indeed, stood between the two frozen vampires.

The gong clanged. Mace snatched away the charms and vanished down the trapdoor, and the fighting began. Jimmy alone looked away, more interested in watching Wang's face. When Turkey's geong si leaped forward and got his long-nailed fingers around his opponent's throat, the kid flinched.

"The Eleventh Tiger strikes!" cried the announcer. "White Lightning, trapped already! But he's — he's away! *Ohhh!*"

The crowd went wild as Turkey's geong si swept the retreating White Lighting's feet out from under him. White Lightning dropped like a stone, but somehow flipped his feet over his head and landed in a crouch, snarling.

This impressive maneuver got everyone's attention, and Jimmy sensed a shift in the crowd's sympathies. But when White Lightning somersaulted forward right at the Eleventh Tiger's feet and then popped up to clock the Eleventh Tiger in the cheek with a hammy fist, the booing began.

"White Lightning catches the Eleventh Tiger off guard!" screamed the announcer, as the robe-wearing geong si took another punch to the nose, this time with White Lightning's left fist. "Could this be the end of the Eleventh Tiger's reign of terror?"

It certainly seemed possible. The Eleventh Tiger was now attempting to extricate itself from White Lightning's bear hug, but White Lightning's teeth were getting ever closer to the Eleventh Tiger's throat as the geong si stuck his leg between White Lighting's legs to keep from going over.

Clearly desperate, the Eleventh Tiger risked it all, bringing a knee into contact with what had been White Lightning's nuts. Jimmy winced as White Lightning crumpled, and The Eleventh Tiger jumped clear. Likely the geong si wasn't feeling the same pain *he'd* feel in such a circumstance, but lots of qi resided in the balls so it effectively crippled the poor bastard. The Eleventh Tiger took advantage of that, pinning the writhing corpse beneath him and sinking his teeth into his neck.

"Another win for the Eleventh Tiger!" The announcer was hard to hear over the cheers of the crowd.

But one person wasn't cheering. Wang, wide-eyed, looked on as the winning geong si drank the invisible essences of his opponent until, maddened by the fresh qi, he rose and began to fling himself up against the mesh, hungry for more. While Jimmy made his way over to Wang's side, Turkey's trainer climbed on top of the mesh screen and used a straw to blow a puff of vermilion dust onto the Eleventh Tiger's face, which quieted him.

"Want some air?" Jimmy muttered in Wang's ear.

"Sure." Wang lurched to his feet.

"Not so fast," said Tiang, stepping over and squeezing Wang's shoulder so hard the kid winced. "Ain't so many half-breeds 'round Chinatown that I can't spot a fraud just because she cuts her hair off," Tiang snarled. "Yeah, I know who you are, Elouise Merriwether."

Jimmy looked over at Wang. He was blushing something fierce.

"What're you saying, Tiang?" asked Turkey.

"I knew I'd seen this brat before. She calls herself Lou, usually — Lou Merriwether," said Tiang. "She's the daughter of Archibald Merriwether — yes, of the Merriwether Agency. Only the most reputable game in town, fucking *Jimmy*."

Jimmy studied the kid's face and in horror saw what he'd missed: The narrowness of her chin, the smoothness of her brow, the tilt of her eyebrows. The absence of an Adam's apple. She was a homely girl-child, that was obvious enough, but girl-child she was — not some punk kid.

"Don't be stupid," said Wang — Lou — whoever. "I'm not —"

"Shut up," said Tiang. "What, so you grew up on *wuxia* tales of girls dressing as boys to do their father's work or whatever?" Tiang squeezed the girl's shoulder until she cried out. "Now you're gonna learn how that *really* ends up, won't she, Turkey?"

Jimmy looked at Wang a final time, hoping against hope it was all a big mistake… but he knew it wasn't. Goddamn, *this* after he'd assured Zeke that if they had to take care of this kid, no one would come looking? Jesus Christ, he was a dead man.

"Sorry, Jimmy," she said, looking up at him sheepishly.

"Get her bag, Zeke," commanded Turkey. "You come too," he said, casting a hard look in Jimmy's direction.

♦

They were in the basement with the un-risen geong si. Turkey had propped Lou in a chair and tied her hands behind her back. Then he'd hit her in the face.

"How'd you hear about us?" he asked pleasantly.

"Fuck you," she said.

Well, she hadn't been faking scrappy. All the same, Jimmy knew she'd fare better if she showed some goddamn respect. Stupid fucking kid.

Turkey hit her again.

"That one almost hurt," she said, tears running down her cheeks.

Turkey, shaking out his hand, shot her a look that sobered her up with the quickness.

"Look," she said, "We heathen Chinee can actually see out of our slanty eyes, you know? Buncha bodies go missing, and most of them through Pacific-American Shipping?" Lou must've noticed Turkey shooting Jimmy a nasty look. "I'm sure Jimmy's been doing his job best he can, but just because lawmen won't listen to Chinamen don't mean we don't listen to *each other*."

"Toldja you were being too greedy," said Tiang. "But no, you had to —"

"Don't be a fool!" said Turkey. "Sheriff wouldn't deputize no teenage girl to go undercover. Hell, I'd bet no one even knows she's here."

Jimmy saw fear flit across Lou's face. Looked like Turkey's hunch was spot-on. Jesus. Scrappy didn't begin to describe this kid!

"She did us a favor, really," Turkey said to Tiang and Zeke. "I've been wanting to try something for a while. The Eleventh Tiger's gonna need some nice fresh qi to do well next time he's in the ring. Everyone else feeds their geong si on qi from the sick and dying. What if we give him a ripe young girl?" He eyed Lou's face. "Well, *some* sort of girl. Easy enough, after, to dump her somewhere the sheriff'll find her. I dunno about you boys, but *I* never saw a girl called Elouise. Or Lou. I might've seen a boy get real drunk and pick fights with his betters, but certainly not a *girl*."

"No!" Jimmy took a step towards Turkey. "You can't do this!"

Turkey didn't even look up. "Take care of Jimmy, will you Zeke?"

Jimmy broke for the door. He hated himself for being such a coward, but he told himself that even if he was running out on the kid, he could find someone to help, before —

He heard a revolver fire; the world went all colorful and fuzzy, and next thing he knew he was on the floor, next to one of the chained geong si. He'd been gut-shot, and heard and saw everything through a fog of pain.

"The real question is," Turkey was musing, "should I let the Tiger eat her now, or keep her here until right before the match?"

Jimmy was trying not to groan as waves of pain hit him, but he heard groaning just the same. When he realized what it was, he startled away from the geong si beside him. It was awake, and staring at him with wide, dead, hungry eyes.

"I say get rid of her soon as possible," opined Tiang.

"Probably best," said Turkey.

Through his panic, it hit Jimmy that he still had the key to the geong si's manacles in his pocket. If he let the creature go it might at least provide enough of a distraction for him to try to make it to the door and call for help. He forced himself to inch back toward the creature, hoping Zeke wouldn't notice. Tiang was already halfway up the stairs. Just one quick turn of the key in the manacles… Jimmy held his breath, hoping against hope —

The geong si rose, and, with a cry, launched itself at Turkey.

"What the," cried Turkey, as long fingers wrapped around his neck. Then the qi-vampire buried its teeth in his throat.

Trying to kick herself away from the feeding vampire, Lou toppled over, her head knocking against the floor. Jimmy laughed; for some reason it was the funniest thing he'd ever seen. Even funnier, Tiang rushed back in to pull the geong si off Zeke, but, instead, the vampire got one hand around each of their necks.

"Jimmy!"

He heard the kid's voice through the fog, and saw Wang — no, *Lou* — looking at him from where she lay on the floor, still tied to the chair. "My bag! The charms!"

Her pleading got through somehow, and Jimmy got to his feet, casting about for the satchel.

"In the corner!" she cried, jutting her chin in the right direction. Spying it, Jimmy stumbled forward, opened the bag, and found the roll of paper charms.

The geong si was feasting on the now-silent Tiang. Jimmy waited for the creature to finish, and, after it took a giant bite out of Zeke, Jimmy lurched over and slapped a ward on its forehead, immobilizing it.

Jimmy sank to his knees. He looked down at his gut wound for the first time. Blood soaked his clothes, flowing out of him in short, pulsing bursts.

"Jimmy," called Lou. "Jimmy, help me!"

"I just did…"

"Jimmy, *please*. Get my hands free, and I'll go find you a doctor."

He made his way over to her on all fours to where she lay on her side.

"There's a jackknife in my pocket. Come on! The faster you move, the faster I can get help!"

"Sure," he said as he sawed at the rope binding her wrists. When he got through it, she sprang to her feet.

"I'll be right back," she promised.

But the basement was already fading away, receding from his view as he watched her flee up the steps and into the mist beyond.

Victimless Crime

John Helfers

I should've known something was wrong the moment I saw her.

I'd just finished dinner in a dingy Subway shop attached to a BP gas station. She stalked into the convenience store and began prowling the aisles. Wearing tan designer slacks, a white blouse, and night-black sunglasses, her artfully tousled hairstyle cost a C-note, or I'm a parking valet. Not even a hint of sweat marred her brow as she loaded up; chips, animal crackers, energy drinks, hand towelettes. She never looked around, just kept adding to the pile in her basket.

I casually glanced at the cashier, where two people waited in line at the counter. Sixty-second window, minimum.

I'd only need half of that.

It was perfect — or so I thought.

I wadded up the paper from my sandwich, slipped on my shades, and headed for the door.

Outside, the heat sucked my breath away for a moment. The late afternoon sun beat down like the gaze of God. It lent a hazy, shimmering unreality to the deserted parking lot. Around me,

Denver smoldered like a shit pancake on a mountaintop griddle. But glorious sanctuary was only a few steps away.

Nearby was a huge black Cadillac Escalade, brand-new and idling. I didn't look over my shoulder as I approached it; she'd parked in the only spot that couldn't be seen from the gas station's windows. My day couldn't get any better.

I hooked the door, which popped open smoother than silk, like it wanted me to come in. With an invitation like that, how could I refuse?

That delicious, indefinable new-car smell wafted over me as I climbed inside. Gentle air-conditioning caressed my face as I checked my fit. I didn't even have to adjust the seat; she was only a few inches shorter than me. A quick glance at the rearview mirror confirmed that she didn't have OnStar, so the boys wouldn't have to hack in and disable it.

That same look also revealed that wherever she was going, it was for a really long time. Suitcases were stacked almost to the roof in the third bench seat, and both middle captain's chairs were loaded as well, the pile behind the driver covered with a blanket. More money, and no problems.

Easing the Caddy into gear, I backed it out of the parking lot. For such a large vehicle, it handled just fine. I'd picked up a 2012 model last Christmas, and remembered it being a bit underpowered, but they must have beefed up the engine this year. Pulling onto the road was a dream. I could almost get used to this. Shame it would be out of my hands in less than an hour, but the bonus I'd get would take most of the sting out.

By now, I'm sure you've guessed what I do for a living. And before you get all righteous, you might as well save your breath. What I just did was the exact and only way I do my job; clean and clear, no weapons, no violence, no complications. That woman's insured up the ass. She'll probably overestimate the loss of her clothes and jewelry anyway; the rich always do. Sure, she'll be inconvenienced for a few days, and her wardrobe might suffer until her next trip to Saks or wherever she buys her overpriced designer clothes, but she'll live. Probably have another SUV, same exact make and model, by the end of the week. And she'll also have a true story of crime in the city to wow her charity group or society club the next time they get together. No one gets hurt; it's as close to a perfect crime as you can find.

As for me, I'm also no one, literally. Five-ten, one hundred sixty-five pounds, brown and blue, black T-shirt, blue jeans, no distinguishing features. Just your average Caucasian male in a sea of millions, a guy who slides across your vision and fades away like he was barely there in the first place. It's an image I work very hard to maintain. Cops and the press call us thieves or carjackers. In the trade, we call ourselves ghosts.

From Alameda I turned north on Highway 225, driving past the scrub prairie and wasteland on the outskirts of Denver. I'd only been here two weeks, but I already hated the place. Imagine about four square miles of relatively decent city, surrounded by an unholy maze of concrete on- and off-ramps spewing endless speeding vehicles. Beyond that sprawled miles and miles of industrial parks gone to seed, warehouses, and abandoned factories, the legacy of Colorado's declining mining and manufacturing base.

Getting the shop set up here took longer than we planned — there were literally too many places to choose from. But Trey got us up and running, and when the mercury climbed above one hundred degrees, I went to work.

I flowed with the traffic onto I-70 west and ran with the commuting metal herd to I-270, heading into a suburb called Commerce City. A smartphone mounted on the dash trilled as I navigated the on-ramp. I shut it off once I was safely in my lane. After four miles I jumped off at Quebec Street and ran north all the way to East 72nd Avenue, then doubled back to Tower Road. I turned north again, admiring the Escalade's all-wheel drive and responsive steering, and continued to 104th Avenue, staying under the speed limit all the way. Turning right, I entered another run-down industrial section, filled with silent warehouses and forlorn equipment looming in dusty, deserted lots.

I pulled up to a corrugated metal building indistinguishable from the dozen others lining both sides of the street. The only thing different about this one was that every window was painted black. I idled the motor for a moment, and the large garage-bay door slid up just high enough for me to ease the SUV inside. As soon as I was in the door closed.

I pulled the behemoth to a stop in the middle of the warehouse floor and rolled the window down, feeling the warm air outside overpower the Escalade's AC. "Whaddaya think, boys?"

I basked in the whistles and smiles on their faces as the guys admired the ride. From an office in the back, the man I was waiting for heard the commotion and came out to take a look.

Trey Hennigan was the brains behind the entire outfit. The story was that he came up with the whole idea supposedly while mailing a letter on a broiling hot summer day just like today.

Some *nuevo* rich jerk yapping on his phone had almost hit Trey while pulling into a parking space right in front of him. The designer asshole got out, not even glancing in Trey's direction, and left his Lexus running with the doors unlocked while he went inside. Leaving Trey alone in an empty parking lot with $80,000 worth of merchandise.

That's when the idea hit him. Trey didn't swipe the car — he just stood there and timed the guy's visit. More than two minutes passed before he came back out. And the rest is history.

Trey was — and many in the business say still is — the best mechanic around. In the course of his work, he made some unconventional contacts, and they helped him start his business. He'd outlined his idea to some like-minded individuals — none of whom I ever want to meet — and the operation had hit the road three months later. That was six years ago, and we were still going strong.

I'd hooked up with them about twelve months ago, referred by a friend of a friend. Before this, I was making the rounds on the dirt-track racing circuit in the Midwest. The racing life was wearing thin, and I was more than ready for a change. That, plus the fact that I'd totaled my car in an illegal street race — no one injured, but I was banned from the sport for life — had me looking for a different line of work.

When I first met Trey, he looked me up and down through his granny glasses, and asked a few questions to ensure that I knew exactly what his crew was about. He also asked about the reckless driving citation. I told him it was out of my system, and I was looking for something more stable.

He nodded. "Bring me a car."

Three hours later, I rolled up in a two-year-old Ford F-150, and that was that. I found out later that he'd run a complete background check on me, which was clean except for the citation. I didn't mind; there was nothing else to find, and it proved that he took the operation very seriously. As do I.

I turned the Caddy off and opened the door while waiting for him. Behind him, I saw the half-dozen tractor-trailers sitting in the other half of the warehouse. They're what Trey, I, and the rest of the crew use to move from city to city all across the nation, never staying in one place for more than six weeks. We breeze in to wherever Trey rents for two months cash up front, take a day to set up shop, and then me and up to three other guys go to work.

The cars, trucks, and SUVs we pick up are cleaned and the VINs altered or erased, depending on if they're getting chopped or not, and then either parted out or shipped to whomever's buying. When a load is ready, Trey makes a call to a friend of his. Within twenty-four hours, an empty auto hauler rolls up with perfect transfer paperwork on every car. We load it up, and never see them again. With the popularity of SUVs on both sides of the US-Mexican border, business was booming.

We have all the action we can handle year-round. When winter rolls in, we hit the slopes, where a bright ski jacket is all the urban camo you need. We lift loaded BMWs, Mercedes, and Lexus sport-utes from the ski bunnies in Colorado, Wyoming, Utah, and any other state with a mountain big enough to ski down. When the big storms roll east from the Rockies, making temperatures plunge across the Great Plains, we run in Minnesota, Iowa, Illinois, picking up cars already running and heated, waiting for their owners to return. After four to six weeks in each location, we pack up and melt away. We never return to an area for at least a year, and never set up shop within five hundred miles of our last job. Getting friendly with the locals isn't in the game plan either; there just isn't time.

Usually we wouldn't hit Denver right now, but our last stretch in Milwaukee had been light. One night Trey said, "We're headin' west," and that was all we needed to hear. His intuition for the best pickings was usually right on the money, our meager haul in Miller country notwithstanding. We headed out the next day, cutting through Madison and across the bottom half of Wisconsin, hopping the Mississippi into Iowa, trying to stay awake through pancake-flat Nebraska till we crossed the Colorado state line into Denver. A day later, we were back at it.

It's a perfect life. I get a grand per car, double that if the vehicle's on our most wanted list, and another thou if it's brand-new like this one. I checked the digital odometer. Four hundred fifty-four miles. I'd just made three thousand bucks in thirty minutes. That may not seem like a lot, but my room and board are taken care of, and my income is tax free, hidden in safety deposit boxes only I know about. I get behind the wheel of at least two cars a day. I don't take days off except for traveling. You do the math.

Trey ambled up and took a look inside, the miniature headphones around his neck pumping out a tinny version of something classical with a lot of French horns. He never went anywhere without that damn iPhone playing. He leaned on the sill and looked at me. "Nice work, Eric. If I didn't know any better, I'd say you were going on vacation. Not the luggage pattern I'd pick, though."

The rest of the crew chuckled. Sonny and Manny Lopez were two identical brothers, mechanics from Detroit, and together they could strip a car, foreign or domestic, clean in sixty minutes. The other guy, Bryan Mello, was a part-time spotter who also handled our computer engraving for the VINs, cracked any locator and antitheft systems, and any online stuff we needed. He was our full-time keyboard jockey, but wanted to branch out, so Trey was starting him off slowly. Our other two full-timers were on duty until they snagged something. The four of us gave the Lopez boys all the work they could handle.

"Well, this one's headed down Mexico way for sure. Bry, get the plates changed, and, since it fills our load, I'll make a call. Good work, everyone."

"Thanks." I slid out of the butter-soft leather seat and was about to walk away when I heard a faint noise, like someone sighing in contentment. "Geez, Manny, it's just a Caddy, you don't have to fall in love with it."

"What? Wasn't me, man," the lean Latino replied.

I looked at Sonny, who shook his head. Bryan was walking away to begin his work up, and I couldn't possibly imagine such a noise ever coming from Trey, which left only one thing.

I slowly turned back towards the SUV. As I did so, I heard the noise again; a soft exhalation, followed by a gentle coo coming from the seat behind the driver.

Oh damn, let that be a puppy, I thought. The Lopez brothers walked up alongside me, ready for anything. I glanced over at Trey, who nodded.

"Your show, ace."

I reached for the passenger door and eased it open. Everything was as I had first found it, the stacked luggage, the blanket-covered pile of —

Almost of their own accord, my fingers whisked the blanket away from what I thought had been a pile of suitcases. Instead, sitting in a large plastic restraint chair was a peaceful, sleeping baby.

♦

No one moved for a moment. Unaware of everything around it, the infant stretched a chubby fist up and rubbed its right eye, then slumped back in its car seat, still out cold. It looked to be about eighteen months old, and was cute enough, if you go for that sort of thing. It also explained the animal crackers and moist wipes.

I tore my gaze away to find Trey already walking to the front of the Cadillac. He squatted down near the bumper. "These plates aren't new." He waved Bryan back over. "Run 'em and find out where they came from. While you're at it, check the local news for anything on an abduction, Amber Alert, anything you can find. You two —" he looked at both Lopezes. "— You're always yakking about your big family, you're on babysitting detail. One of you wipes the car clean and watches the kid, the other one's packing. Pull the others back in ASAP, they're on cleanup. No matter how this goes down, we're out of here tonight —"

"The cell phone —" I blurted.

Trey turned to me. "What about it?"

"Uh, sorry, there's a cell phone mounted in the front. I turned it off, as usual."

"Let's take a look."

Manny produced four pairs of latex gloves from his coverall pockets, and we all yanked them on. I walked to the passenger side door, Trey right behind me. Opening the door, I removed the inert phone and jabbed at the power button, but Trey stopped me before it could power up.

"Let's do this away from the vehicle," he said. We walked over to the office, and I turned the phone on. A picture of the woman driver and the baby appeared on the touch screen. It jingled immediately, something soft and classical.

"*Eine Kleine Nachtmusic*," Trey said. "I like her already. Why don't you answer it?"

I realized I was staring at the trilling device like I'd never seen a phone before. "Uh, right," I replied.

I was already rattled enough, and Trey's calm demeanor wasn't helping any. No one had fucked up this bad in a long time, not since one of our boys got drunk three years ago, stole a car, and was chased by five state troopers and a helicopter for forty miles. The footage had eventually ended up on *World's Scariest Police Chases*. We haven't returned to Arizona since. When Trey had gotten that news, he just pulled his phone out and stepped outside. Needless to say, that guy's no longer working for us, or anyone else, for that matter. I prayed I hadn't just made a similar mistake.

"What should I say?"

"Your haul, your call," Trey answered. "You can turn that phone off and walk away right now."

The rule was anything in the car belonged to the ghost who lifted it. Our only exceptions were guns or drugs, both of which we destroyed as our little contribution to public safety. Clothes, jewelry, laptops, phones, CD players, anything else was moved through Trey's connections. One time, he told us about a ghost who'd lifted a car with a minor Renoir painting in the trunk. The guy had retired on his share of that sale.

The scary thing was that I knew if I chose not to answer the phone, or that if she and I couldn't reach an agreement, Trey would make a call, and that baby would disappear like it never existed. If he turned a profit on it, I'd get half of whatever the kid went for, but I wouldn't be able to live with myself. Hot cars are one thing; this was completely different. No way, no day.

I stabbed the *talk* button. "H-hello?" I said, angling it so Trey could listen as well.

"Is this the person who stole my Cadillac?"

"Yes," I said.

"You can have the car and everything in it, I just want my daughter back," said the voice on the other end. It was a woman — *the woman*, I thought. I imagined her sitting at that BP parking lot, feeding quarter after quarter into the pay phone in the back until she got through. Her tone was calm, but I could feel the stress coming across the line. I sensed she was stretched to the breaking point, but for some reason it wasn't just because of her missing kid. The way she spoke actually sounded — familiar, but

I didn't know why. *Something else is going on here,* I thought. Whatever was going down, she was way too calm for a parent who just lost her child.

"Okay, she wasn't what I wanted anyway. How do you suggest we handle this?"

"There's an abandoned quarry twenty miles north of Arvada off Highway 72. Meet me there in an hour."

"We'll be there. Any sign of the police, and you'll never see her again," I said, despising the words as they came out.

When I heard a faint sob, I thought I'd broken through her unruffled facade. "I've only called this number, no one else. I — I don't need the attention." Except for that noise and her odd choice of words, she might have been ordering a pizza. "Anything else?"

"Hang on." I covered the mouthpiece. "We're giving everything back, right?" I asked Trey.

He nodded. "Too risky not to."

All right, the exchange will happen at the quarry in one hour," I said.

She didn't reply, just hung up.

"That was — weird. She wasn't crying or hysterical — nothing like that," I said. "She was too ready, too cool — like she'd already figured all of this out before she talked to us. You think this is some kind of sting?"

"No, just a whole shitload of trouble," Bryan said behind us.

"What do you mean?" Trey asked.

Bryan jerked a thumb at the SUV. "Those plates are registered to one Thomas Carlucci. Of the New England Carluccis."

The already sinking feeling in my stomach plummeted right through my feet and slammed into the floor. "You mean a relative of Michael 'Crusher' Carlucci, in New Hampshire?" I asked.

Everybody knew of Crusher — although only a handful would admit that in public. He controlled a string of junkyards along the East Coast where, for the right price, you could dispose of anything. And I mean *anything*. My gut tightened at that thought.

Bryan nodded. "Uh, the same — I got a number." He said. "Also, I can't find a peep about a missing baby anywhere. No news story, no Amber Alert, nothing."

Trey digested all of this while sucking in a slow breath through his teeth, the only sign he was truly agitated. "She hasn't called this in yet. Interesting. Let's see if I can get us all out of this in one piece. Gimme the number." Once he had it, he drew his own phone and walked a few paces away.

I rubbed my face with both hands, wishing I could somehow turn back time and avoid this whole mess. Finding a car that's ready to be stolen takes a bit of prowling, but more often it's just a knack for being in the right place at the right time. I hadn't thought anything of it when I saw her in the store and the SUV outside, it was just my usual luck for picking a good spot to find an unattended car. My regular targets were banks, post offices, and smaller supermarkets, although I've swiped cars from just about everywhere, including being mistaken as a valet in a performing arts center parking lot. But this one was a cardinal mistake. No one was ever supposed to be put in danger because of anything I did.

I glanced at Trey, who stood with his ear welded to his cell. His lips weren't moving, except in very short bursts, which I took to mean he was saying yes or no to whomever was on the other end. The rest of us tried to busy ourselves with something, anything, but we wouldn't have fooled anyone. We all knew the operation, and perhaps our lives, hung on what was being said only a few yards away.

After a few more minutes, Trey lowered his phone and walked over to us. "All right, here's what's going down. You and I —" he pointed at me, "— will take the Caddy to the drop in —" he checked his watch. "— fifty-one minutes. Manny, you'll follow us in the company car — we'll probably need a ride home. Mr. Carlucci himself will meet us there to reacquire his family. We hand over the kid, the wife comes back into the fold, and we're out of here tonight, never to return. Denver is now officially off limits forever."

"Even though we got his kid and wife ba—" Bryan began, but was stopped by Trey's upraised hand.

"No rocking the boat, we're getting off easy." The corner of our boss's mouth crooked in what passed for a smile. "Never liked Denver much anyway, and I really hate it now."

"Amen," Manny said, crossing himself in reflex. The twin brothers trotted to the work bay and began packing tools.

"Bryan, when can we expect Jim and Steve back?" Trey asked.

"Steve called in and said he was on the outskirts of Westminster, figured he'd be back in a half hour or so," Bryan replied. "Jimmy was downtown, and said he'd be here inside twenty minutes."

Trey nodded. "All right, start breaking everything down. I wanna be out of here by ten, not a minute later." He draped an arm around my shoulder. "Let's go find out where this hole in the ground is."

I pulled on a windbreaker and exchanged the latex for a pair of leather driving gloves, then slid behind the Escalade's wheel, with Trey getting in on the passenger side. I started the engine, and checked the backseat. The baby girl was still sleeping, designer bags all around her.

Sonny hit the garage door and we eased out into the early evening twilight. Behind us, Manny followed in an older, nondescript SUV. He would stop about a half mile away from the meeting point and wait for Trey's call to pick us up.

Neither of us were in the mood for conversation, but after a few miles I had to say something. "Sorry about the fuck up, Trey."

He just stared out into the deepening night. "Nothing to apologize for. You saw what looked like a sweet ride and went for it. Woulda done the same thing in your place. What's done is done, now we've got to fix the problem, not the blame." He leaned back in the seat, adjusted the air-conditioning. "As long as neither Mr. or Mrs. Carlucci do anything stupid, this should go down smooth. But in case it doesn't —"

He unzipped his fanny pack and pulled out a small revolver. "I want you to hold this at the meeting."

"You know how I feel about guns."

"And you know how often I give any of you guys a direct order," he replied.

"How'd I know you were gonna say that?" My smile faltered as I glanced at him. I held his unblinking stare for a few moments before looking back at the road. "All right, all right." I took the pistol and shoved it into my jacket pocket, its weight uncomfortable on my leg.

"It's clean, so you don't have anything to worry about. I don't think they'll expect either of us to carry. If they wanna search you, let it go, and let me do the talking. Just remember, always follow my lead. Except for her, we're basically all on the same side, so I'm not expecting trouble, but — "

"Better to have it and not need it than need it and not have it," I said, almost hiding the tremor in my voice.

With Trey navigating on his iPhone, I circled the city until I reached Highway 72, then accelerated north out of town. After fifteen minutes of scrubland, I saw a giant, gaping pit in the ground, more evidence of Colorado's abandoned mining heritage. Although there were *No Trespassing* signs on posts all around, the crumpled gate lay on one side of the road, smashed off its hinges and never replaced.

Trey called Manny. "We're here. Wait for my call. You know the drill if I don't." The standard rule was that if Trey ever went off the grid or got into trouble, we were to wait two hours for him to contact us. If he didn't, we were to shut everything down and scatter to the four winds.

I exchanged a glance with him. He nodded. I drove in.

A broad gravel road led down into the quarry, with huge twin tire treads indicating where hundreds of truckloads of stone and ore had been carried out. Now it was a symbol of better times gone by, leaving only gaping, empty holes behind.

We hit the bottom and drove out onto the rough plain. I turned the Escalade around and left the headlights on and aimed where the road entered the quarry. We both got out and looked around at the scarred walls rising several stories above us, resembling a huge grave. Not the most comforting thought.

Trey checked his phone, then dialed a number again. "Yes, we're here… no sign of her yet. When I call again, you can move in. Yes, sir… yes, sir — there won't be any problems. All right."

He looked over at me. "I take it you got the meaning of that conversation."

I nodded, a lump growing in my throat.

With the SUV's engine off, it was absolutely silent, not even the wind blowing down here. The sun was gone too, slipping behind the horizon as if unwilling to witness what was about to happen. As the light receded, darkness crept down the walls, held off only by the twin headlight beams, bringing with it a chill that stole through our clothes.

The minutes ticked past, and both of us tensed during the infrequent times we heard a car pass by overhead. Finally one slowed, and we saw the faint glimmer of headlights over the lip of the quarry. Trey strolled around to the rear of the vehicle, his hand close to his mouth. I strained my eyes, trying to spot anyone coming down the walk. After only a few seconds, the headlights disappeared, leaving only the Caddy's lights illuminating our surroundings.

For a moment, all was silent, then, faint at first, we heard the crunch of footsteps on gravel. Trey hit a button on his phone, waited a few seconds, then slipped it into his pocket.

The steps grew louder, and I saw the woman from the store enter the pool of light thrown by the SUV. When she saw us, she paused and threw her hand up to shield her eyes, then started forward again.

She walked up to me. "I want to see my daughter."

I opened the passenger door. "She's here, safe and sound."

She walked over to look. For a moment her features softened, and I saw a mother whose only concern was for her child. Then she straightened, and the hard veneer was back in an instant. "All right, let's get this over with."

Trey came around from the other side of the SUV. "I'm afraid it's not that easy, Mrs. Carlucci."

The woman stiffened as she looked at him. Trey nodded at the quarry's edge behind her. A row of eight headlights pulled up to the lip, and a long black car turned onto the access road, heading down to the three of us. When she saw it, her features turned completely blank.

At that moment, I realized exactly where I'd heard that tone in her voice and seen that look on her face before.

The limousine pulled up a few yards away, and a man got out of the back. He was dressed in a tailored suit that almost hid his paunch, and his short, iron-gray hair was perfectly coiffed. He shot his cuffs and strode over to the woman, his mouth set in a tight slash. She watched him approach, her shoulders slumping. He didn't say a word, just raised his hand and delivered a vicious backhand that spun her around. One hand went to her reddening cheek as she turned back to him.

"Get in the car," he growled.

"No."

Everyone turned at the sound of my voice.

"What?" Carlucci asked, his eyes narrowing when he saw the gun in my hand.

"What the fuck is this? What's going on, Trey?"

"I have no clue," my boss said as he stepped away from me.

The woman remained silent, her gaze flicking between her husband and me.

"She's not going anywhere with you," I said, waving him toward me with the pistol. "Come here."

The expression on his face told me everything — no one had talked back to him like that in years. I had to keep going, while he was still confused. "You —" I still didn't know her name. "Get in the Caddy. Now."

She scrambled over to the driver's seat and got in while Carlucci walked to me. When he was a couple yards away, I held up a hand, hoping she wouldn't leave me high and dry in the next few seconds.

"Don't be stupid, kid," Carlucci said. "I don't know what you think you're doing, but you're making a very big mistake."

I shook my head. "You'd never understand. Raise your hands."

As he did, the driver's door of the limo opened.

"Is everything all right, sir?" his driver asked.

"You know what to say." I patted him down; he was unarmed — I imagined this was the last thing he expected to happen. I did grab his cell phone.

"It's fine, Johnny. Get back in the car."

"All right, now you're going to walk ahead of me." I led him around the other side of the SUV. Keeping the pistol on him, I opened the front passenger door. "Get in."

"What are you doing?" she asked, her eyes wide.

"Trust me." I opened the rear passenger door and waved him into the front. "Get in. I won't ask again."

"And if I don—"

Before he could finish, I smacked his head with the gun butt, hard enough to snap it to the side. "Next time, it'll be worse. Now *get in.*"

He did. I got into the backseat and pressed the muzzle of the pistol hard into the back of his neck. "Don't even think of trying anything."

I glanced at Trey, who was still staring at me with a stunned look on his face. "Trey had nothing to do with this — as far as he knew, we were coming here to give you your wife and baby back."

"I don't give a fuck about him," Carlucci said. "Look, kid, you can still walk away from this. Put the gun away and let us go right now."

"Nope." I tapped him with his cell phone. "Call your guys and tell them to let us through and not to follow us."

"All right, this has gone fucking far enough —" He twisted in the seat to glare at me, and that's when I let him have the butt right between the eyes. His head snapped back; a red welt rose on his forehead.

"That's two. One more, and I will put a bullet into you."

He barked a short, bitter laugh. "Are you kidding? You kill me, you got no insurance."

"I didn't say I was going to kill you," I replied, tapping him with the phone again. "Make the call."

Seething, he grabbed the phone and dialed, snapping out orders. He hung up, and I snatched the phone out of his hand and looked at his wife. "Let's go."

She put the SUV in gear and drove out of the quarry. At the top of the excavation, the highway ahead of us was deserted.

"Which way?" she asked.

"Head north and turn left at the first intersection."

With the muzzle of the pistol jammed back into Carlucci's neck, I kept an eye on the four bodyguard cars, but they stayed put as she pulled onto the road. We accelerated fast, and soon left the quarry and everything behind, heading out into the Colorado scrub and the endless night.

To his credit, Carlucci didn't waste his breath with any more threats. We drove for a good twenty minutes, until the city was far behind us. Finally, I judged we were far enough away. "Pull over here."

When she did, I opened the front passenger door. "Get out," I said, letting my hand holding the pistol rest on the top of the front seat.

Carlucci did, trying his best to maintain his dignity. He shook his head. "You got balls, kid — remember I said that when I find you and feed 'em to you."

I reached out to close the door. "Good luck."

"You're letting him go?" she asked.

"Yeah —" was all I got out before she snatched the gun. I went for her, but she was already aiming at her husband. I barely turned away in time as she squeezed the trigger twice.

The flash and blast felt like a bomb had gone off in my face. My ears rang, and I saw the afterimage of the gunshot every time I blinked. When my vision returned, I saw her aiming the pistol at me. The shots woke the baby; I could faintly hear her wails through the ringing in my ears.

"Get out," she said, having to repeat herself before I got what she was saying. I complied, shivering in the cold night air.

She rolled the passenger window down. "He's got a money roll," she said loud enough for me to understand. "Get it and toss it to me."

I stared at Carlucci's body, the look of surprise still on his face, his chest covered in blood. Bending down, I patted his pockets, finding a roll of bills that would have choked a python. I stood and tossed it to her through the open window.

"Why?" she asked, pistol still pointed at me. "Why'd you do it?"

"The last time I knew a woman in trouble, I couldn't help her. This time, I could."

She stared at me for a moment, her face expressionless. "That's the only reason you're still alive. But if I ever see you again, you'll be next." Then she drove off, leaving me alone in the dark with a dead man.

I looked around the deserted road, then walked away fast. As I did, I pulled out my own phone and figured out where the hell I was. As soon as I knew, I turned south, into a large, empty field. I'd come across a road soon enough, and then find a car, and get the hell out of the state as fast as I could.

I hadn't expected any thanks from her — after all, I was the one who'd gotten her into the mess in the first place. I suppose I was just lucky she hadn't killed me, too. I'd thrown away my job, and would probably have to leave the country, but it had been worth it.

As I walked, I couldn't forget the look on her face when she saw that car coming down into the quarry. When I saw it, I knew what I had to do.

It was the same look on my mother's face during every single day of her marriage.

Buried

Gareth Ryder-Hanrahan

"In the old days," and Nikolai makes a gun with his thumb and forefinger, "bang, back of the head."

"So why did you come in today?" I ask.

"Someone has to hold the gun," he replies.

"You old Chekist! I came in for the pornography." Vasily is the embodiment of a bad night out in Tverskaya — booze, grease, a taste for expensive women, and secret police all in one ugly package. He's tapped the phones of half the prostitutes in Moscow, and gets off on heavy breathing and sex chats.

The last member of our little third-floor office quartet scowls in distaste from the doorway. Comrade Irina is of the opinion that Vasily does not carry out his duties with the professionalism and zeal for Marxism-Leninism that his exalted position in the KGB requires. She sweeps into the office like a snowstorm, puts on her headphones, and makes a very great show of ignoring us.

Vasily ambles to the window and looks out at the square. I join him. "And you, comrade?" he asks me.

I see graffiti on the wall opposite the Lubyanka — an unthinkable transgression up until a few days ago. *FUCK THE KGB*.

"I wanted to see how fucked we are."

A week ago, certain would-be heroes of the Soviet Union formed a junta and assumed power over the nation. They claimed President Gorbachev was *tired* — exhausted by his busy schedule of reforming the institutions that had kept those would-be heroes and their ilk in power since Lenin's day. Our boss's boss's boss — Chairman Vladimir Kryuchkov, head of the KGB — belonged to the would-be junta.

Their coup failed. Demonstrations on the streets, chanting and placards and public order offences, strikes, all the stuff we'd seen in Europe last year.

We are intimately familiar with this dance; we've learned the steps from tapped telephones and reports from stations in Budapest and Berlin and Kraków. The hardliners make their grab, but the proles discover their collective spines and don't back down. Cue either reform or revolution.

Comrade Kryuchkov thought things would be different here in the Motherland, but three demonstrators got themselves run over, and became martyrs. Suddenly, we hear Yeltsin declaring them Heroes of the Soviet Union, and the hardliners retreated. Kryuchkov gambled the KGB's reputation of invincibility, and lost, and was forced to resign. We were in dangerous territory now. The top floor of the Lubyanka building was no longer the third house of government.

We know the next step. The KGB will be reformed, remade, neutered, worse than any purge. The only question is which of us will be trampled.

Irina is already hard at work, the clatter of her typewriter testament to her diligence. We're the afternoon shift in the Bureau of Telephone Monitoring. When one of the bulbs on the big board lights up, signifying that one of the monitored telephones is in use, we are supposed to tap the signal and note any suspect conversations. Nikolai and I spend most of the afternoon speculating about Kryuchkov's fate — the basement or the gulag — and only put on our headphones when we hear footsteps in the corridor outside. Vasily, the dirty goat, listens in on his girls: some of their telephones stay live even when on the hook.

As night falls across Moscow, Vasily sits bolt upright in his chair.

"A screamer?" I ask.

"Listen to this!" he says to me. "Quick!"

I press my head to the proffered earpiece. To my surprise, I immediately recognise one of the speakers.

Frogface Yuri.

Yuri Karbainov, deputy director of the KGB. Special chief, counter-subversion. Occupies the office two storeys up and three rooms to the left of the one in which I stand. Like any good spy agency, the KGB is clinically paranoid and spends a large proportion of its resources spying on itself, but our office isn't remotely authorised to eavesdrop on a deputy director. If he knew we were listening, he'd have us both killed.

Then again, it's a lesson on why one shouldn't conspire on an unsecure line.

Yuri certainly shouldn't be arranging a clandestine meeting with an unidentified American. I mouth "number?" at Vasily; he scribbles the name of one of his girls, then crosses it out and writes down an address as Yuri gives our mysterious American the location for their hookup — a bar in the city centre. They're to meet there in half an hour. I put the headphones back down, careful to keep my hand from shaking.

Vasily fishes a packet of cigarettes out of his pocket and slams it on the table. I don't smoke, but I still take one and follow him out the door.

Nikolai watches us with his cold eyes. Irina doesn't look up, but her typewriter is silent, and I know she was listening.

♦

Up on the roof, in the forest of the satellite dishes and aerials. Vasily smokes the first cigarette in a single long drag, then takes the other one from my hand and puffs away on that.

"Fuck me," he says.

By rights, we should report this immediately. But to who? Frogface is head of counter-subversion. Frogface's superior, Comrade-General Kryuchkov, is among the walking dead. We can't trust anyone else, not yet. I can see Vasily's come to the same conclusions.

"Tell you what," I say, "one of us goes to the girl and finds out who the American is. The other goes to that bar and watches the meeting."

We agree this is a good plan. I suggest we toss a coin for who goes where, but Vasily points out that only he knows who the prostitute is, so that's his job, and I get to spy on Frogface.

In the twilight, the grey snow underfoot is slick and uncertain. I skirt round a blocked underpass, still choked with the remains of cars and buses that were used as barricades by Yeltsin's supporters. A column of tanks came through here, crushing the barricade with their terrible strength, and they still lost. Power isn't everything — you have to be willing to use it, and those tank gunners couldn't bring themselves to fire on their own countrymen.

Patriotism and love of one's fellow comrades was never a big thing for me. This may shock you, but Irina is something of an exception in our line of work. Most members of the KGB are men who know which side their bread is buttered on, or hardliners like Kryuchkov, or those who don't fit anywhere else, like me. I was bright but undisciplined, and there weren't many places in the system for people like that. Nikolai would say they didn't so much recruit me as preemptively arrest me. I started out forging documents and papers, then got transferred here to the Fifth Directorate.

And then there are people like Frogface. I quicken my step.

♦

I spot the two of them in the hotel bar. Frogface has bags under his froggy eyes, and his uniform is creased and grimy, but he talks animatedly, energetically, his hands chopping the air and hammering on the table for emphasis. His bodyguards look even more exhausted, watching the crowd with hollow expressions. Andrei, an Afghan veteran, he looks like he must have after the retreat from Kabul. By contrast, the American is the cat who not only ate the cream but has an ironclad alibi for the time of the theft. I see Frogface hand him an envelope.

Frogface stands up, and the two shake hands. Meeting over. I sidle back into the lobby, loitering with the intent of following the American when he leaves. I pick up a newspaper as cover, but it's actually an interesting read. A week ago, they wouldn't have dared write such things about members of the *nomenklatura*. I see Frogface's car draw up outside, and he and his goons march out. The American heads towards the street; I idly walk in the same general direction.

Suddenly, Andrei is right next to me. "Keep walking", he says, and he moves his hand inside his coat pocket so I can see the outline of the gun.

"What are you doing? I just came out for a drink!"

"Shut up."

Outside, he drags me to the left when the American turns right. We pass other people on the street, and they look away, unwilling to acknowledge our existence. The mob may be able to defy the KGB, but individuals shy away from Andrei, recognizing him for what he is.

He leads me towards another car. My stomach hurts, like I've already been gun-shot. The car, I know, will bring me to some deserted alleyway, and there Andrei will kill me. I can't bring myself to run. My mind has fled my body in fear, and it's as if I'm observing on my own impending death.

"Get in."

I climb into the passenger seat. Andrei walks around the car, opens the driver's door, then crumples when someone hits him from behind. Practised hands rifle through Andrei's coat for the keys, and then old Nikolai slides in beside me, grunting with the effort. He drives off, slamming the door as he accelerates down the street. I see Andrei dwindle in the rear-view mirror, a black shape outlined against grey slush in the gutter.

Nikolai drives fast, but with unhurried calm. He takes turns at random. He drives down side streets and tunnels I don't recognize. He checks the rear-view mirror every ten seconds. Without looking at me, he tells me my tradecraft is shit.

I really can't argue with him. The only question is what to do next.

♦

Vasily comes to my apartment smelling of vodka and cheap cologne. Nikolai invites himself in without a word, and perches on a stool by the kitchen window. He drinks black tea; without asking, Vasily digs a bottle of vodka out of the cupboard. He glances at Nikolai, asking me in eyebrow semaphore what the older spy is doing there, but I'm too shaken to explain. Vasily doesn't mind: it's a bigger audience for his bravura performance of *Vasily the Brilliant, and how he found out everything from the girl.*

The American, Vasily tells us, is called Harrison. Works for an oil company. He flew in from Riyadh two days ago. Here on a commercial visa, approved by Frogface's office. Nothing on him in any files that Vasily could find, so he's clean.

Is Frogface passing state secrets to the Americans? Running his own network? Or does he see the writing on the wall, and he's setting up a bolt-hole for himself in the Middle East? Vasily and Nikolai swap theories, but I've got more pressing concerns.

"Andrei made me at the bar. Frogface will want to know what I was doing there."

"I can cover for you," says Vasily, "it'll just take a while to set up. You should both disappear for the night."

"Those documents," says Nikolai, "we need to see what they were. This American, he took a taxi to your whore?" Vasily nods.

"But he left the bar on foot, and turned right, down Petrovka. He's probably staying at the Metropol. All the Saudis stay there."

Within an hour, I'm wriggling through the crawlspace between the fifth and sixth floors of the Metropol, smearing my shirt in rat droppings and dust. The American's in the room below. Through the spyhole, I can see him lying on the bed, shoes off, the folder of documents open next to him. Maps, geological surveys, pages of charts and closely typed text. Several sections are heavily redacted. I can't see any immediate military application — as far as I can make out, it's all empty tundra, a million miles from nowhere. Hardly worth all the secrecy.

I watch him get up, walk across the room, dial a number. International, which means it'll be logged. And would be recorded, were it not for the fact that three of the four technicians in charge of eavesdropping on international telephone calls in the Moscow area are playing truant. I get half the conversation through a microphone, though.

"I've made contact… it all looks good… yes. Yes. November. Good."

November. He said November. But everything changed in three days in August, so who knows what November will bring?

◆

Who knows? Turns out it's Irina. She's got connections. Nikolai and I drop some hints in the office, disguised as office gossip. She tells us that one of her Party friends told her about Yeltsin's reform package. With the premier sidelined and the hardliners routed, Yeltsin's seizing the moment and pushing through changes in the law. Notably, opening up private ownership of corporations, liberalizing trade, changing the rules in investment and shareholdings: all the groundwork for the new Communism, the one that looks like Capitalism in a fur hat. Irina's full of venom about it, and blames both Yeltsin and Kryuchkov for betraying the Union.

I spend my first hour in the office waiting for the axe to fall. No sign of Vasily. There's nothing for me to do but sit there at my desk and worry. Will I be called up to Yuri's office, or will they skip that and bring me straight down to the basement? I try to talk to Nikolai, but he brushes me off.

If Yuri's passing intelligence to the CIA, he's being brazen about it. That American must be clean. There's no way he'd risk such overt contact with the enemy, even with the KGB in disarray. At the same time, it's clearly an off-the-books operation, and Yuri's thug Andrei pulled a gun on me to protect his boss. My best guess is that he's positioning himself for the post-perestroika world. Vasily said that the American worked for Standard Oil — if that's his actual job, and not a CIA cover, then Yuri could be arranging some deal with them, a deal that will become possible in November.

That's all perfectly plausible. Unfortunately, it means that I can't count on anyone to protect me. If Yuri was a traitor, then I could convince some of the other generals to act, but he's selling out to the private sector. Like I said, we're in uncharted territory.

I hear footsteps in the corridor. It's going to be Andrei, isn't it? Andrei and a short walk downstairs. The Lubyanka, they say, is the tallest building in Moscow, because you can see Siberia from the basement. I'll be lucky to see Siberia.

The door opens, and Vasily barges in, accompanied by the stench of cigar smoke. He stumbles and falls across my desk, and drops a tape from his coat onto my lap. "Andrei's just behind me", he whispers, "use this." And he grins at me like all this is tremendous fun.

Scrawled on the tape are the words "Room 502, Hotel Metropol, August 21st."

The door opens again, in comes Andrei, and out I go. He escorts me towards the stairs without a word. There's a lovely purple-blue lump like a duck's egg on the back of his shaved head, and while he's not carrying a gun this time, I know he could still snap my neck with those leathery hands of his. Fortunately for my continued existence, we go upstairs.

Frogface waits for us behind his desk, squatting like some pagan god on an altar. Andrei grabs my shoulder and forces me down into the seat in front of the desk.

"What were you doing at the bar last night?" he asks. He speaks in a light, solicitous tone, as though we were old friends meeting for a drink.

"Comrade. I was brought there by... intercepted intelligence. You should be aware of this." I take Vasily's tape out of my pocket and lay it on the desk. Frogface watches it like a frog watches a juicy fly, then his tongue darts out and picks it up.

His arm. His arm darts out and puts it into a machine in his desk drawer. My mouth is very dry, and I can barely hear the tape over the pounding of my heart.

There's the sound of a phone dialing out, and then an electronic squeal like a modem. I know that sound, and so does Frogface. I plunge ahead.

"This is a recording of a telephone call from the Hotel Metropol, from the room of a foreign visitor named Harrison. As you can clearly hear, the conversation is encrypted, and that encryption sounds identical to other transmissions we intercepted from CIA stations in Europe and Asia." I pray that Vasily is sober enough to fiddle with the logs, so that when Frogface checks, there's a note of us tapping the hotel phone on the right date.

Frogface can't stop blinking. "This visitor isn't on the watch list. Why did you intercept his call?"

"A random sweep," I lie.

"We haven't broken this encryption. How did it lead you to that bar?"

Before I can answer, the door behind me opens. "Comrade," booms a voice, "a word, please. You can finish this later." I don't dare take my eyes off Yuri until he lets me go.

On the way out I brush past an older man in a general's uniform. His eyes twinkle merrily as he puffs away on his cigar.

♦

Downstairs, things are moving fast. Vasily drags me into an empty office and asks me how the interview went. He curses me for my stupidity when I get to the end.

"Idiot! You should have said you suspected the American, and that why you followed him. And then we'd have blamed a protestor for hitting Andrei."

"Who was that general?" I asked. I don't add "the one who smokes the same cigars as you do."

"Never you mind." Vasily speaks rapidly. "The tape will spook Frogface, make him think that he didn't vet the American properly, and that he's been talking to the CIA. He'll back off for a few days, and that gives us time to get some leverage."

As always, Vasily has a plan.

♦

Back in the office, we wait until a light on the big board flashes. An outgoing call from Yuri's office. Vasily listens in. It goes to a little office deep in the Ministry of Oil and Gas, to some junior clerk in the archives. We hear Yuri order the clerk to sit tight and do nothing, that there was a delay.

About an hour later, I show up at the clerk's door. "My boss, Yuri Karbainov, sent me," I tell him, "he called you earlier, right? There's been another change of plan." After the last few days, it's oddly nostalgic to terrify some poor apparatchik with the dread name of the KGB. He lets me into the archive, and assures me that the files are still secure.

I ask to be left alone with them, and he obliges. I can hear him waiting outside the door, and when I leave he'll check to make sure I haven't stolen anything.

I check the dusty cover. This document's been buried in the archive since the 50s, and checked out only a handful of times since then. It's been copied once — presumably, that's the redacted copy I saw in the Hotel Metropol.

I'm not a geologist. I don't understand a lot of it, but I understand enough. Back in the 50s, the Ministry of Oil and Gas conducted a huge and largely fruitless survey inside the Arctic Circle. They found something — an oilfield, I guess, or something like that. Gold, maybe, or diamonds. Immensely valuable, but conditions were too tough to extract it, so it got ignored, then buried. Maybe by accident, maybe deliberately in some internal power play that went sour. Maybe everyone who knew about it got killed by Stalin. Such things were not uncommon back then. The fact that this document is the only trace of the find suggests a cover-up.

How did Yuri find out? I don't know that either. Maybe he had some kindly old uncle who told him the secret on his deathbed as he died of miner's lung. Maybe the clerk stumbled across it by accident and reported it, or some doomed suspect offered it to Yuri as he pleaded for mercy in Lubyanka Prison.

Vasily guessed it would be something like this as soon as he saw where Yuri's call went, and it only takes me a few minutes to make the changes he suggested. There are hundreds of thousands of square kilometres of tundra; why not let Yuri search them? I change a few numbers, shifting the location six hundred kilometres west. My tradecraft may be poor, but I'm a good forger.

My part of Vasily's plan done, I head home to wait. I make myself dinner, and listen to the sound of fire engines wailing in the distance. That's part two of the plan. Nikolai's job is to eliminate the American's copy of the map, so only Vasily and I know what the original said. We then trade that information to Yuri for a payoff and protection.

My phone rings. Vasily, panicked.

"That bitch! It's all gone wrong! Irina — she reported us. Nikolai's dead. They shot him outside the hotel…"

"Who did?"

"Third Directorate men. I think. I wasn't there." Third Directorate: military police. We're being purged, like Nikolai said would happen. On the street instead of the basement, but still bang, back of the head.

"Shit. I made the changes. Vasily, did Nikolai get the other copy? If he did, then we can threaten Yuri, get him to intercede maybe."

"I don't know. Look, stay right where you are for the moment. Don't move. I'll come round."

I put the phone down. My hands shake so much it falls off the receiver. I check the window. The snowy street outside is empty, apart from one badly parked car. I look closer — I know that car. It's Nikolai's.

I sprint downstairs, rush up to the car, pull open the door. The floor's a sea of blood. Nikolai's dead in the driver's seat. On the dashboard is a passport and a plane ticket to Riyadh in Harrison's name.

Another car turns into my street. I duck down, and pull Nikolai's still-warm body down too. The car drives past us, and I spot Andrei at the wheel. He stops outside my apartment, climbs out, walks towards my front door. I see him plunge his right hand into his pocket, and I know he's armed. Andrei isn't Third Directorate. Vasily was wrong.

Vasily lied.

I shove Nikolai's body out of the car and drive.

♦

I was a forger, remember?

I flew out of Moscow a day later, on Harrison's ticket. Moscow to Riyadh, Riyadh to Schipol, Schipol to anywhere. By the time they identified the burnt corpse in the hotel room as Harrison, I was halfway around the world.

All that was, what, twenty years ago? A lot changes in twenty years. Look at Russia now; look at Putin and his FSB. FSB, KGB, whatever, they're all Chekists, all cut from the same dark cloth. Lots of people say things would have been better if Kryuchkov's coup had worked, if the oligarchs had never bought and sold the Motherland.

I never went home to Russia, but I heard stories.

Yuri ended up in Matrosskaya Tishina prison, along with Kryuchkov. I don't know what happened to him after that.

Irina — I heard she was fired when Yeltsin's hatchet men took over in November of 91. She probably lives in some little apartment in Moscow now, lighting candles in front of a shrine to Putin.

That general, the cigar-smoking one? He's dead. They found his body in a gutter in Tverskaya in 1995, throat cut.

And Vasily, Vasily — you know he survived. He's a fixer for the oligarchs now — but he's not one of them, and that eats him alive. I've seen photos of him, and the smile's gone. He's still on the outside, listening in but not able to fuck the girl.

See, I lied too. Like Vasily told me to, I changed the records in the Ministry archive — but I didn't make the changes Vasily suggested. The real site isn't six hundred kilometres east of the patch of worthless tundra that Vasily and his cigar-smoking buddy wasted their money on. It's actually…

Well, that would be telling. The oil field is still there, though, and they say this global warming will make it economical to develop in a few years.

I think we can make a deal, you and I.

The Weapon At Hand

Elizabeth A. Vaughan

"You are new come to the King's Hall, are you not?" the warrior asked, his voice rough with a barely hidden air of command.

I turned slightly, the silk of my sleeve catching on the rough edge of the table as a warrior settled on the bench beside me. He was a bigger man than I, but not so large as the other warriors that surrounded us in King Saer's feasting hall. Still, of a solid build, bearded, long-haired, blond, as were all the rest, and blue-eyed, as were all the men of the north. Truth tell, I was sometimes hard-pressed to distinguish one Wesorix from another.

It would not be diplomatic to mention that, of course. As rough as this land was, as harsh as life here was, my position required that the niceties be observed.

"I am new come, yes, Warrior." I still stumbled over the phrasing of their language at times. So as to distinguish him in my mind, I made note of the man's armor, heavy fur cloak, and weapon, a fine axe with a long hooked blade placed within easy reach of his right hand. These details aided memory; armor and weapons varied as much as faces did in my homeland. "May I ask…?"

"Artheran Thirdson," was the response.

I was too skilled to allow my eyebrow to rise. The youngest of King Saer's brothers then, which explained his seating at this table. And his ease at arriving late.

"I am Oaeton, of —"

"Ambassador from Uyole, far in the southern climes." Artheran flashed a wicked grin and gestured toward my dark skin and face. "Your look betrays you. How do you find our winters, Ambassador?"

One of the main doors opened at that moment, and a bone-chilling wind whipped through the hall, cutting through my robes. "Bracing," I replied loudly, to be heard over the protests from the other warriors filling the feasting hall.

Artheran snorted, and leaned back as ale and bread were placed before him. "And this is but the start of winter, Oaeton. Wait until its depths, when the snow reaches your balls."

"Hard to believe it can get even colder," I said, letting the truth slip. "I'd never in my life slept so cold as last night."

Artheran narrowed his eyes. "How so?" he asked.

"I am sure it's a matter of adjusting," I assured him. That and a few more blankets on the bed. "I look forward to it," I continued, not without a degree of truth. I'd heard such fabulous tales that I could not bring myself to believe. But then I'd stepped from my ship to see such mountains, their peaks covered in white, beneath a sky filled with stars I didn't recognize. Such unexpected beauty in a rough, raw land. Who knew what else might be true?

Artheran was frowning, scanning the hall. "I was not told you had arrived. Does Saer know that you are here?"

"I arrived very late and was shown to a room," I said simply. "I fear that I have only just woken, and was escorted to this place. I was told that King Saer was involved in ceremonial rites, and would be informed of my presence later."

Artheran's frown deepened into a scowl. "You've not had the welcome you are entitled to, and, for that, I apologize. Things have changed, southerner, since you left your home to travel here."

"In what way?" I asked, concealing my concern. My mission was to negotiate a marriage agreement for the hand of our Princess Bryilwa between Saer and my king. Much depended on the outcome of my mission; I feared anything that might put it in jeopardy.

"Saer's daughter, Princess Annaella, died in childbirth not a week past. Her rites were observed today."

The wind cut through the hall again as the main doors opened and closed, and caught me unaware. A shiver went down my spine as I drew my robes close. "A terrible thing," I said. "To lose a beloved child. No wonder my arrival drew no attention. There is no need to apologize."

"Your understanding does not excuse our neglect." Artheran looked to the high table and rose. "Come. I will make the introductions."

"Perhaps later," I hesitated. "King Saer might not wish to be disturbed at such a time."

"And perhaps," Artheran put his hand at my elbow and bid me rise. "He'd wish nothing better."

He led the way to the high table, and I followed, conscious of the attention I was drawing. "King Saer, may I introduce Ambassador Oaeton, of Uyole," Artheran announced. "Newly come to your hall and table."

King Saer lifted his head from his cup, and greeted me with a nod. A handsome man, I was relieved to see, but with the look of one in sorrow and pain.

"You are welcome, Ambassador." King Saer's voice was low, but pleasant.

The lie was thick in his mouth, but I ignored that. "I thank you, your majesty." I bowed my head low. "I have learned of your loss, and grieve with you. I would also offer my king's regrets. He has many daughters, and would sympathize with your pain."

"My thanks," King Saer replied. "I know that we are to begin to talk, but I would ask your understanding if we delay the matter for a while."

"Or not discuss it at all," the man to his right muttered.

I ignored that as well. "I am at your majesty's service." I bowed again. "Let it be as you desire."

"Ambassador," Artheran said. "Let me present Derik Secondson," gesturing toward the man who had spoken so rudely.

Derik frowned; I suspected that Artheran had offered a subtle insult in the manner of introduction, but I wasn't certain how.

"Other introductions can wait," Artheran said abruptly, looking at his brother the king. The man to the king's left narrowed his gaze; it would appear that Artheran Thirdson had a gift for offending. "I simply wished to make Oaeton known to you, Saer. I fear his welcome was not all it might have been."

"Not so," I said, shaking my head.

"Still, we are grateful for your sympathy and patience," King Saer said.

"And to that end," Artheran took his cloak off with a flourish, and settled it around my shoulders. Its weight and warmth enveloped me, along with the scent of oiled mail and leather. "Allow us to gift you with this. More suitable than those robes, Ambassador."

That brought a smile to King Saer's eyes, however slight. "We will have a high feast, to offer you formal welcome, Oaeton. For now, Artheran will see to your comfort."

I bowed low, and returned with Artheran to our seats.

♦

My chamber was cold and dark when Artheran escorted me back to it. No windows, no fire, no lamp.

"What is this?" Artheran pushed his way into my chamber from behind me. "Pah," he said with disgust. "There should be a woman," he growled. "Wait."

He went back through the door, barking commands, and returned in an instant, with three women, talking so rapidly I could not understand their words. The women seemed to offer apologies and explanations, but he would have none of it.

"This is an honored guest," he declared. "See to his comforts and needs."

He drew out the chairs by the table where I'd already set out my papers and inks. "Here," he said. "Let them work."

I seated myself as the women scurried in, bearing lamps, and setting up a brazier filled with coals. Artheran stood in the center, surveying with an eagle eye.

"This explains it," Artheran said, yanking the silk coverlet I had brought with me from the bed. "You see this?" He lifted the blanket below it, and shook it so that the feathers within expanded inside the cloth. "This, it must be on top. The down catches the heat. But if they are pressed flat —"

"Ah," I said, not really understanding.

He laughed. "No, it's true. You will see this night." He settled in the other chair, and the women brought us mulled wine, rich and spicy.

"Make sure you prepare the bed as well," he called after them, then focused on me. "Be sure to tell them each night before you wish to sleep, and they will bring warmers."

I hesitated, not wanting to offend. "The offer is kindly met, but I have no desire for companionship —"

He looked puzzled for a moment, then burst into laughter. "No, no, although the women will offer that as well, if they choose. You are an exotic, eh? They simply bring covered pans of warm coals and set them between the blankets. Otherwise, your bedding will steal your heat, and leave you the worse off."

I nodded my understanding, wrapped in my new cloak, warm wine in my belly, feeling much more comfortable. "I am grateful, Prince Artheran."

"It is the courtesy owed a guest," Artheran said. He glanced at the women, then continued in my language. "But it is more than that. I believe that a marriage alliance will benefit both our countries, Oaeton. I wish to see it prosper. King Saer needs an heir."

"Is not Derik Secondson an heir now?" I asked, also in my native tongue. "With the death of Annaella?"

"Our Council of Eorals has a voice in the matter, so long as the bloodline is followed," Artheran grimaced. "If Annaella had borne a son, he'd have been Saer's heir."

"I had not wanted to inquire before," I hinted delicately. "But —"

"The child died with her," Artheran said softly. "The midwives say a male child."

"An even greater loss," I said.

"Especially for Karid, her husband," Artheran pointed out. "He'd hoped to rule through his son."

I glanced about, but the women had finished their work and left us in peace. Still, I couched my question in my tongue. "Karid was the one seated by King Saer at the high table? He didn't seem particularly saddened."

"Princess Annaella adored him," Artheran said flatly. "And he adored her title. Karid is the second son of Eoral Bernt, with not much in the way of prospects."

"Ah," I said.

"Derik opposes an alliance," Artheran warned. "He couches it in talk of distant lands and strange ways, but he really fears that Saer will have another male child." Artheran snorted. "Derik's a poor breeder. There's been no bastards born of the woman he sleeps with. His beard came in late — always a bad sign."

"And what of you?" I asked, lulled by the warmth that surrounded me to ask direct questions.

"I take no pleasure in women," he said. "Men are my preference."

Again, long experience kept me from reacting. That confidence could easily be a trap for the unwary, luring into a trust later betrayed. But I could not help my curiosity. "Are such ways tolerated here?"

His blue eyes were sharp as the corners crinkled. "We are ever a practical people. It's too damn cold to worry about who one sleeps with."

That made me laugh. Of all the reasons… and yet it made sense. Still, it felt odd to find such understanding in so barbaric a land.

"Your Princess Bryilwa, she is a smart one? Trained in writing and in sums, isn't she?" Artheran asked as he gestured vaguely at the papers I'd scattered over the table.

"Yes," I let my pride reflect in my voice. "She is skilled in mathematics and the literary arts."

He nodded in satisfaction. "I have traveled, in my youth, enough to learn your language, see other places. Wesorix, our kingdom, it makes us strong. Our lives, our ways, force us to strength." He held up his hand, clenched tight. "But this fist? It only goes so far. Only lasts so long."

I raised my eyes in a question, trying to understand.

"Princess Bryilwa will teach her children, or see that they are taught. And the Eorals? They will see the royal children taught, and want the same for their children. And Wesorix will grow stronger still." Artheran smiled. "Both our lands will benefit from this marriage. But we will benefit even more."

Not as much as my people would, but I concealed that thought. "If we can come to terms," I pointed out.

"If so," Artheran laughed and rose. "We'll see what comes of our talks, Ambassador. Sleep well."

With that, he departed, and two blue-eyed, blonde-haired women came in, with large pans with wooden handles, slipping them between the covers. I settled at my desk with a clean piece of parchment and started to prepare my pens.

One of the women coughed to get my attention. She smiled, and then offered herself for my pleasure. I declined with thanks and feigned regret. I learned long ago to suppress my passions when in foreign lands. And for all of Artheran's apparent honesty, this was not the time or place to surrender to desires, wherever they may fall.

She took her leave, with a backwards look that spoke of regret, and closed the door behind her.

The room was warm enough that I let my new cloak fall off my shoulders, the better to reach for my pens and ink. I wouldn't let the bed cool, but I wanted to get my thoughts on paper. My king needed to be informed of the recent events.

My dearest Uncle,…

♦

Diplomacy teaches the fine art of waiting, and using time to one's advantage. My formal welcome having been delayed, I decided one night to indulge in one of my safer interests. I slipped out on a clear night, when the moon was gone from the sky, to gaze my fill of their stars. So bright, so clear, they filled the heavens.

I went out a distance from the King's Hall, away from the torches that burned outside, and found a place where I could sit and stare to my heart's content. But it was not so much as pleasure that drove me, it was a burning curiosity, for all the patterns I had studied in my land were shattered here. What place was this that even the stars were so very different?

A crunch of snow, and a warrior approached, wrapped in a new cloak. "Oaeton?"

"Artheran," I said and shifted over so that he could sit as well.

"What do you out here?" he asked, his breath hanging in the starlight.

"Stargazing," I said. Seeing his eyes bright with curiosity, I explained about the patterns that the stars dance in the sky, and the stories they tell.

"You know their dance?" he asked finally, when I'd run out of breath and words.

"Those of my home," I laughed. "These? These would take weeks, months, years, a lifetime even, to track and learn. But know you not the names of some?"

"A few," he shrugged. "The Wounded Hunter, the Enraged Boar. The skuld would know more, and all their tales."

"I'll talk to him," I said. "Perhaps he'd be kind enough to point them out."

"He would if you write down some of his epics," Artheran grinned. "He's already hinted to the king of his interest in your written word."

"I'll start to chart them too," I said. "It will take some time to come to agreements."

"Perhaps longer than you think," Artheran laughed.

♦

King Saer stared at the small portrait of Princess Bryilwa, one that I had carried with me on my long journey. "In truth, I have no heart for this, Artheran."

Artheran put his hand on the King's shoulder. "I know," he said. He stood at his brother's side, and only I could see that his face was a mixture of brotherly affection and determination.

King Saer had finally extended an invitation to me to meet with him and Artheran privately to discuss the commencement of the talks. But if ever there was a man more torn between love and duty, I'd not seen it before.

"Elsela has only been gone this past year." King Saer caught my eye and looked away. "My wife," he said softly.

"Elsela understood expediency, Saer. And the need." Artheran said softly. "Oaeton has traveled far, and we would offer no insult to his king. Let us at least start talks. Summon the eorals. It will be some time for them to gather, and probably a season or two before we can come to terms, and in that time you will… your resolve will have strengthened."

"There is no need," King Saer set aside the portrait and took up his cup. "I will declare you my heir, and the matter is done."

"No, Saer." Artheran sighed. "We have talked of this too, late into the night and our cups, and it would accomplish nothing. Our bloodline has ruled since our grandfather's grandfather, and I would not see it falter on my shoulders. Nor on Derik's, who's sired no children in all this time. You need an heir, my king."

"That's not the only reason you oppose Derik." Saer took a drink.

Artheran glanced at me. I saw his hand squeeze on the king's shoulder, as a reminder perhaps, to my presence in the room.

King Saer drew a heavy sigh. "Very well," he conceded. "I will summon the Council of Eorals."

♦

The eorals were to a man blond-haired, blue-eyed warriors. Their weapons and armor varied as much as the insects of my land, thank the kindly spirits. Their faces may have all looked the same, but their attitudes differed as much as their weaponry. Caution, disdain, hostility, indifference, friendliness, and the spark in the eye that every diplomat knows. The desire for something for nothing, the taste for getting the better of a deal that lingers deep in every trader's heart.

It reminded me of home, and I settled into the talks with a will. But whereas I would willingly discuss terms for hours on end, these men were not of that kind. After even a short discourse, they'd grow restless, and if the talk stretched out one would have thought they were all children straining to be released from lessons.

So I developed new skills as the months progressed. Negotiating during a deer hunt, as we rode through thick woods of new green leaves. Addressing issues while tracking the wild boar. Talking at the side of a forge as weapons were sharpened. Discussing terms at the edge of a sparring circle. Deflecting hostilities while bathing in a nearly frozen high-mountain pool in the worst of the summer's heat. Conferring on trade details as we feasted among leaves turned vivid shades of red and yellow.

I learned much in this way, and the eorals took the measure of me, both in our differences and our similarities, our strengths and weaknesses. And if there was much laughter in my inability to wield a great sword, there was also respect. For when the final terms were decided and the bargain sealed, they learned that my weapons were my voice and my pen, and the skill with which I wielded them.

All the while, I sent missives to my king with the details of my work, along with descriptions of the land and its people. I wrote to Bryilwa too, telling her of King Saer, of his people and their customs, and sending her language lessons.

And when once again the snow did in fact "reach my balls" as Artheran had put it in the poetry of the north, I wrote of that as well. I thought it best to be honest about Wesorix and speak truthfully about the land and conditions. To warn them both. Not that princesses are given choices; such is not their lot in life. Bryilwa would know that. So I wrote of all I saw and experienced and hoped for the best.

Until the day in late summer when the final agreements were reached, and I could send word that all was in readiness for the wedding.

◆

Our princess arrived late enough that a threat of first snow hung in the air. I met Bryilwa's ship, boarding the moment it met the wood of the dock.

She was sequestered in her warm cabin, surrounded by handmaidens. Their lovely dark faces all turned toward me, and brought a rush of homesickness in their strange unfamiliarity.

"My dearest princess," I smiled to see her lovely face.

"Dearest cousin." She seemed weary, but she smiled. "It is so good to see you."

"King Saer awaits you in his hall to give you formal greetings." I replied. At her puzzled look I repeated the sentence in our language. "Have you not studied the words I sent you?" I asked.

"Has he not learned my language?" she countered.

I sighed.

She laughed. "Come, Cousin. Show me this land you write so eloquently about. From your description, gods and angels surely roam this place. And what is this thing called snow?"

She learned on the way to the King's Hall.

◆

The first seven days of their meeting were an unmitigated disaster.

On the final day, Artheran and I watched from behind one of the giant pillars in the Great Hall. I in growing despair, he almost doubled over in mirth, as King Saer and the princess sat by the hearth and attempted to talk.

"What I particularly like," he choked out. "Is that when she thinks he doesn't understand her, she just talks louder." Artheran leaned against a pillar, and snorted into his arm.

"This is not funny," I snapped. "They have had a week now, and it's not —"

King Saer's head was up, as if he were scanning the hall, looking for escape as he had each time before, after a few minutes in her presence.

"You're right." Artheran stood, and took a deep breath. "This has been going on long enough."

"What?" But he left me standing there as he marched the length of the hall to the King's side.

"Sire, m'lady, I'd ask for private conversation, if you'd permit," Artheran said, executing a fairly formal bow.

"Of course," King Saer said, rising quickly.

"With both of you," Artheran continued. As the king's face fell, Artheran gestured to his chambers. He made the request again, in my language. Princess Bryilwa cast me a puzzled glance, then rose as well.

King Saer led the way, the princess following. But as I approached the door, Artheran stepped within and gave me an odd look. "Your services as a translator will not be needed."

With that, he closed the door in my face.

♦

"You perfidious, manipulative, lying —"

Artheran sprawled in the chair by my table, his hands laced over his stomach with every indication of contentment. "I didn't lie," he protested.

"— treacherous *raskullin*," I spat.

"You haven't taught me that word," he tilted his head, his grin even wider. "It sounds like one I should know."

"It's in ruins now. The marriage, the alliance, the trade agreements, all shattered." I gestured to the documents scattered over the table. "All that work, wasted. Even now, the princess packs for the voyage home, her handmaidens all fluttering about like —"

"They never stop talking, do they?" Artheran leaned his head back as if studying the ceiling. "Saer was right about that."

"What does it matter?" I paced the room. "We shall return home with nothing accomplished, and —"

"You'll go with them?"

I stopped dead in my pacing, and spun on my heel to stare at Artheran. Who sat there and regarded me with his calm, cool, blue eyes.

"You knew this would happen," I seethed. "All this time. You never intended that —"

"No," his denial was firm. "The eorals were pressuring Saer to name an heir. I proposed a foreign alliance to keep them at bay, with trade seeded in to whet their greed. At best, I hoped to pull him from his grief with a new wife, a new hope. At worst, to stall, to delay, at least until he could see the need." Artheran dropped his gaze. "Then Annaella died, and I thought we'd lose Saer with her."

"But you talked to King Saer and the princess for hours, let them slip out from under their obligations, let them break their engagement when they should have been held to the terms of —"

"Really?" he raised an eyebrow. "To bind them to a marriage without any mutual attraction, other than a signed document?" He shifted one of the papers on the table. "That is not what I wanted for my brother. I suspect you didn't want it for your cousin as well."

My anger dissipated like the mist. "No," I said simply. "I'd hoped they'd find each other acceptable. At least find some common ground."

"She is too young," he said abruptly. "Saer sees his dead daughter in her every move, every gesture. He sends her home with good wishes, no offense offered or taken."

"But he needs an heir, you said that yourself —"

"He does," Artheran said calmly. "And I suspect that in the next few months, his attention will turn to some of our noble ladies. Older, but still in their fertile years. Someone comfortable. Familiar. Who knows, perhaps even someone he can love. Now that there is heart in him again," and there was that wicked grin. "After his fortunate escape."

I bristled, and he shrugged what he must have thought was an apology. "Well, your goals are met, and my mission is a failure." I rose, and went to the table. Artheran pulled his legs back to make room. I started to gather up the parchments. "Without a wedding, without trade agreements, without —"

"Oh, we still have trade agreements."

"What?" I paused, looking into his dancing eyes.

"And an alliance. I suspect your uncle will even allow us to keep the dower price."

"What?" I frowned at him, since he was certainly pleased with himself for a reason I could not fathom. "Why?"

"Because there is still a suitable candidate for a marriage to bind our countries together."

"Who?"

"One of royal blood," he sat up in the chair.

"There is no one." I dismissed his foolishness. "My other cousins are all too young to be wed. My uncle will never allow —"

"One who is learned in math, and science, and the art of writing." Artheran rose.

I continued to gather the parchments, rolling them tightly together. "You are mad. And as thick as the posts that support the Great Hall."

Artheran chuckled. "One who is skilled at the hunt. One who understands the ways of Wesorix and its people. Even enjoys them."

"You'll be hard pressed to find such a woman among the noble ladies. Even the —"

Artheran leaned close and whispered in my ear. "One who studies the stars."

I froze.

He shifted. I was suddenly conscious of the heat he radiated.

"One who once told me that he needed… weeks… months… years to learn their patterns. A lifetime, even."

"But —" I stood, stunned, yet with a heart racing within my chest. I could feel the pulse in my neck, beating under my skin.

Artheran's gaze locked on my throat, that slow smile starting in the corner of his mouth. His gaze lifted to mine from under his golden lashes. "I formally asked Princess Bryilwa for your hand in marriage, with the great good wishes and permission of my brother, King Saer."

"I —" I closed my eyes, not daring to breathe.

His hand cupped the back of my neck, his sword-callused thumb rubbing the skin behind my ear. "Look at me," he said.

My mouth was dry as I met his gaze. "My king… my uncle… will not permit —" I swallowed hard. "My people do not —"

"The princess said that she thought her father would care more for your happiness than aught else. She seemed particularly pleased that I asked for your hand formally." Artheran's fingers trailed down my neck and lifted my chin. "Such is the lot of princes, to make sacrifices for their people."

"It would not be a sacrifice," I blurted out.

His smile deepened. "She will carry the request to your Uncle, with all the documents signed and witnessed. All that needs done is to change a name, and all the *her*'s to *his*'s."

He leaned in closer, his lips close to mine. "A simple matter, really."

"In truth," I turned my head slightly toward his. "And in the best interests for both our peoples."

He pulled back slightly. "And in ours, yes?"

"Yes," I whispered.

He pulled the rolled parchments from my hand, and let them drop to the table. They unrolled as he pushed me down into the chair. "Best be about it, then," he gestured to my pens. "Take up your weapon."

I looked up into sparking blue eyes. "You're about to make some sort of crude joke, aren't you?"

"Not at all," he managed to keep his face straight, but his laughter was in his eyes. "I thought to save that for later."

I reached for the weapon at hand.

The Bridgehouse Game

Kathryn Kuitenbrouwer

A t the time, I was a student of anthropology with a particular interest in primordial sacrificial ritual — a Flemish academic I was, surrounded by decay. Paradoxically, I had for years patiently waited for the slow and unpleasant death of a grand-aunt, anticipating a handsome financial legacy. It was not, incidentally, *nothing* to guard her bedside during the convalescence, and no small gratitude to bring her favourite things to her — *koek*, Tierentijn's famous mustard, *matte taart* from the right bakery. She was a lovely individual, and, when she finally passed away, to honour her life, I designed and had built a living space, quite modern in function, which served me well.

♦

It was cherry-red painted steel and spanned the ancient Leie, in Gent, België, acting as both house for me, and bridge for the people. The roof was well insulated though I could feel the reverberation of foot traffic sometimes, revelers during the Gentse Feesten, and the cyclists who used my house to get from one side of the canalized waterway to the other. Melissa lived here with me at the time. She was an opportunist, yes, but she was sad — bitchy and beautiful in her sorrow — and I fell for that.

The water of the Leie barely flowed and smelled horribly. It seeped into our waking dreams, but we became used to it.

I was studying one night, occasionally looking up from my book to tell Melissa about a series of barrows in England that were vaginal in configuration, and absolutely monstrous in size, and thought to have been tributes to some sort of earth goddess. They had got me thinking about the enclosed tunnel under the house — the tunnel my bridge house created! — and the water causeway as a sexual avenue. It was, I told her, "a sacred place where ancients sacrificed in the hope of cyclical fecundity."

"And you the dryad," she muttered. She was writing in her journal, something I found later and kept away from the authorities. It read, for example: *My fingers along her trachea.*

"Centaur," I corrected, noting that dryads were for sissies.

"Ah," she said, "because you are half-assed."

I did not bother to tell her that centaurs were in fact a hybrid of Homo sapiens and Equus, not donkey. There was really no point once she got punning. "Neigh," she would say, or something along those lines. Instead, I pointed out, "If you boat down there, you'll notice the fetid water, the rotting carcasses of intoxicated wildlife, and the composting *excrementum* that represents hundreds of years of bad European plumbing. And then you'll think of human sacrifice."

"Tell me, Bart," Melissa segued. "If you had to kill someone, how would you go about it?" She was such a one for changing the topic.

♦

Later I would read this in her journal, along with many more such tracts: *How far can one go? How close to the line? Veerla's throat was long, white and soft like the throat of a swan. She never talked when a gesture would suffice. Her white, quiet throat. My fingers on her trachea. And her arching her brow over at Bart, which meant, Who does he think he is?*

I'd never fallen for a girl, and wasn't even sure that's what this was. It was something, though, yes.

♦

I coyly answered, "Petit mort, of course, a hundred of them amounting to one big one."

"A-mounting! Darling. That's very funny," she said, "but you cannot kill by orgasm. Not without pre-existing heart condition or epilepsy or some such." She did not even look over at me when she suggested alternatives, "Knife, strangulation, bullet, or poison?"

"This is —"

"Hypothetical. How would you make the sacrifice?" Her voice sounded exacerbated, but you never knew with Melissa. It might have been a grand act, like so much she did.

I sighed. "It would certainly be half-assed," I said.

♦

If one opened the front and rear entrance of the bridgehouse, as we had come to call it, as indeed all of Gent had come to call it, there would be a thin suck of air, initially, and then, whoosh, the centuries-old dust, the pollen of ancient recycling life forms, the bleach of my neighbour's daily cleaning rituals would eddy through, one odour upon the next, until a person might almost swoon with sensory confusion. I liked to stand in the front-door threshold and press up against it in the evenings, and this is what I did then. I got up from my studies and pulled first the back and then the front door open, holding on to the jamb for the resistance I knew I would need. It was a time of great European winds. There had been deaths, to be sure. And the reek of humanity ran through the place like an entity.

"Bart," Melissa said, not even looking up from her task, "you make a conduit. This house is the asshole of all Europe. The stink pipe of the Lowlands. Wake up and smell the methane —"

♦

I had no idea what the word conduit meant at the time so I smiled and turned back to the open door. She went on like this all the time, and there was no sense listening to it all — I knew it was grief talking, how mourning must work its way out through the vocabulary, and, less grandly, through sleep, illness, and defecation. Time, in other words. The air was sweet this night, edging my skin where it was bare and pulling up the little arm and leg hairs. In light of my studies, I wondered what small bits of skin and human dust, what minute parasites were lifted from me to join the breeze, and its swoop away from me.

The bridgehouse itself, I now considered, was more a barrow, open like this, than ever the passage beneath it, which let all things through it, and therefore weakened its sacred aspect. I felt I was getting somewhere in this line of thinking. I was getting nowhere, as it turned out, nowhere.

"Why Hank?" I said, surprising even myself with the boldness of the question, as well as the suddenness of it.

"Why not Hank?" I could tell she was irritated. She added, "He was kind."

"I meant why did they call him that. Was it short for Henry, then? It's hardly a name."

She pushed her jottings to the side and stretched out on the leather couch. I bought the couch for its clean modern lines, for its clinical sterility, and that is the effect it now gave her, and, instantly, I regretted the purchase. It visually highlighted her worst personality inclinations. I was sideways in the door, communing both out and in, or so I thought.

"He wasn't short for anything. Hank always said the name was between a shank and a hankie. And that so was he. I have no idea what he meant." She added, "It was never Henry."

"Did you see his body?"

"I saw his casket."

"He was an ugly man, or so I have heard."

"Yes, he was hideous. Such a heinous thing, I was ashamed of being seen with him in public. I'd pace myself so that I looked as if I was with the man in front or the one behind."

♦

Aside: I, on the other hand, was beautiful. And like all beautiful people, I felt it afforded me leeway in all manner of things. Even my feet were lovely.

So I said, "From the ridiculous to the sublime," meaning me, that I was sublime and that Hank had been ridiculous.

But Melissa said, "To the subliminal, you mean."

"I don't understand." I didn't. Really, I didn't.

"Sometimes you present as advertising copy, that's all. Only I haven't figured out what the product is."

"It isn't my fault —"

"— It's no one's fault, ever," she said, as if this were another conversation with another man in another town in another time. That was Melissa. She lived everywhere at once, and never anywhere properly. Advertising copy? Jesus wept.

She admitted to playing a certain game, then. She would pick out a face on the bus or in the market, then try to attach it metaphorically to what it was that face would best sell. The butcher, who had ears that looked chewed, and tiny beaded eyes, and skin the soft pinkness of a fresh born piglet, she said would sell dolls. "Dolls," she said, "to pedophiles." I worried when she said this.

"Do pedophiles buy dolls?" I asked, but the question was ignored, for it was boring or not au courant in her momentary antic quest.

"You," she said. "I can't place. Costume jewelry on one of those late-night infomercials, maybe. Or laundry soap. Or hope to starving nations. I can't decide."

I thought of my poor aunt, then, and the terrified look that swept her face as grim death came for her. I was not prepared for this, had not expected (nor wanted) to be there at the final second. She did not go gently. Her face contorted into an asymmetrical hyena, selling, I supposed, despair, and then she screamed a scream so shrill and demonic, I feared for her soul. I thought how the mustard and the almond custards offered no solace in this final moment, and how all I'd managed to do was distract her. I could no more sell hope than jewelry.

Melissa's journal entry: *Veerla was the last person to touch Hank.*

It's landscape I am after for you here but I shall not achieve it. I'm only capable, under the circumstances, of portraiture. You can't get at a person entirely. You can only get snippets of them. As much as I detest Impressionism, this will only work if you stand way back and completely give over.

Melissa's hair was thick only when she remembered to add hairspray. She was not tenacious except when she thought she would not be allowed to have what she wanted. In other words, there was nothing she wanted until she found out she couldn't have it. She lacked initiative. She made up for this in bed. She loathed autobiography. She disliked the truth when a story would suffice. She loved Hank: a soldier, a lover, a slow take. And according to some who knew about these things, she was always the main suspect in his unresolved death.

"We loved each other like George and Martha in *Who's Afraid of Virginia Woolf.*"

"They were like wild animals at each other's throats."

"Exactly. We loved like wild animals at each other's throats."

"Were you —?"

"I was Martha."

"Did you —?"

"I have regrets."

"You feel you pushed him away." I had heard this version through the grapevine and like a half-ass I pursued it to see where it might lead. She draped one of her arms languidly off the couch and I was, from a distance, examining the curve of her armpit, an area not normally associated with ardour, but there you go — there is never any accounting for taste. "You shouldn't have pushed him away, Martha."

"Don't be foolish. It was he who pushed me. I loved him too dearly to ever, ever push. It was me who was the pushover."

"But he who drowned." I should never have said this. Or muttered it. Or whatever I dared do. Mentioning the event always made her tetchy.

"Drowned by alcohol," — Oh, she was spitting angry — "if that's what you mean. Drowned in sorrow. In misery. In country and western radio." This bit was contestable. She did say it, but I believe it to be a lie. Not one of his friends and relations would corroborate, for example, that he drank excessively, or that he listened any more than anyone else to country and western music. Veerla claimed he admired electronica, and that he had a penchant for John Cage.

"He liked the silences," she said, and added a meaningful tilt of the head to her comment, which I could in no way read.

◆

Aside: are we not all tired of coy women? Are we not up to our ears in coyness? I would, personally, give all I own for a practical girl. A slow romp under the sheets with a girl who considered for one minute what I might want, for Christ's sake.

◆

Melissa's journal entry: *Hank said, "Pretend like I haven't been away. Pretend like no time has passed. Pretend you can't assume or surmise or even imagine what hells I have witnessed. Pretend for me," he said. "So as I can forget."*

◆

I'd shut the door by this point and made a roaring fire in the hearth. Along the floor of the living room and trailing into the kitchen and beyond was all manner of debris. Curl of leaf, and crunch of grit. The wind had driven it into an erratic pattern, a wild shifting line right down the centre of my home.

It appeared as art to me, defining my space from hers, as I sat opposite the lounger, in my red-tweed-and-chrome rocker. I watched her stare absently at the ceiling, thinking, I supposed, of Hank, or Veerla, or sudden death, or war. She had every right, but still it crept up on me, made me jealous. It made me wish I had met him, or even gently brushed up once against him, so that she would send some small thought in my direction. I see now how already I was a goner.

◆

"Between a rock and a hard place," I said. It occurred to me that that's what these barrows were, at least to the sacrifices themselves, that they left very little room for maneuvering, if one happened to be a vestal virgin or a plump and chosen toddler. What didn't occur to me — at least not until it came out of my mouth and she gave me her infamous long suffering look — was the rhythm: a rock and a hard place / a shank and a hankie, but then it hit me, and I shook myself and glared at her. "I didn't mean it like that. I didn't —"

"Bart?" she said. She was lying so still. She was like a small, disappointed child, one who has lost much, and hasn't a clue how to regain it, and then her lips opened just ever-so-slightly, and even in this tiny movement, she had such a capacity for cruelty. "Have you ever *done* anything?"

I had the impression of being dead in that moment, a déjà vu dead, in which one has never felt more alive. It was a split second of dire expectation. It took me a while to put a voice to my apprehension and when I did it came out as shaky as one might expect. "Yes, certainly. I've done many things," I said, though I could think of not one single occurrence in my life worth citing.

"I mean real things." Still, she did not move and neither did I.

◆

Melissa's journal entry: *But I wanted to know the tiniest details of Hank's psychology. I wanted to see the things he had seen. I wanted to have done what he had done, or at least know of it. What is love? I did love him. And so I decided I would have to piece him together from this person and that, from this memory, and that photograph, and that walk we had together reconstructed. Again and again, I would loop through certain sequences of our lovemaking, trying to get them right, trying to get them down. And then very soon, this wasn't enough. I wanted something substantial.*

◆

"Have I done anything?" I knew she wanted to know if I had ever killed anyone. Or if I had hated anyone. If I had held a gun and felt the connection. "You mean like enlist and wantonly go against all my principals?"

Melissa gestured, her palms flippering. She said, "Like anything?" She wanted to know if I knew that war could lead to peace, and that annihilation to Paradise. "I could love you," she added, then, a little too needily, too faux lustily, a little too up-my-alleyish, "if only you'd *act* a certain way." Her lips charmed me as she said this, that red lipstick she always wore glinting in the light from the wood fire. You have no idea how alluring she could be on that lounger, with her lips parted just so, demanding things, suggesting she might love me. Suggesting some incremental movement in our story.

"You could love me?"

And she turned then, and smiled. "In a certain way, yes. I could." She had his uniform, she said then.

◆

Melissa had somehow retrieved the fatigues from his effects, even though the bulk of his belongings would have gone to his parents, with perhaps a token or two making their way into Veerla's hands. I knew where things were going within seconds. It was her excitement that revealed everything. She was brimming over with energy and possibility, and that is how I knew, too, that she had been thinking this up for some time, that things never were spontaneous with her, or hadn't been since Hank.

She leapt off the lounger and scurried to the back of the house, scattering the line drawn so nicely by nature between us, and was gone for long enough I had forgotten her mention of the uniform, and had gone off in my head along some more rational romantic path, so that when she returned cradling it — a small, vile, digital-camouflage bundle — it took some seconds to assemble my thoughts.

"Oh God," I said. "This is horrible."

"Yes!" Her eyes glistened with plans unfolding.

"Was it cleaned, at least?"

"No." She nodded solemnly down at it. "It will be a touch big, I expect."

And then things truly hit home. And I was undone by the realization. Undone to the point of poor decision-making. I accepted the filthy packet when she pressed it on me. I held it as reverently as I had just watched her do. I looked from it to her. "Really, I can't," I said.

"You can. Really." And that smile satellited around me so that I knew what it took to be central, and also the particular stunning warmth of that centrality. She stood there waiting, knowing and waiting. I'd not ever seen her so engaged.

◆

In the time it took for me to strip down, stand briefly naked, and, almost automatically, robotically, pull on the jacket, the cargo pants, the army issue socks, and the heavy boots, I heard two cyclists pass over the building, the tires jolting at each riveted section, and a man singing Pergolesi's *Stabat Mater*. When I was done, she had me sit back down, and then she also sat back down. The mess on the floor was now everywhere and had no meaning. It was just a dirty floor, and I did not care, for now I had her attention and I had his boots on. It was impossible not to feel this transformed space between us.

"What do you want me to do?"

"Shh," she said. "Let me think for a minute." Her eyes were shining up and down my body. I knew I existed in a way I hadn't before. I was being newly created. After some time, she said, "I want you to talk. I want you to tell me the awful things you saw. Tell me what you did. What was done to you."

"Melissa," I said. "I won't play this game. I do have some self resp—"

"Please," she said. She was desperate, whining. "For once in your life, be alive. Be fucking something. You're spoiling a perfectly good —"

Opportunity. And so I was. And so I stopped protesting and sat there for an hour recounting my mission in Afghanistan. And every time I stalled, having run out of things to say, having run out of made-up atrocities or kind memories of children I had saved, or moments of existential panic late at night in my tent, she would smile and urge me on, "Tell me more," she would say. "I want to know about the sergeant. I want to know about the corporal you slept with. I want to know about her body odour, and how she touched you, and how for her, you touched yourself. Tell me, too," she would say, "how the dust sprayed up at you when she died. Tell me how in that moment you missed me," and she leaned over and really truly and properly watched me.

I carried on for another hour, making things up, and then the hours mounted and the night cued the day. I was exhausted. I was unfolding another man inside myself inside this narrative. I can't explain it any other way.

She said, "Don't move. Don't move your face just for a minute. Oh God —"

And I watched her watch him, the thin heat from the morning sunlight moving across my cheek, my eyes, and she was beautiful, her face full of longing and remembering and sorrow. And I did not move, at all.

◆

Melissa's journal entry: *Everyone was there for the funeral. We splayed out through the grounds. The graveyard was called EverRest Community, as if the dead played euchre together, or argued labour law, or built parkettes for their living children. The funeral director gave me Hank's uniform. He must have thought I was higher up the kin ladder. Veerla came up behind me as he handed the parcel to me, and ran her nail down my neck. She had come from Europe to witness the burial, and to talk. But I didn't want to talk. I wanted him back. I began then to accumulate and press the pieces back into something resembling him.*

◆

A week passed, and then another. I spent a little time on my studies and in between — an in-between that widened like a river during flood season — I googled. There were plenty of blogs on the topic and plenty of media reports. I practiced to memory some slang, and current weapons training, and I downloaded a lengthy application. I renewed my passport and went to my family doctor for a full physical. I coughed, and he nodded. I was healthy, and young, and purposeful. It was the easiest thing in the world to enlist.

◆

Melissa's journal entry: *Veerla arched her back into a bridge underneath the white linens of my bed. I yawned, and said, "There are things you do in war you wouldn't dream of doing in any other situation. You might find someone in mortal pain begging you to shoot him, and you might shoot him." I had read about all these* things. I said, "You might mistake a woman for a suicide bomber and react too quickly. The Russians left toy-shaped IEDs that looked like butterflies. You might see a child stoop to pick one up, a toy, they are thinking, and you can see the joy in their eyes. Veerla, the military has access to all sorts of depravity."

"Access?" she said. "You make it sound like an entitlement issue."

♦

And then it was like in a cartoon, when a character saws a hole in the floor and you fall down, only in this case, I fell from the house the death of my grand-aunt financed, into a world that makes no sense to me even now. I looked up and saw Melissa holding the saw, grinning from ear to ear, leaning in the hole, and she became smaller and smaller until she was nothing but a speck. I was a warrior in any war I chose. Sometimes I was in the American Civil War, sharpening my bayonet, and marching. Sometimes I was in a trench in the First World War, sometimes I was in Vietnam. I had been in the Crusades, and I had been in Afghanistan. I had been in Sarajevo. I had been in Rwanda. I had been in a small family skirmish in Friesland one hundred years before.

It didn't matter. For in war, I was never *there* there. The blood from the shot-off hand, the bone sticking out of the donkey's leg, the missing eye, and its infection, the noise and the reek of spent uranium, and the orders from above, and the smiling so they didn't hate me so much they might kill me, was not me, and I was not it. The dust in my every orifice was just that, and not the dust unto which I would expect to become.

♦

Melissa's journal entry: *The last time Hank and I fucked, I said to him, "When I was young I made up a story about a giant owl who lived in the next property over. I told this story to the girl who lived in the house on this property. I took her on a tour of her property showing her where the owl lived and the markings it had left. I half believed myself when we walked through the forest that we were tracking it. The story made me large just as it made her small. Before I knew it, I was as big as God, and she was sobbing and running as fast as she could away.*

♦

So it was I came to know sacrifice.

♦

Melissa's journal entry: *I said, "Tell me what you did over there. It'll be good for you to speak about it — good to unload this."*

I watched the words, Tell me, reverberate back and forth between us: Tell me, tell me, tell me, until it began to sound maudlin, insinuating, hurtful. It was too late to take it back, and I knew it would echo unresolved and un-dissipated forever.

Veerla arched her eyebrows, watching us.

"I can't remember," he said. He wore the camouflage duds. He seemed to always have them on. There was a glass with scotch in it in front of him and then it was finished and he was reaching to the bottle for another. People are clichés when they are in pain. They are country and western music. They drink. They don't remember the details of their pain.

♦

When I returned, I quit the military. I went back to my studies, this time privately, the enclosed space of the university classrooms proving within weeks of my registration to be claustrophobic. Yes, I moved home, and the house was changed by my changed self, and I lived in it, transformed, with Melissa when she was home, and with her journal when she wasn't. No one had ever said not to flip through it. I read *him*, and *he*, and *Hank* and *Bart*, and I swear I did not always know which one was Hank and which one me — it was not clear whether Melissa distinguished either, anymore. Things were muddled. I did not go out much.

◆

Honestly, I hardly left.

◆

Veerla came by to visit Melissa regularly. I could not parse their relationship. It seemed to consist of glances, and gestures and nods of approval. They wanted to engage me in all manner of conversation, to learn what had transpired in my — what they called — "war experience," and seemed almost pleased that I had nothing to say. I had nothing to add to the conversation in that regard. I had gone down the rabbit hole, and though things had happened, the amplitude and resonance of those things had canceled themselves out — the dust, the blood, the anger, the ballyhoo of it was a darkness, for in the rabbit hole there is no light source.

◆

I was the house through which all things flowed. I was the conduit of nothing to Nothing. If sex is an offering, it fled me faster than if I had immolated in Afghanistan along with Cpl. Stanley, and Cpl. J. Haddows and the beautiful Sgt. we all called Madonna, even after we slept with her.

◆

Aside: sleeping with the Sgt. we all called Madonna was like sleeping with a childhood secret. The intimacy was talismanic. We would be safe. We would survive. But we were not all safe. I recall the pieces of the Sgt. we called Madonna more clearly than I remember her. The blast was minor, and I was tasked with gathering her up — a hand, a mess of intestine, there were large and small pieces, her hair, my tears, and that feeling you get as your insides harden against it. And afterward, I would re-evaluate safety, for it was an illusion. I had done something, and it had undone me. There was nothing more to say about it.

Melissa said, "Remember when he left to Kabul?" and I did not know whether she referred to me, or whether to Hank, or whether she referred to someone I had never met. But anyway, she was speaking to Veerla, not to me.

"He had the world on his lips," Veerla responded.

"His lips?"

"Yes."

"Tell me." And Veerla turned away, and Melissa smiled.

Melissa's journal entry: *For two years I catalogued details about Hank. And whenever I needed to feel whole, I recalled these gestures, or snippets of conversation, and sometimes images that resided in photographs or memories — and Veerla, of course — and if I could not have Hank, I would rebuild him.*

And then when Veerla would leave, a regular ritual would unfold. Melissa would sit opposite me, in a way that reminded me of before except that now I had her attention, and she would look not at me but *into* me, and she would ask me questions that I could not answer, and this not answering made her smile. Sometimes she would pet my hand as if I was a child. "Bart," she said. "Don't move. Don't change. This is how I want you to stay forever. Dear Bart."

Melissa's journal entry: *It seems impossible, but it isn't.*

I did not take my fatigues off for six months.

Melissa's journal entry: *And then Veerla wanted to quit. She came by and would not contribute. Things became difficult among us then.*

♦

Six months is a long time to sit still and fetid and war-torn in a house financed by one's lovely dead aunt and to let the thoughts meander through one. The thoughts were like a breeze through me. My friends came by initially but if you even consider for one second the situation you will know in your heart that even were you my friend, you too would have fallen away. There was nothing there for anyone, and no matter what people thought they might do to help — bring food, sweep, clean the dishes — the essential problem of me remained the same. I overheard Veerla say, "Remnant," in relation to me, and when I heard this, for the first time in weeks and weeks I smiled, recalling the line of leaves through my house, and the accumulation of debris and the significance I felt it had as a boundary between Melissa and me — a *grenzen* demarcating our territories. Yes, I supposed I was a remnant. A sacrifice to some unknown purpose — the greater good, what have you.

♦

Then, one day when Melissa was not home, Veerla stopped by and seduced me. It was inconsequential in the big scheme of things. I was a puppet and she the puppeteer. I sat in a chair as she touched my face. When she saw I was ready, she unzipped my fatigues and tugged them down; she slipped her panties off and maintained a kind of plaintive eye contact while she fucked me. And when the sex was done, she looked sad and defeated, and I realized she had meant to heal me somehow, and the medicine had failed.

♦

Melissa returned after Veerla had left and said, "I love you."

She was looking at me and saying it to Hank. It didn't matter to me that when she said this or that, she thought of Hank. I nodded, and she sat down at the kitchen table and opened her journal, and set it ready with a pen on one side of her, and on the other she opened a photo album of mementos, and pictures of him and pictures that reminded her of him. There were shots of places he had traveled before she met him, and business cards of companies he had had tenuous, sometimes almost non-existent, dealings with. It was a portfolio. It was an infrastructure upon which to hang her longings — and in that it was something. She asked me to stay still while she looked three ways, to my form, to the drawing she was making of me, to the album. And when she was done, she tore out the drawing and added it to the album. "Thank you," she said.

Melissa's journal entry: *It took time to fall in love with Bart, but I was determined. Then, when I knew it was real and authentic, I told him. I no longer needed Veerla's gestures. I wanted only him. I wanted to collect it all on him.*

Veerla came by once a week at least after that first time. She brought ice cream once, and another time she brought a wind-up car, and set it motoring along my chest — these things were meant to make me laugh. She lay beside me naked and asked me what I liked. At first I couldn't think of a thing. She touched me, asking, did I like this? or this? She ran her finger along every part of me until she found the good places. My tailbone, the spot near the tip of my penis, the inside of my mouth.

Was I healing? Maybe. Maybe.

◆

Melissa's journal entry: *And then he began to change.*

◆

Aside: A husk of a man. Between a rock and hard place. Half-assed. One thing I learned is that it is harder to live outside a role than inside one. It is not enough to have done something. It is only enough to have been thought to have done something. You are only as whole as the stories told about you. And I have no one. What is love? I do not know the answer to that question. I do not. The bicycles clatter by, and the bicycles clatter by. That is all.

◆

Melissa's journal entry: *And then I discovered Veerla there. I knew her. I knew her, and then this. The beautiful neck of a swan. My fingers. Death is uglier than I imagined, and more barbaric. She had no breath to scream, but her face contorted to nasty dismay. Afterward I let go, and she dropped into the Leie, and was not found for ages, her body decaying, splitting off into the still water, the compost of millennia aching for one more gift. My gift was like a keening and wailing. What is love? Love is an illness.*

Biographies

Jesse Bullington is the critically acclaimed author of the novels *The Sad Tale of the Brothers Grossbart, The Enterprise of Death*, and most recently, *The Folly of the World*. All three are historically set oddities that are sure to offend somebody, but maybe not for the usual reasons. His short fiction and articles have appeared in numerous magazines, anthologies, and websites. He can be found physically in Colorado, and more ephemerally at www.jessebullington.com.

Born in the Caribbean, **Tobias S. Buckell** is a New York *Times* best-selling author. His novels and over fifty short stories have been translated into seventeen languages, and he has been nominated for the Hugo, Nebula, and Prometheus Awards, and John W. Campbell Award for Best New Science Fiction Author. He currently lives in Ohio.

John Helfers is an author and award-winning editor currently living in Green Bay, Wisconsin. During his sixteen years working at Tekno Books, he edited numerous fiction anthologies and more novels than he can count. His short fiction has appeared in more than forty anthologies, including *If I Were An Evil Overlord*,

Time Twisters, and *Places to Be, People to Kill*. He's also written fiction in the *Dragonlance®*, *Transformers®*, *BattleTech®* and *Shadowrun®* universes.

Tania Hershman is the author of two story collections: *My Mother Was an Upright Piano: Fictions* (Tangent Books, 2012), a collection of fifty-six very short fictions, and *The White Road and Other Stories* (Salt, 2008; commended, 2009 Orange Award for New Writers). Tania's short stories and poetry are published or forthcoming in, among others, *Five Dials*, *The Stinging Fly*, *Tears in the Fence*, PANK *Magazine*, *SmokeLong Quarterly*, *The London Magazine*, and New Scientist, and on BBC Radio. She has just begun a PhD in creative writing, exploring the intersection between fiction and physics, and is editor of the journal *The Short Review* and the new UK short story listings site *ShortStops*. www.taniahershman.com

Jonathan L. Howard has been a game designer and scripter for the last twenty years, and a full-time author for the past four. He is the author of the Johannes Cabal novels and the Russalka Chronicles series. He lives in the south-west of England.

Kathryn Kuitenbrouwer is the author of the novels *The Nettle Spinner* and *Perfecting*, as well as, the short fiction collection *Way Up*. Her short stories have appeared in *Granta* magazine, *The Walrus* and *Storyville*, where they won the Sidney Prize. Her novel *All The Broken Things* is forthcoming from Random House of Canada in 2014.

Editor and Stone Skin Press Creative Director **Robin D. Laws** is an author, game designer, and podcaster. Robin's previous editorial work can be seen in such Stone Skin anthologies as *The Lion and the Aardvark* and *Shotguns v. Cthulhu*. His fiction includes *New Tales of the Yellow Sign*, *Pierced Heart*, and *Blood of the City*. Robin created the GUMSHOE investigative roleplaying rules system and such games as *Feng Shui*, *Hillfolk*,

HeroQuest and *Ashen Stars*. He comprises the Canadian half of the podcasting team behind "Ken and Robin Talk About Stuff."

Laura Lush is the author of four collections of poetry, including *Carapace*, which was released in 2011 by Palimpsest Press, and a collection of short stories entitled *Going to the Zoo* by Turnstone Press. She teaches creative writing and academic English at the University of Toronto's School of Continuing Studies. She lives in Guelph with her son, Jack.

Nick Mamatas is the author of a number of novels, including the fantasy-noir *Bullettime* and the full-on noir *Love is the Law*. His short fiction has appeared in *Asimov's Science Fiction*, *Weird Tales*, and *Best American Mystery Stories*, among many other venues, and his art criticism has appeared in *New Observations*, *Art Papers*, and *Artbyte*. A native New Yorker, Nick now lives in California.

Gareth Ryder-Hanrahan (@mytholder) is a writer and game designer. He wrote the Paranoia novel *Reality Optional* and has contributed stories to several anthologies, including *The Lion and the Aardvark* from Stone Skin Press. He's worked on more award-winning roleplaying games than he can readily recall, notably Paranoia, Traveller, The One Ring, Doctor Who and The Laundry Files. He lives in Ireland with more children, spaniels and Apple products than he ever expected.

Robyn Seale is a freelance creator born before the era of the Internet, memes, pictures of cute animals, and terrible cartooning. She has embraced all of these things. When not creating or talking to her cats, she practices awkwarding at people (with varying degrees of success) and attempting to avoid all of the things aforementioned (with less success). You can find her on twitter @ robynseale or through her website NoodlyAppendage.com.

Ekaterina Sedia resides in the Pinelands of New Jersey. Her critically acclaimed novels, *The Secret History of Moscow*, *The*

Alchemy of Stone, *The House of Discarded Dreams*, and *Heart of Iron* were published by Prime Books. Her short stories have sold to *Analog*, *Jim Baen's Universe*, *Subterranean*, and *Clarkesworld*, as well as numerous anthologies, including *Haunted Legends* and *Magic in the Mirrorstone*. She is also the editor of *Paper Cities* (World Fantasy Award winner), *Running with the Pack*, and *Bewere the Night*, as well as forthcoming *Bloody Fabulous*. Visit her at www.ekaterinasedia.com.

Molly Tanzer lives in Boulder, Colorado, along the front range of the Mountains of Madness, or maybe just the Flatirons. Her debut, *A Pretty Mouth*, was published by Lazy Fascist Press in September 2012, and was singled out by *The Guardian* as the favorite among eight hundred indie novels of 2012. Her short fiction has appeared in *The Book of Cthulhu* and *The Book of Cthulhu II*, *The Lovecraft eZine*, and *Fungi*, and is forthcoming in *The Starry Wisdom Library* and *Zombies: Shambling Through the Ages*. She blogs — infrequently — about writing, hiking, cocktail mixing, vegan cooking, movies, and other stuff at mollytanzer. com, and tweets as @molly_the_tanz.

Elizabeth A. Vaughan, *USA Today* best-selling author, writes fantasy romance. Her first novel, *Warprize*, the first book in the Chronicles of the Warlands, was re-released in April, 2011. Learn more about her books at www.eavwrites.com.

Kyla Lee Ward is a Sydney-based creative who works in many modes. Her latest release is *The Land of Bad Dreams*, a collection of poetic nightmares. Her novel *Prismatic* (co-authored as Edwina Grey) won an Aurealis. Her short fiction has appeared on Gothic. net and in the *Macabre* and *New Hero* anthologies, amongst others. Roleplaying games, short films and plays — if it can be done darkly she probably has, to the extent of programming the horror stream for the 2010 Worldcon. A practicing occultist, she likes raptors, swordplay, and the Hellfire Club. To see some very strange things, try http://www.tabula-rasa.info.

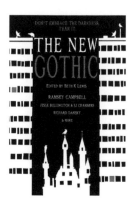

The New Gothic

The Gothic is the most enduring literary tradition in history, but in recent years friendly ghosts and vegetarian vampires threaten its foundations.

The New Gothic is a collection of short stories which revisits the core archetypes of the Gothic - the rambling, secret-filled building, the stranger seeking answers, the black-hearted tyrant - and reminds us not to embrace but to fear the darkness. A dozen tales of terror fill this anthology including an original, never-before-seen story from the godfather of modern horror, **Ramsey Campbell**.

ISBN: 9781908983053

Available from the Stone Skin Press website

www.stoneskinpress.com

The Lion and the Aardvark
Aesop's Modern Fables

These confusing times of Internet trolls, one-percenters, toxic fame, and impending singularity cry out for clarity—the clarity found in Aesop's 2,500 year old fables. Over 60 writers from across the creative spectrum bring their modern sensibilities to this classic format. Zombies, dog-men and robot wasps mingle with cats, coyotes and cockroaches. Parables ranging from the punchy to the evocative, the wry to the disturbing explore eternal human foibles, as displaced onto lemmings, trout, and racing cars. But beware—in these terse explorations of desire, envy, and power, certitude isn't always as clear as it looks.

ISBN: 9781908983022

Available from the Stone Skin Press website

www.stoneskinpress.com

Shotguns v. Cthulhu

Pulse-pounding action meets cosmic horror in this exciting collection from the rising stars of the New Cthulhuiana. Steel your nerves, reach into your weapons locker, and tie tight your running shoes as humanity takes up arms against the monsters and gods of H. P. Lovecraft's Cthulhu Mythos. Remember to count your bullets...you may need the last one for yourself.

Relentlessly hurtling you into madness and danger are:

Natania **BARRON** • Steve **DEMPSEY** • Dennis **DETWILLER**
Larry **DiTILLIO** • Chad **FIFER** • A. Scott **GLANCY**
Dave **GROSS** • Dan **HARMS** • Rob **HEINSOO**
Kenneth **HITE** • Chris **LACKEY** • Robin D. **LAWS**
Nick **MAMATAS** • Ekaterina **SEDIA** • Kyla **WARD**

ISBN: 9781908983015
Available from the Stone Skin Press website
www.stoneskinpress.com